"Are you hurt?"

"No. No, not really," Deborah said. There would be plenty of bruises on both her skin and her emotions, but she would worry about them later. "Just shaken up." In the faint backsplash from the streetlight, she saw that his face was masked. "Nemesis," she murmured. "I thought you were the product of someone's overworked imagination. I am grateful."

"I don't look for gratitude."

Her chin came up as he threw her words back in her face. "For what, then?"

He stared at her. "For justice. Weren't you going to call the police?"

"Yes. I have a phone in my car."

"Then I suggest you use it."

She was too tired to argue. Shivering a bit, she started down the alley. Five minutes later, after calling 911 and giving her location and the situation, she walked back into the alley.

He was gone.

Dear Reader,

I hope you enjoyed last month's new authors, and I know you are looking forward to this month's lineup of books. What better way to begin the month than with one of your all-time favorites, Nora Roberts? Nora is back with a sequel to *Night Shift* entitled *Night Shadow*. This is a very special—even magical—book, with a hero you won't soon forget. I don't want to give anything away, so let me say only that everyone who reads this book is going to be clamoring for a "Nemesis" of her very own.

The rest of the authors this month are terrific, too. Mary Anne Wilson's *Child of Mine* deals with a wrenching custody suit and a man who has to prove his right to raise his own son. You'll be on his side right from the start, pulling for him to win his child—and the woman he loves. Lynn Bartlett's *Heart and Soul* is set on a university campus where there's a lot more than learning going on. High-level espionage and very adult passion are certainly ingredients that were missing when I went to school! Finally, try Sandy Steen's *The Simple Truth,* the story of a mother searching for her lost son—and running head-on into love, along with a little boy who *might* be hers but is absolutely adorable no matter what.

In months to come, look for Dallas Schulze, Marilyn Pappano, Ann Williams, Heather Graham Pozzessere and more. In fact, starting later in the year, we'll bring you two stories you've waited a very long time for—those of the remaining Marshall brothers, from talented Kristin James, who has been missing from the line for far too long.

There's always something exciting happening at Silhouette Intimate Moments, so join us every month for the best in contemporary romance fiction.

Leslie Wainger
Senior Editor and Editorial Coordinator

NORA ROBERTS

Night Shadow

SILHOUETTE·INTIMATE·MOMENTS®

Published by Silhouette Books New York

America's Publisher of Contemporary Romance

With thanks to Isabel and Dan

SILHOUETTE BOOKS
300 East 42nd St., New York, N.Y. 10017

NIGHT SHADOW

ISBN: 0-373-07373-9

First Silhouette Books printing March 1991

Printed in the U.S.A.

NORA ROBERTS

lives in western Maryland with her husband and two children. Nora's book, *Irish Thoroughbred*, a Silhouette Romance, was published in 1981 to universal acclaim. Mid-1988 marked the publication of her *fiftieth* Silhouette and the beginning of a new series. A charter member of the Romance Writers of America, Nora Roberts is the first author to win six Golden Medallions, and she entered the RWA Hall of Fame in 1986.

One of Silhouette's most popular and prolific authors, Nora has appeared on CNN and *Good Morning, America*, as well as in articles in the *Washington Post*, the *Baltimore Sun*, the *New York Times*, and the *Wall Street Journal*.

AWARDS:

Romance Writers of America,
First Place/Golden Medallion:
The Heart's Victory, Silhouette Special Edition. 1983.
Best category sensuous romance.
Untamed, Silhouette Romance. 1984.
Best traditional romance.
This Magic Moment, Silhouette Intimate Moments. 1984.
Best contemporary romance.
Opposites Attract, Silhouette Special Edition. 1985.
Best contemporary romance under 70,000 words.
A Matter of Choice, Silhouette Intimate Moments. 1985.
Best contemporary romance over 70,000 words.
One Summer, Silhouette Special Edition. 1987.
Best long contemporary book.
Georgia Romance Writers of America "Maggie":
Partners, Silhouette Intimate Moments. 1985.
Best category contemporary romance.
Romantic Times "Artie":
1984 Best category contemporary author.
Romantic Times "Best Continuing Series":
1986 The MacGregor Series.
Romantic Times Reviewers' Choice Awards
Reflections, Silhouette Special Edition. 1984.
Partners, Silhouette Intimate Moments. 1985.
One Summer, Silhouette Special Edition. 1986.

Dear Reader:

We need heroes. One of the reasons writing romances appeals to me is it gives me the opportunity to create heroes—male and female. You know, those people who are able to triumph over adversity, emotional pain and yes, bad guys.

In *Night Shadow* I wanted to create a different kind of hero, someone a little beyond the realm of the usual. You'll find he's not the kind of guy you might meet at a party or on a train or the checkout counter at the supermarket. In fact, the heroine meets him . . . Well, you only have to turn a few pages to find out, so I won't spoil it.

The point is, heroes come in all sizes and shapes. In *Night Shadow* he's just a little more, and less, than average. But he's still vulnerable to the love of a good woman. He's still forced to face the problems and joy of forging an emotional bond with that one special person. He falls in love, he makes mistakes, and he learns to compromise. *And* he chases bad guys. That's my kind of hero.

I hope he's yours.

Love,
Nora

Chapter 1

He walked the night. Alone. Restless. Ready. Clad in black, masked, he was a shadow among shadows, a whisper among the murmurs and mumbles of the dark.

He was watchful, always, for those who preyed on the helpless and vulnerable. Unknown, unseen, unwanted, he stalked the hunters in the steaming jungle that was the city. He moved unchallenged in the dark spaces, the blind alleys and violent streets. Like smoke, he drifted along towering rooftops and down into dank cellars.

When he was needed, he moved like thunder, all sound and fury. Then there was only the flash, the optical echo that lightning leaves after it streaks the sky.

They called him Nemesis, and he was everywhere.

He walked the night, skirting the sound of laughter, the cheerful din of celebrations. Instead he was drawn to the whimpers and tears of the lonely and the hopeless pleas of the victimized. Night after night, he clothed himself in black, masked his face and stalked the wild, dark streets. Not for the law. The law was too easily manipulated by those who scorned it. It was too often bent and twisted by those who claimed to uphold it. He knew, oh, yes, he knew. And he could not forget.

When he walked, he walked for justice—she of the blind eyes.

With justice, there could be retribution and the balancing of scales.

Like a shadow, he watched the city below.

Deborah O'Roarke moved quickly. She was always in a hurry to catch up with her own ambitions. Now her neat, sensible shoes clicked rapidly on the broken sidewalks of Urbana's East End. It wasn't fear that had her hurrying back toward her car, though the East End was a dangerous place—especially at night—for a lone, attractive woman. It was the flush of success. In her capacity as assistant district attorney, she had just completed an interview with a witness to one of the drive-by shootings that were becoming a plague in Urbana.

Her mind was completely occupied with the need to get back to her office and write her report so that the wheels of justice could begin to turn. She believed in justice, the patient, tenacious and systematic stages of it. Young Rico Mendez's murderers would answer for their crime. And with luck, she would be the one to prosecute.

Outside the crumbling building where she had just spent an hour doggedly pressuring two frightened young boys for information, the street was dark. All but two of the streetlights that lined the cracked sidewalk had been broken. The moon added only a fitful glow. She knew that the shadows in the narrow doorways were drunks or pushers or hookers. More than once she had reminded herself that she could have ended up in one of those sad and scarred buildings—if it hadn't been for her older sister's fierce determination to see that she had a good home, a good education, a good life.

Every time Deborah brought a case to trial, she felt she was repaying a part of that debt.

One of the doorway shadows shouted something at her, impersonally obscene. A harsh feminine cackle followed it. Deborah had only been in Urbana for eighteen months, but she knew better than to pause or to register that she had heard at all.

Her strides long and purposeful, she stepped off the curb to get into her car. Someone grabbed her from behind.

"Ooh, baby, ain't you sweet."

The man, six inches taller than she and wiry as a spring, stank. But not from liquor. In the split second it took her to read his glassy eyes, she understood that he wasn't pumped high on whiskey but on chemicals that would make him quick instead of sluggish. Using both hands, she shoved her leather briefcase into his gut. He grunted and his grip loosened. Deborah wrenched away and ran, digging frantically for her keys.

Even as her hand closed over the jingling metal in her pocket, he grabbed her, his fingers digging in at the collar of her jacket. She heard the linen rip and turned to fight. Then she saw the switchblade, its business end gleaming once before he pressed it against the soft skin under her chin.

"Gotcha," he said, and giggled.

She went dead still, hardly daring to breathe. In his eyes she saw a malicious kind of glee that would never listen to pleading or logic. Still she kept her voice low and calm.

"I've only got twenty-five dollars."

Jabbing the point of the blade against her skin, he leaned intimately close. "Uh-uh, baby, you got a lot more than twenty-five dollars." He twisted her hair around his hand, jerking once, hard. When she cried out, he began to pull her toward the deeper dark of the alley.

"Go on and scream." He giggled in her ear. "I like it when they scream. Go on." He nicked her throat with the blade. "Scream."

She did, and the sound rolled down the shadowed street, echoing in the canyons of the buildings. In doorways people shouted encouragement—to the attacker. Behind darkened windows people kept their lights off and pretended they heard nothing.

When he pushed her against the damp wall of the alleyway, she was icy with terror. Her mind, always so sharp and open, shut down. "Please," she said, though she knew better, "don't do this."

He grinned. "You're going to like it." With the tip of the blade, he sliced off the top button of her blouse. "You're going to like it just fine."

Like any strong emotion, fear sharpened her senses. She could feel her own tears, hot and wet on her cheeks, smell his stale breath and the overripe garbage that crowded the alley. In his eyes she could see herself pale and helpless.

She would be another statistic, she thought dully. Just one more number among the ever increasing victims.

Slowly, then with increasing power, anger began to burn through the icy shield of fear. She would not cringe and whimper. She would not submit without a fight. It was then she felt the sharp pressure of her keys. They were still in her hand, closed tight in her rigid fist. Concentrating, she used her thumb to push the points between her stiff fingers. She sucked in her breath, trying to channel all of her strength into her arm.

Just as she raised it, her attacker seemed to rise into the air, then fly, arms pinwheeling, into a stand of metal garbage cans.

Deborah ordered her legs to run. The way her heart was pumping, she was certain she could be in her car, doors locked, engine gunning, in the blink of an eye. But then she saw him.

He was all in black, a long, lean shadow among the shadows. He stood over the knife-wielding junkie, his legs spread, his body tensed.

"Stay back," he ordered when she took an automatic step forward. His voice was part whisper, part growl.

"I think—"

"Don't think," he snapped without bothering to look at her.

Even as she bristled at his tone, the junkie leaped up, howling, bringing his blade down in a deadly arc. Before Deborah's dazed and fascinated eyes, there was a flash of movement, a scream of pain and the clatter of the knife as it skidded along the concrete.

In less than the time it takes to draw and release a single breath, the man in black stood just as he had before. The junkie was on his knees, moaning and clutching his stomach.

"That was..." Deborah searched her whirling brain for a word, "impressive. I—I was going to suggest that we call the police."

He continued to ignore her as he took some circular plastic from his pocket and bound the still-moaning junkie's hands and ankles. He picked up the knife, pressed a button. The blade disappeared with a whisper. Only then did he turn to her.

The tears were already drying on her cheeks, he noted. And though there was a hitch in her breath, she didn't appear to be ready to faint or shoot off into hysterics. In fact, he was forced to admire her calm.

She was extraordinarily beautiful, he observed dispassionately. Her skin was pale as ivory against a disheveled cloud of ink-black hair. Her features were soft, delicate, almost fragile. Unless you looked at her eyes. There was a toughness in them, a determination that belied the fact that her slender body was shaking in reaction.

Her jacket was torn, and her blouse had been cut open to reveal the icy-blue lace and silk of a camisole. An interesting contrast to the prim, almost mannish business suit.

He summed her up, not as man to woman, but as he had countless other victims, countless other hunters. The unexpected and very basic jolt of reaction he felt disturbed him. Such things were more dangerous than any switchblade.

"Are you hurt?" His voice was low and unemotional, and he remained in shadow.

"No. No, not really." There would be plenty of bruises, both on her skin and her emotions, but she would worry about them later. "Just shaken up. I want to thank you for—" She had stepped toward him as she spoke. In the faint backsplash from the streetlight, she saw that his face was masked. As her eyes widened, he saw they were blue, a brilliant electric blue. "Nemesis," she murmured. "I thought you were the product of someone's overworked imagination."

"I'm as real as he is." He jerked his head toward the figure groaning among the garbage. He saw that there was a thin trickle of blood on her throat. For reasons he didn't try to understand, it enraged him. "What kind of a fool are you?"

"I beg your pardon?"

"This is the sewer of the city. You don't belong here. No one with brains comes here unless they have no choice."

Her temper inched upward, but she controlled it. He had, after all, helped her. "I had business here."

"No," he corrected. "You have no business here, unless you choose to be raped and murdered in an alley."

"I didn't choose anything of the sort." As her emotions darkened, the faint hint of Georgia became more prominent in her voice. "I can take care of myself."

His gaze skimmed down, lingered on the shredded blouse then returned to her face. "Obviously."

She couldn't make out the color of his eyes. They were dark, very dark. In the murky light, they seemed black. But she could read the dismissal in them, and the arrogance.

"I've already thanked you for helping me, even though I didn't need any help. I was just about to deal with that slime myself."

"Really?"

"That's right. I was going to gouge his eyes out." She held up her keys, lethal points thrusting out. "With these."

He studied her again, then gave a slow nod. "Yes, I believe you could do it."

"Damn right I could."

"Then it appears I've wasted my time." He pulled a square of black cloth from his pocket. After wrapping the knife in it, he offered it to her. "You'll want this for evidence."

The moment she held it, she remembered that feeling of terror and helplessness. With a muffled oath, she bit back her temper. Whoever, whatever he was, he had risked his life to help her. "I am grateful."

"I don't look for gratitude."

Her chin came up as he threw her words back in her face. "For what then?"

He stared at her, into her. Something came and went in his eyes that made her skin chill again as she heard his words, "For justice."

"This isn't the way," she began.

"It's my way. Weren't you going to call the police?"

"Yes." She pressed the heel of her hand to her temple. She was a little dizzy, she realized. And more than a little sick to her stomach. This wasn't the time or the place to argue morality and law enforcement with a belligerent masked man. "I have a phone in my car."

"Then I suggest you use it."

"All right." She was too tired to argue. Shivering a bit, she started down the alley. At the mouth of it, she saw her briefcase. She picked it up with a sense of relief and put the switchblade in it.

Five minutes later, after calling 911 and giving her location and the situation, she walked back into the alley. "They're sending a cruiser." Weary, she pushed the hair back from her face. She saw the junkie, curled up tight on the concrete. His eyes were wide and wild. Nemesis had left him with the promise of what would happen to him if he was ever caught again attempting to rape.

Even through the haze of drugs, the words had rung true.

"Hello?" With a puzzled frown, she looked up and down the alley.

He was gone.

"Damn it, where did he go?" On a hiss of breath, she leaned back against the clammy wall. She hadn't finished with him yet, not by a long shot.

He was almost close enough to touch her. But she couldn't see him. That was the blessing, and the curse, the repayment for the lost days.

He didn't reach out and was curious why he wanted to. He only watched her, imprinting on his memory the shape of her face, the texture of her skin, the color and sheen of her hair as it curved gently beneath her chin.

If he had been a romantic man, he might have thought in terms of poetry or music. But he told himself he only waited and watched to make certain she was safe.

When the sirens cut the night, he could see her rebuild a mask of composure, layer by layer. She took deep, steadying breaths as she buttoned the ruined jacket over her slashed blouse. With a final breath, she tightened her grip on her briefcase, set her chin and walked with confident strides toward the mouth of the alley.

As he stood alone in his own half world between reality and illusion, he could smell the subtle sexiness of her perfume.

For the first time in four years, he felt the sweet and quiet ache of longing.

Deborah didn't feel like a party. In her fantasy, she wasn't all glossed up in a strapless red dress with plastic stays digging into her sides. She wasn't wearing pinching three-inch heels. She wasn't smiling until she thought her face would split in two.

In her fantasy, she was devouring a mystery novel and chocolate chip cookies while she soaked in a hot bubble bath to ease the bruises that still ached a bit three days after her nasty adventure in the East End alley.

Unfortunately, her imagination wasn't quite good enough to keep her feet from hurting.

As parties went, it was a pretty good one. Maybe the music was a bit loud, but that didn't bother her. After a lifetime with her sister, a first-class rock and roll fanatic, she was well indoctrinated into the world of loud music. The smoked salmon and spinach canapés weren't chocolate chip cookies, but they were tasty. The wine that she carefully nursed was top-notch.

There was plenty of glitz and glamour, lots of cheek bussing and glad-handing. It was, after all, a party thrown by Arlo Stuart, hotel magnate, as a campaign party for Tucker Fields, Urbana's mayor. It was Stuart's, and the present administration's hope, that the campaign would end in November with the mayor's reelection.

Deborah was as yet undecided whether she would pull the lever for the incumbent, or the young upstart challenger, Bill Tarrington. The champagne and pâté wouldn't influence her. Her choice would be based on issues, not party affiliations—either social or political. Tonight she was attending the party for two reasons. The first was that she was friends with the mayor's assistant, Jerry Bower. The second was that her boss had used the right combination of pressure and diplomacy to push her through the gilded swinging doors of the Stuart Palace.

"God, you look great." Jerry Bower, trim and handsome in his tux, his blond hair waving around his tanned, friendly face, stopped beside Deborah to press a quick kiss to her cheek. "Sorry I haven't had time to talk. There was a lot of meeting and greeting to do."

"Things are always busy for the big boss's right arm." She smiled, toasting him. "Quite a bash."

"Stuart pulled out all the stops." With a politician's eye, he scanned the crowd. The mix of the rich, famous and influential pleased him. There were, of course, other aspects to the campaign. Visibility, contact with shop owners, factory workers—the blue, the gray and the white collars, press conferences, speeches, statements. But Jerry figured if he could spend a small slice of one eighteen-hour day rubbing silk elbows and noshing on canapés, he'd make the best of it.

"I'm properly dazzled," Deborah assured him.

"Ah, but it's your vote we want."

"You might get it."

"How are you feeling?" Taking the opportunity in hand, he began to fill a plate with hors d'oeuvres.

"Fine." She glanced idly down at the fading bruise on her forearm. There were other, more colorful marks, hidden under the red silk.

"Really?"

She smiled again. "Really. It's an experience I don't want to repeat, but it did bring it home, straight home to me that we've got a lot more work to do before Urbana's streets are safe."

"You shouldn't have been out there," he mumbled.

He might as well have nudged a soapbox under her feet. Her eyes lit up, her cheeks flushed, her chin angled. "Why? Why should there be any place, any place at all in the city where a person isn't safe to walk? Are we supposed to just accept the fact that there are portions of Urbana that are off-limits to nice people? If we're—"

"Hold it, hold it." He held up a surrendering hand. "The only person someone in politics can't comfortably outtalk is a lawyer. I agree with you, okay?" He snagged a glass of wine from a passing waiter and reminded himself it could be his only one of the long evening. "I was stating a fact. It doesn't make it right, it just makes it true."

"It shouldn't be true." Her eyes had darkened in both annoyance and frustration.

"The mayor's running on a tough anticrime campaign," Jerry reminded her, and gave smiling nods to constituents who wandered by. "Nobody in this city knows the statistics better than I do. They're nasty, no doubt, and we're going to push them back. It just takes time."

"Yeah." Sighing, she pulled herself away from the brink of the argument she'd had with Jerry more times than she could count. "But it's taking too much time."

He bit into a carrot slice. "Don't tell me you're going to step over to the side of this Nemesis character? 'If the law won't deal with it quickly enough, I will'?"

"No." On that she was firm. The law would mete out justice in a proper fashion. She believed in the law, even now, when it was so totally overburdened. "I don't believe in crusades. They come too close to vigilantism. Though I have to admit, I'm grateful he was tilting at windmills in that alley the other night."

"So am I." He touched her lightly on the shoulder. "When I think of what might have happened—"

"It didn't." That helpless fear was still much too close to the surface to allow her to dwell on it. "And in spite of all the romantic press he's been getting, up close and in person, he's rude and abrupt." She took another sip of wine. "I owe him, but I don't have to like him."

"Nobody understands that sentiment more than a politician."

She relaxed and laughed up at him. "All right, enough shoptalk. Tell me who's here that I should know and don't."

Jerry entertained her. He always did. For the next few minutes he gulped down canapés and put names and tax brackets to the faces crowding the Royal Stuart ballroom. His clever and pithy comments made her chuckle. When they began to stroll through the crowd, she hooked her arm easily through his. It was a matter of chance that she turned her head and, in that sea of people, focused on one single face.

He was standing in a group of five or six, with two beautiful women all but hanging on his arms. Attractive, yes, she thought. But the room was filled with attractive men. His thick, dark hair framed a long, lean, somewhat scholarly face. Prominent bones, deep-set eyes—brown eyes, she realized, dark and rich like bittersweet chocolate. They seemed faintly bored at the moment. His mouth was full, rather poetic looking, and curved now in the barest hint of a smile.

He wore his tux as if he'd been born in one. Easily, casually. With one long finger he brushed a fiery curl off the redhead's cheek as she leaned closer to him. His smile widened at something she said.

Then, without turning his head, he merely shifted his gaze and locked on Deborah.

". . . .and she bought the little monsters a wide-screen TV."

"What?" She blinked, and though she realized it was absurd, she felt as though she had broken out of a spell. "What?"

"I was telling you about Mrs. Forth-Wright's poodles."

"Jerry, who is that? Over there. With the redhead on one side and the blonde on the other."

Glancing over, Jerry grimaced, then shrugged. "I'm surprised he doesn't have a brunette sitting on his shoulders. Women tend to stick to him as though he was wearing flypaper instead of a tux."

She didn't need to be told what she could see with her own eyes. "Who is he?"

"Guthrie, Gage Guthrie."

Her eyes narrowed a bit, her mouth pursed. "Why does that sound familiar?"

"It's splashed liberally through the society section of the *World* almost every day."

"I don't read the society section." Well aware it was rude, Deborah stared stubbornly at the man across the room. "I know him," she murmured. "I just can't place how."

"You've probably heard his story. He was a cop."

"A cop." Deborah's brows lifted in surprise. He looked much too comfortable, much too much a part of the rich and privileged surroundings to be a cop.

"A good one, apparently, right here in Urbana. A few years ago, he and his partner ran into trouble. Big trouble. The partner was killed, and Guthrie was left for dead."

Her memory jogged then homed in. "I remember now. I followed his story. My God, he was in a coma for..."

"Nine or ten months," Jerry supplied. "He was on life-support, and they'd just about given him up, when he opened his eyes and came back. He couldn't hack the streets anymore, and turned down a desk job with UPD.

He'd come into a plump inheritance while he was in the *Twilight Zone,* so I guess you could say he took the money and ran.''

It couldn't have been enough, she thought. No amount of money could have been enough. ''It must have been horrible. He lost nearly a year of his life.''

Jerry picked through the dwindling supply on his plate, looking for something interesting. ''He's made up for lost time. Apparently women find him irresistible. Of course that might be because he turned a three-million-dollar inheritance into thirty—and counting.'' Nipping a spiced shrimp, Jerry watched as Gage smoothly disentangled himself from the group and started in their direction. ''Well, well,'' he said softly. ''Looks like the interest is mutual.''

Gage had been aware of her since the moment she'd stepped into the ballroom. He'd watched, patient, as she'd mingled then separated herself. He'd kept up a social patter though he'd been wholly and uncomfortably aware of every move she'd made. He'd seen her smile at Jerry, observed the other man kiss her and brush a casually intimate hand over her shoulder.

He'd find out just what the relationship was there.

Though it wouldn't matter. Couldn't matter, he corrected. Gage had no time for sultry brunettes with intelligent eyes. But he moved steadily toward her.

''Jerry,'' Gage smiled. ''It's good to see you again.''

''Always a pleasure, Mr. Guthrie. You're enjoying yourself?''

''Of course.'' His gaze flicked from Jerry to Deborah. ''Hello.''

For some ridiculous reason, her throat snapped shut.

"Deborah, I'd like to introduce you to Gage Guthrie. Mr. Guthrie, Assistant District Attorney Deborah O'Roarke."

"An A.D.A." Gage's smile spread charmingly. "It's comforting to know that justice is in such lovely hands."

"Competent," she said. "I much prefer competent."

"Of course." Though she hadn't offered it, he took her hand and held it for a brief few seconds.

Watch out! The warning flashed into Deborah's mind the instant her palm met his.

"Will you excuse me a minute?" Jerry laid a hand on Deborah's shoulder again. "The mayor's signaling."

"Sure." She summoned up a smile for him, though she was ashamed to admit she'd forgotten he was beside her.

"You haven't been in Urbana long," Gage commented.

Despite her uneasiness, Deborah met his eyes straight on. "About a year and a half. Why?"

"Because I'd have known."

"Really? Do you keep tabs on all the A.D.A's?"

"No." He brushed a finger over the pearl drop at her ear. "Just the beautiful ones." The instant suspicion in her eyes delighted him. "Would you like to dance?"

"No." She let out a long, quiet breath. "No, thanks. I really can't stay any longer. I've got work to do."

He glanced at his watch. "It's already past ten."

"The law doesn't have a time clock, Mr. Guthrie."

"Gage. I'll give you a lift."

"No." A quick and unreasonable panic surged to her throat. "No, that's not necessary."

"If it's not necessary, then it must be a pleasure."

He was smooth, she thought, entirely too smooth for a man who had just shrugged off a blonde and a redhead. She didn't care for the idea of being the brunette to round out the trio.

"I wouldn't want to take you away from the party."

"I never stay late at parties."

"Gage." The redhead, her mouth pouty and moist, swayed up to drag on his arm. "Honey, you haven't danced with me. Not once."

Deborah took the opportunity to make a beeline for the exit.

It was stupid, she admitted, but her system had gone haywire at the thought of being alone in a car with him. Pure instinct, she supposed, for on the surface Gage Guthrie was a smooth, charming and appealing man. But she sensed something. Undercurrents. Dark, dangerous undercurrents. Deborah figured she had enough to deal with; she didn't need to add Gage Guthrie to the list.

She stepped out into the steamy summer night.

"Hail you a cab, miss?" the doorman asked her.

"No." Gage cupped a firm hand under her elbow. "Thank you."

"Mr. Guthrie," she began.

"Gage. My car is just here, Miss O'Roarke." He gestured to a long sleek limo in gleaming black.

"It's lovely," she said between her teeth, "but a cab will suit my needs perfectly."

"But not mine." He nodded at the tall, bulky man who slipped out of the driver's seat to open the rear door. "The streets are dangerous at night. I'd simply like to know you've gotten where you want to go, safely."

She stepped back and took a long careful study, as she might of a mug shot of a suspect. He didn't seem as dangerous now, with that half smile hovering at his mouth. In fact, she thought, he looked just a little sad. Just a little lonely.

She turned toward the limo. Not wanting to soften too much, she shot a look over her shoulder. "Has anyone ever told you you're pushy, Mr. Guthrie?"

"Often, Miss O'Roarke."

He settled beside her and offered a single long-stemmed red rose.

"You come prepared," she murmured. Had the blossom been waiting for the blonde, she wondered, or the redhead?

"I try. Where would you like to go?"

"The Justice Building. It's on Sixth and—"

"I know where it is." Gage pressed a button, and the glass that separated them from the driver slid open noiselessly. "The Justice Building, Frank."

"Yes, sir." The glass closed again, cocooning them.

"We used to work on the same side," Deborah commented.

"Which side is that?"

"Law."

He turned to her, his eyes dark, almost hypnotic. It made her wonder what he had seen when he had drifted all those months in that strange world of half life. Or half death.

"You're a defender of the law?"

"I like to think so."

"Yet you wouldn't be adverse to making deals and kicking back charges."

"The system's overburdened," she said defensively.

"Oh, yes, the system." With a faint movement of his shoulders, he seemed to dismiss it all. "Where are you from?"

"Denver."

"No, you didn't get cypress trees and magnolia blossoms in your voice from Denver."

"I was born in Georgia, but my sister and I moved around quite a bit. Denver was where I lived before I came east to Urbana."

Her sister, he noted. Not her parents, not her family, just her sister. He didn't press. Not yet. "Why did you come here?"

"Because it was a challenge. I wanted to put all those years I studied to good use. I like to think I can make a difference." She thought of the Mendez case and the four gang members who had been arrested and were even now awaiting trial. "I have made a difference."

"You're an idealist."

"Maybe. What's wrong with that?"

"Idealists are often tragically disappointed." He was silent a moment, studying her. The streetlamps and headlights of oncoming traffic sliced into the car, then faded. Sliced, then faded. She was beautiful in both light and shadow. More than beauty, there was a kind of power in her eyes. The kind that came from the merging of intelligence and determination.

"I'd like to see you in court," he said.

She smiled and added yet one more element to the power and the beauty. Ambition. It was a formidable combination.

"I'm a killer."

"I bet you are."

He wanted to touch her, just the skim of a fingertip on those lovely white shoulders. He wondered if it would be enough, just a touch. Because he was afraid it wouldn't, he resisted. It was with both relief and frustration that he felt the limo glide to the curb and stop.

Deborah turned to look blankly out of the window at the old, towering Justice Building. "That was quick," she murmured, baffled by her own disappointment. "Thanks for the lift." When the driver opened her door, she swung her legs out.

"I'll see you again."

For the second time, she looked at him over her shoulder. "Maybe. Good night."

He sat for a moment against the yielding seat, haunted by the scent she had left behind.

"Home?" the driver asked.

"No." Gage took a long, steadying breath. "Stay here, take her home when she's finished. I need to walk."

Chapter 2

Like a boxer dazed from too many blows, Gage fought his way out of the nightmare. He surfaced, breathless and dripping sweat. As the grinding nausea faded, he lay back and stared at the high ornate ceiling of his bedroom.

There were 523 rosettes carved into the plaster. He had counted them day after day during his slow and tedious recuperation. Almost like an incantation, he began to count them again, waiting for his pulse rate to level.

The Irish linen sheets were tangled and damp around him, but he remained perfectly still, counting. Twenty-five, twenty-six, twenty-seven. There was a light, spicy scent of carnations in the room. One of the maids had placed them on the rolltop desk beneath the window. As he continued to count, he tried to guess what vase had been used. Waterford, Dresden, Wedgwood. He concentrated on that and the monotonous counting until he felt his system begin to level.

He never knew when the dream would reoccur. He supposed he should have been grateful that it no longer came nightly, but there was something more horrible about its capricious visits.

Calmer, he pressed the button beside the bed. The drapes on the wide arching window slid open and let in the light. Carefully he flexed his muscles one by one, assuring himself he still had control.

Like a man pursuing his own demons, he reviewed the dream. As always, it sprang crystal clear in his mind, involving all his senses.

They worked undercover. Gage and his partner, Jack McDowell. After five years, they were more than partners. They were brothers. Each had risked his life to save the other's. And each would do so again without hesitation. They worked together, drank together, went to ball games, argued politics.

For more than a year, they had been going by the names of Demerez and Gates, posing as two high-rolling dealers of cocaine and its even-more lethal offspring, crack. With patience and guile, they had infiltrated one of the biggest drug cartels on the East Coast. Urbana was its center.

They could have made a dozen arrests, but they, and the department, agreed that the goal was the top man.

His name and face remained a frustrating mystery.

But tonight they would meet him. A deal had been set painstakingly. Demerez and Gates carried five million in cash in their steel-reinforced briefcase. They would exchange it for top-grade coke. And they would only deal with the man in charge.

They drove toward the harbor in the customized Maserati Jack was so proud of. With two dozen men for backup, and their own cover solid, their spirits were high.

Jack was a quick-thinking, tough-talking veteran cop, devoted to his family. He had a pretty, quiet wife and a young pistol of a toddler. With his brown hair slicked back, his hands studded with rings and the silk suit fitting creaselessly over his shoulders, he looked the part of the rich, conscienceless dealer.

There were plenty of contrasts between the two partners. Jack came from a long line of cops and had been raised in a third-floor walk-up in the East End by his divorced mother. There had been occasional visits from his father, a man who had reached for the bottle as often as his weapon. Jack had gone straight into the force after high school.

Gage had come from a business family filled with successful men who vacationed in Palm Beach and golfed at the country club. His parents had been closer to working class by the family standard, preferring to invest their money, their time, and their dreams in a small, elegant French restaurant on the upper East side. That dream had ultimately killed them.

After closing the restaurant late one brisk autumn night, they had been robbed and brutally murdered not ten feet from the doorway.

Orphaned before his second birthday, Gage had been raised in style and comfort by a doting aunt and uncle. He'd played tennis instead of streetball, and had been encouraged to step into the shoes of his late father's brother, as president of the Guthrie empire.

But he had never forgotten the cruelty, and the injustice of his parents' murder. Instead, he had joined the police force straight out of college.

Despite the contrasts in their backgrounds, the men had one vital thing in common—they both believed in the law.

"We'll hang his ass tonight," Jack said, drawing deeply on his cigarette.

"It's been a long time coming," Gage murmured.

"Six months prep work, eighteen months deep cover. Two years isn't much to give to nail this bastard." He turned to Gage with a wink. "Course, we could always take the five mil and run like hell. What do you say, kid?"

Though Jack was only five years older than Gage, he had always called him "kid." "I've always wanted to go to Rio."

"Yeah, me, too." Jack flicked the smoldering cigarette out of the car window where it bounced on asphalt and sputtered. "We could buy ourselves a villa and live the high life. Lots of women, lots of rum, lots of sun. How 'bout it?"

"Jenny might get annoyed."

Jack chuckled at the mention of his wife. "Yeah, that would probably tick her off. She'd make me sleep in the den for a month. Guess we'd just better kick this guy's butt." He picked up a tiny transmitter. "This is Snow White, you copy?"

"Affirmative, Snow White. This is Dopey."

"Don't I know it," Jack muttered. "We're pulling in, Pier Seventeen. Keep a bead on us. That goes for Happy and Sneezy and the rest of you dwarfs out there."

Gage pulled up in the shadows of the dock and cut the engine. He could smell the water and the overripe odor of fish and garbage. Following the instructions they'd been given, he blinked his headlights twice, paused, then blinked them twice again.

"Just like James Bond," Jack said, then grinned at him. "You ready, kid?"

"Damn right."

He lit another cigarette, blew smoke between his teeth. "Then let's do it."

They moved cautiously, Jack holding the briefcase with its marked bills and microtransmitter. Both men wore shoulder holsters with police issue .38s. Gage had a backup .25 strapped to his calf.

The lap of water on wood, the skitter of rodents on concrete. The dim half-light of a cloudy moon. The sting of tobacco on the air from Jack's cigarette. The small, slow-moving bead of sweat between his own shoulder blades.

"Doesn't feel right," Gage said softly.

"Don't go spooky on me, kid. We're going to hit the bell tonight."

With a nod, Gage fought off the ripple of unease. But he reached for his weapon when a small man stepped out of the shadows. With a grin, the man held up his hands, palms out.

"I'm alone," he said. "Just as agreed. I am Montega, your escort."

He had dark shaggy hair, a flowing moustache. When he smiled, Gage caught the glint of gold teeth. Like them, he was wearing an expensive suit, the kind that could be tailored to disguise the bulk of an automatic weapon. Montega lowered one hand carefully and took out a long, slim cigar. "It's a nice night for a little boat ride, *sí?*"

"*Sí.*" Jack nodded. "You don't mind if we pat you down? We'd feel better holding all the hardware until we get where we're going."

"Understandable." Montega lit the cigar with a slender gold lighter. Still grinning, he clamped the cigar between his teeth. Gage saw his hand slip the lighter casually back into his pocket. Then there was an explosion, the sound, the all too familiar sound of a bullet ripping out of a gun. There was a burning hole in the pocket of the fifteen-hundred-dollar suit. Jack fell backward.

Even now, four years later, Gage saw all the rest in hideous slow motion. The dazed, already dead look in Jack's eyes as he was thrown backward by the force of the bullet. The long, slow roll of the briefcase as it wheeled end over end. The shouts of the backup teams as they started to rush in. His own impossibly slow motion as he reached for his weapon.

The grin, the widening grin, flashing with gold as Montega had turned to him.

"Stinking cops," he said, and fired.

Even now, Gage could feel the hot tearing punch that exploded in his chest. The heat, unbearable, unspeakable. He could see himself flying backward. Flying endlessly. Endlessly into the dark.

And he'd been dead.

He'd known he was dead. He could see himself. He'd looked down and had seen his body sprawled on the bloody dock. Cops were working on him, packing his wound, swearing and scrambling around like ants. He had watched it all passionlessly, painlessly.

Then the paramedics had come, somehow pulling him back into the pain. He had lacked the strength to fight them and go where he wanted to go.

The operating room. Pale blue walls, harsh lights, the glint of steel instruments. The beep, beep, beep of monitors. The labored hiss and release of the respirator.

Twice he had slipped easily out of his body—like breath, quiet and invisible—to watch the surgical team fight for his life. He'd wanted to tell them to stop, that he didn't want to come back where he could hurt again. Feel again.

But they had been skillful and determined and had dragged him back into that poor damaged body. And for a while, he'd returned to the blackness.

That had changed. He remembered floating in some gray liquid world that had brought back primordial memories of the womb. Safe there. Quiet there. Occasionally he could hear someone speak. Someone would say his name loudly, insistently. But he chose to ignore them. A woman weeping—his aunt. The shaken, pleading sound of his uncle's voice.

There would be light, an intrusion really, and though he couldn't feel, he sensed that someone was lifting his eyelids and shining a bead into his pupils.

It was a fascinating world. He could hear his own heartbeat. A gentle, insistent thud and swish. He could smell flowers. Only once in a while, then they would be overpowered by the slick, antiseptic smell of hospital. And he would hear music, soft, quiet music. Beethoven, Mozart, Chopin.

Later he learned that one of the nurses had been moved enough to bring a small tape player into his room. She often brought in discarded flower arrangements and sat and talked with him in a quiet, motherly voice.

Sometimes he mistook her for his own mother and felt unbearably sad.

When the mists in that gray world began to part, he struggled against it. He wanted to stay. But no matter how deep he dived, he kept floating closer to the surface.

Until at last, he opened his eyes to the light.

That was the worst part of the nightmare, Gage thought now. When he'd opened his eyes and realized he was alive.

Wearily Gage climbed out of bed. He had gotten past the death wish that had haunted him those first few weeks. But on the mornings he suffered from the nightmare, he was tempted to curse the skill and dedication of the medical team that had brought him back.

They hadn't brought Jack back. They hadn't saved his parents who had died before he'd even known them. They hadn't had enough skill to save his aunt and uncle, who had raised him with unstinting love and who had died only weeks before he had come out of the coma.

Yet they had saved him. Gage understood why.

It was because of the gift, the curse of a gift he'd been given during those nine months his soul had gestated in that gray, liquid world. And because they had saved him, he had no choice but to do what he was meant to do.

With a dull kind of acceptance, he placed his right hand against the pale green wall of his bedroom. He concentrated. He heard the hum inside his brain, the hum no one else could hear. Then, quickly and completely, his hand vanished.

Oh, it still existed. He could feel it. But even he couldn't see it. There was no outline, no silhouette of knuckles. From the wrist up, the hand was gone. He had only to focus his mind, and his whole body would do the same.

He could still remember the first time it had happened. How it had terrified him. And fascinated him. He made his hand reappear and studied it. It was the same.

Wide palmed, long fingered, a bit rough with callus. The ordinary hand of a man who was no longer ordinary.

A clever trick, he thought, for someone who walks the streets at night, searching for answers.

He closed the hand into a fist, then moved off into the adjoining bathroom to shower.

At 11:45 a.m., Deborah was cooling her heels at the twenty-fifth precinct. She wasn't particularly surprised to have been summoned there. The four gang members who had gunned down Rico Mendez were being held in separate cells. That way they would sweat out the charges of murder one, accessory to murder, illegal possession of firearms, possession of controlled substances, and all the other charges on the arrest sheet. And they could sweat them out individually, with no opportunity to corroborate each other's stories.

She'd gotten the call from Sly Parino's public defense attorney at nine sharp. This would make the third meeting between them. At each previous encounter, she had held firm against a deal. Parino's public defendant was asking for the world, and Parino himself was crude, nasty and arrogant. But she had noted that each time they sat in the conference room together, Parino sweated more freely.

Instinct told her he did indeed have something to trade but was afraid.

Using her own strategy, Deborah had agreed to the meeting, but had put it off for a couple of hours. It sounded like Parino was ready to deal, and since she had him cold, with possession of the murder weapon and two eye witnesses, he'd better have gold chips to ante up.

She used her time waiting for Parino to be brought in from lockup by reviewing her notes on the case. Because she could have recited them by rote, her mind wandered back to the previous evening.

Just what kind of man was Gage Guthrie? she wondered. The type who bundled a reluctant woman into his limo after a five-minute acquaintance. Then left that limo at her disposal for two and a half hours. She remembered her baffled amusement when she had come out of the Justice Building at one o'clock in the morning only to find the long black limo with its taciturn hulk of a driver patiently waiting to take her home.

Mr. Guthrie's orders.

Though Mr. Guthrie had been nowhere to be seen, she had felt his presence all during the drive from midtown to her apartment in the lower West End.

A powerful man, she mused now. In looks, in personality, and in basic masculine appeal. She looked around the station house, trying to imagine the elegant, just slightly rough-around-the-edges man in the tuxedo working here.

The twenty-fifth was one of the toughest precincts in the city. And where, Deborah had discovered when she'd been driven to satisfy her curiosity, Detective Gage Guthrie had worked during most of his six years with UPD.

It was difficult to connect the two, she mused. The smooth, obstinately charming man, with the grimy linoleum, harsh fluorescent lights, and odors of sweat and stale coffee underlaid with the gummy aroma of pine cleaner.

He liked classical music, for it had been Mozart drifting through the limo's speakers. Yet he had worked for years amid the shouts, curses and shrilling phones of the twenty-fifth.

From the information she'd read once she'd accessed his file, she knew he'd been a good cop—sometimes a reckless one, but one who had never crossed the line. At least not on record. Instead, his record had been fat with commendations.

He and his partner had broken up a prostitution ring which had preyed on young runaways, were given credit for the arrest of three prominent businessmen who had run an underground gambling operation that had chastised its unlucky clients with unspeakable torture, had tracked down drug dealers, small and large, and had ferreted out a crooked cop who had used his badge to extort protection money from small shop owners in Urbana's Little Asia.

Then they had gone undercover to break the back of one of the largest drug cartels on the eastern seaboard. And had ended up broken themselves.

Was that what was so fascinating about him? Deborah wondered. That it seemed the sophisticated, wealthy businessman was only an illusion thinly covering the tough cop he had been? Or had he simply returned to his privileged background, his years as a policeman the aberration? Who was the real Gage Guthrie?

She shook her head and sighed. She'd been thinking a lot about illusions lately. Since the night in the alley when she'd been faced with the terrifying reality of her own mortality. And had been saved—though she firmly believed she would have saved herself—by what many people thought was no more than a phantom.

Nemesis was real enough, she mused. She had seen him, heard him, even been annoyed by him. And yet, when he came into her mind, he was like smoke. If she had reached out to touch him, would her hand have passed right through?

What nonsense. She was going to have to get more sleep if overwork caused her mind to take fantasy flights in the middle of the day.

But somehow, she was going to find that phantom again and pin him down.

"Miss O'Roarke."

"Yes." She rose and offered her hand to the young, harried-looking public defendant. "Hello again, Mr. Simmons."

"Yes, well . . ." He pushed tortoiseshell glasses up on his hooked nose. "I appreciate you agreeing to this meeting."

"Cut the bull." Behind Simmons, Parino was flanked by two uniformed cops. He had a sneer on his face and his hands in cuffs. "We're here to deal, so let's cut to the chase."

With a nod, Deborah led the way into the small conference room. She settled her briefcase on the table and sat behind it. She folded her hands. In her trim navy suit and white blouse she looked every inch the Southern belle. She'd been taught her manners well. But her eyes, as dark as the linen of her suit, burned as they swept over Parino. She had studied the police photos of Mendez and had seen what hate and an automatic weapon could do to a sixteen-year-old body.

"Mr. Simmons, you're aware that of the four suspects facing indictment for the murder of Rico Mendez, your client holds the prize for the most serious charges?"

"Can we lose these things?" Parino held out his cuffed hands. Deborah glanced at him.

"No."

"Come on, babe." He gave her what she imagined he thought was a sexy leer. "You're not afraid of me, are you?"

"Of you, Mr. Parino?" Her lips curved, but her tone was frigidly sarcastic. "Why, no. I squash nasty little bugs every day. You, however, should be afraid of me. I'm the one who's going to put you away." She flicked her gaze back to Simmons. "Let's not waste time, again. All three of us know the score. Mr. Parino is nineteen and will be tried as an adult. It is still to be determined whether the others will be tried as adults or juveniles." She took out her notes, though she didn't need them as more than a prop. "The murder weapon was found in Mr. Parino's apartment, with Mr. Parino's fingerprints all over it."

"It was planted," Parino insisted. "I never saw it before in my life."

"Save it for the judge," Deborah suggested. "Two witnesses place him in the car that drove by the corner of Third and Market at 11:45, June 2. Those same witnesses have identified Mr. Parino, in a lineup, as the man who leaned out of that car and fired ten shots into Rico Mendez."

Parino began to swear and shout about squealers, about what he would do to them when he got out. About what he would do to her. Not bothering to raise her voice, Deborah continued, her eyes on Simmons.

"We have your client, cold, murder one. And the state will ask for the death penalty." She folded her hands on her notes and nodded at Simmons. "Now, what do you want to talk about?"

Simmons tugged at his tie. The smoke from the cigarette Parino was puffing was drifting in his direction and burning his eyes. "My client has information that he would be willing to turn over to the D.A.'s office." He cleared his throat. "In return for immunity, and a reduction of the current charges against him. From murder one, to illegal possession of a firearm.''

Deborah lifted a brow, let the silence take a beat. "I'm waiting for the punch line.''

"This is no joke, sister.'' Parino leaned over the table. "I got something to deal, and you'd better play.''

With deliberate motions, Deborah put her notes back into her briefcase, snapped the lock then rose. "You're slime, Parino. Nothing, nothing you've got to deal is going to put you back on the street again. If you think you can walk over me, or the D.A.'s office, then think again.''

Simmons bobbed up as she headed for the door. "Miss O'Roarke, please, if we could simply discuss this.''

She whirled back to him. "Sure, we'll discuss it. As soon as you make me a realistic offer.''

Parino said something short and obscene that caused Simmons to lose his color and Deborah to turn a cold, dispassionate eye on him.

"The state is going for murder one and the death penalty,'' she said calmly. "And believe me when I say I'm going to see to it that your client is ripped out of society just like a leech.''

"I'll get off,'' Parino shouted at her. His eyes were wild as he lunged to his feet. "And when I do, I'm coming looking for you, bitch.''

"You won't get off.'' She faced him across the table. Her eyes were cold as ice and never wavered. "I'm very good at what I do, Parino, which is putting rabid little animals like you away in cages. In your case, I'm going to pull out all the stops. You won't get off,'' she repeated. "And when you're sweating in death row, I want you to think of me.''

"Murder two," Simmons said quickly, and was echoed by a savage howl from his client.

"You're going to sell me out, you sonofabitch."

Deborah ignored Parino and studied Simmons's nervous eyes. There was something here, she could smell it. "Murder one," she repeated, "with a recommendation for life imprisonment rather than the death penalty—if you've got something that holds my interest."

"Let me talk to my client, please. If you could give us a minute."

"Of course." She left the sweaty public defendant with his screaming client.

Twenty minutes later, she faced Parino again across the scarred table. He was paler, calmer, as he smoked a cigarette down to the filter.

"Deal your cards, Parino," she suggested.

"I want immunity."

"From whatever charges might be brought from the information you give me. Agreed." She already had him where she wanted him.

"And protection." He'd begun to sweat.

"If it's warranted."

He hesitated, fiddling with the cigarette, the scorched plastic ashtray. But he was cornered, and knew it. Twenty years. The public defendant had said he'd probably cop a parole in twenty years.

Twenty years in the hole was better than the chair. Anything was. And a smart guy could do pretty well for himself in the joint. He figured he was a pretty smart guy.

"I've been doing some deliveries for some guys. Heavy hitters. Trucking stuff from the docks to this fancy antique shop downtown. They paid good, too good, so I knew something was in those crates besides old vases." Awkward in the cuffs, he lit one cigarette from the smoldering filter of another. "So I figured I'd take a look myself. I opened one of the crates. It was packed with coke. Man, I've never seen so much snow. A hundred, maybe a hundred and fifty pounds. And it was pure."

"How do you know?"

He licked his lips, then grinned. "I took one of the packs, put it under my shirt. I'm telling you, there was enough there to fill up every nose in the state for the next twenty years."

"What's the name of the shop?"

He licked his lips again. "I want to know if we got a deal?"

"If the information can be verified, yes. If you're pulling my chain, no."

"Timeless. That's the name. It's over on Seventh. We delivered once, maybe twice a week. I don't know how often we were taking in coke or just fancy tables."

"Give me some names."

"The guy I worked with at the docks was Mouse. Just Mouse, that's all I know."

"Who hired you?"

"Just some guy. He came into Loredo's, the bar in the West End where the Demons hang out. He said he had some work if I had a strong back and knew how to keep my mouth shut. So me and Ray, we took him up on it."

"Ray?"

"Ray Santiago. He's one of us, the Demons."

"What did he look like, the man who hired you?"

"Little guy, kinda spooky. Big mustache, couple of gold teeth. Walked into Loredo's in a fancy suit, but nobody thought to mess with him."

She took notes, nodded, prompted until she was certain Parino was wrung dry. "All right, I'll check it out. If you've been straight with me, you'll find I'll be straight with you." She rose, glancing at Simmons. "I'll be in touch."

When she left the conference room, her head was pounding. There was a tight, sick feeling in her gut that always plagued her when she dealt with Parino's type.

He was nineteen, for God's sake, she thought as she tossed her visitor's badge to the desk sergeant. Not even old enough to vote—a privilege she would see he never attained—yet he'd viciously gunned down another human being. She knew he felt no remorse. The Demons considered drive-bys a kind of tribal ritual. And she, as a representative of the law, had bargained with him.

That was the way the system worked, she reminded herself as she stepped out of the stuffy station house into the steamy afternoon. She would trade Parino like a poker chip and hope to finesse bigger game. In the end, Parino would pay by spending the rest of his youth and most of his adult life in a cage.

She hoped Rico Mendez's family would feel justice had been served.

"Bad day?"

Still frowning, she turned, shaded her eyes and focused on Gage Guthrie. "Oh. Hello. What are you doing here?"

"Waiting for you."

She lifted a brow, cautiously debating the proper response. Today he wore a gray suit, very trim and quietly expensive. Though the humidity was intense, his white shirt appeared crisp. His gray silk tie was neatly knotted.

He looked precisely like what he was. A successful, wealthy businessman. Until you looked at his eyes, Deborah thought. When you did, you could see that women were drawn to him for a much more basic reason than money and position.

She responded with the only question that seemed apt. "Why?"

He smiled at that. He had seen her caution and her evaluation clearly and was as amused as he was impressed by it. "To invite you to lunch."

"Oh. Well, that's very nice, but—"

"You do eat, don't you?"

He was laughing at her. There was no mistaking it. "Yes, almost every day. But at the moment, I'm working."

"You're a dedicated public servant, aren't you, Deborah?"

"I like to think so." There was just enough sarcasm in his tone to put her back up. She stepped to the curb and lifted an arm to hail a cab. A bus chugged by, streaming exhaust. "It was kind of you to leave your limo for me last night." She turned and looked at him. "But it wasn't necessary."

"I often do what others consider unnecessary." He took her hand and, with only the slightest pressure, brought her arm down to her side. "If not lunch, dinner."

"That sounds more like a command than a request." She would have tugged her hand away, but it seemed foolish to engage in a childish test of wills on a public street. "Either way, I have to refuse. I'm working late tonight."

"Tomorrow then." He smiled charmingly. "A request, Counselor."

It was difficult not to smile back when he was looking at her with humor and—was it loneliness?—in his eyes. "Mr. Guthrie. Gage." She corrected herself before he could. "Persistent men usually annoy me. And you're no exception. But for some reason, I think I'd like to have dinner with you."

"I'll pick you up at seven. I keep early hours."

"Fine. I'll give you my address."

"I know it."

"Of course." His driver had dropped her off at her doorstep the night before. "If you'll give me back my hand, I'd like to hail a cab."

He didn't oblige her immediately, but looked down at her hand. It was small and delicate in appearance, like the rest of her. But there was strength in the fingers. She kept her nails short, neatly rounded with a coating of clear polish. She wore no rings, no bracelets, only a slim, practical watch that he noted was accurate to the minute.

He looked up from her hand, into her eyes. He saw curiosity, a touch of impatience and again, the wariness. Gage made himself smile as he wondered how a simple meeting of palms could have jolted his system so outrageously.

"I'll see you tomorrow." He released her and stepped away.

She only nodded, not trusting her voice. When she slipped into a cab, she turned back. But he was already gone.

It was after ten when Deborah walked up to the antique store. It was closed, of course, and she hadn't expected to find anything. She had written her report and passed the details of her interview with Parino on to her superior. But she hadn't been able to resist a look for herself.

In this upscale part of town, people were lingering over dinner or enjoying a play. A few couples wandered by on their way to a club or a restaurant. Streetlights shot out pools of security.

It was foolish, she supposed, to have been drawn here. She could hardly have expected the doors to have been opened so she could walk in and discover a cache of drugs in an eighteenth-century armoire.

The window was not only dark, it was barred and shaded. Just as the shop itself was under a triple cloak of secrecy. She had spent hours that day searching for the name of the owner. He had shielded himself well under a tangle of corporations. The paper trail took frustrating twists and turns. So far, every lead Deborah had pursued had come up hard at a dead end.

But the stop was real. By tomorrow, the day after at the latest, she would have a court order. The police would search every nook and cranny of Timeless. The books would be confiscated. She would have everything she needed to indict.

She walked closer to the dark window. Something made her turn quickly to peer out at the light and shadow of the street behind her.

Traffic rolled noisily by. Arm in arm, a laughing couple strolled along the opposite sidewalk. The sound of music through open car windows was loud and confused, punctuated by the honking of horns and the occasional squeak of brakes.

Normal, Deborah reminded herself. There was nothing here to cause that itch between her shoulder blades. Yet even as she scanned the street, the adjoining buildings, to assure herself no one was paying any attention to her, the feeling of being watched persisted.

She was giving herself the creeps, Deborah decided. These little licks of fear were left over from her night in the alley, and she didn't care for it. It wasn't possible to live your life too spooked to go out at night, so paranoid you looked around every corner before you took that last step around it. At least it wasn't possible for her.

Most of her life she had been cared for, looked after, even pampered by her older sister. Though she would always be grateful to Cilla, she had made a commitment when she had left Denver for Urbana. To leave her mark. That couldn't be done if she ran from shadows.

Determined to fight her own uneasiness, she skirted around the building, walking quickly through the short, narrow alley between the antique store and the boutique beside it.

The rear of the building was as secure and unforthcoming as the front. There was one window, enforced with steel bars, and a pair of wide doors, triple bolted. Here, there were no streetlamps to relieve the dark.

"You don't look stupid."

At the voice, she jumped back and would have tumbled into a line of garbage cans if a hand hadn't snagged her wrist. She opened her mouth to scream, brought her fist up to fight, when she recognized her companion.

"You!" He was in black, hardly visible in the dark. But she knew.

"I would have thought you'd had your fill of back alleys." He didn't release her, though he knew he should. His fingers braceleted her wrist and felt the fast, hot beat of her blood.

"You've been watching me."

"There are some women it's difficult to look away from." He pulled her closer, just a tug on her wrist, and stunned both of them. His voice was low and rough. She could see anger in the gleam of his eyes. She found the combination oddly compelling. "What are you doing here?"

Her mouth was so dry it ached. He had pulled her so close that their thighs met. She could feel the warm flutter of his breath on her lips. To insure some distance and some control, she put a hand to his chest.

Her hand didn't pass through, but met a warm, solid wall, felt the quick, steady beat of a heart.

"That's my business."

"Your business is to prepare cases and try them in court, not to play detective."

"I'm not playing—" She broke off, eyes narrowing. "How do you know I'm a lawyer?"

"I know a great deal about you, Miss O'Roarke." His smile was thin and humorless. "That's my business. I don't think your sister worked to put you through law school, and saw you graduate at the top of your class to have you sneaking around back entrances of locked buildings. Especially when that building is a front for some particularly ugly commerce."

"You know about this place?"

"As I said, I know a great deal."

She would handle his intrusion into her life later. Now, she had a job to do. "If you have any information, any proof about this suspected drug operation, it's your duty to give that information to the D.A.'s office."

"I'm very aware of my duty. It doesn't include making deals with scum."

Heat rushed to her cheeks. She didn't even question how he knew about her interview with Parino. It was enough, more than enough, that he was holding her integrity up to inspection. "I worked within the law," she snapped at him. "Which is more than you can say. You put on a mask and play Captain America, making up your own rules. That makes you part of the problem, not part of the solution."

In the slits of his mask, his eyes narrowed. "You seemed grateful enough for my solution a few nights ago."

Her chin came up. She wished she could face him on her own ground, in the light. "I've already thanked you for your help, unnecessary though it was."

"Are you always so cocky, Miss O'Roarke?"

"Confident," she corrected.

"And do you always win in court?"

"I have an excellent record."

"Do you always win?" he repeated.

"No, but that's not the point."

"That's exactly the point. There's a war in this city, Miss O'Roarke."

"And you've appointed yourself general of the good guys."

He didn't smile. "No, I fight alone."

"Don't you—"

But he cut her off swiftly, putting a gloved hand over her mouth. He listened, but not with his ears. It wasn't something he heard, but something he felt, as some men felt hunger or thirst, love or hate. Or, from centuries ago when their senses were not dulled by civilization, danger.

Before she had even begun to struggle against him, he pulled her aside and shoved her down beneath him behind the wall of the next building.

"What the hell do you think you're doing?"

The explosion that came on the tail of her words made her ears ring. The flash of light made her pupils contract. Before she could close her eyes against the glare, she saw the jagged shards of flying glass, the missiles of charred brick. Beneath her, the ground trembled as the antique store exploded.

She saw, with horror and fascination, a lethal chunk of concrete crash only three feet from her face.

"Are you all right?" When she didn't answer, only trembled, he took her face in his hand and turned it to his. "Deborah, are you all right?"

He repeated her name twice before the glassy look left her eyes. "Yes," she managed. "Are you?"

"Don't you read the papers?" There was the faintest of smiles around his mouth. "I'm invulnerable."

"Right." With a little sigh, she tried to sit up. For a moment he didn't move, but left his body where it was, where it wanted to be. Fitted against hers. His face was only inches away. He wondered what would happen—to both of them—if he closed that distance and let his mouth meet hers.

He was going to kiss her, Deborah realized and went perfectly still. Emotion swarmed through her. Not anger, as she'd expected. But excitement, raw and wild. It pumped through her so quickly, so hugely, it blocked out everything else. With a little murmur of agreement, she lifted her hand to his cheek.

Her fingers brushed his mask. He pulled back from her touch as if he'd been slapped. Shifting, he rose then helped her to her feet. Fighting a potent combination of humiliation and fury, she stepped around the wall toward the rear of the antique shop.

There was little left of it. Brick, glass and concrete were scattered. Inside the crippled building, fire raged. The roof collapsed with a long, loud groan.

"They've beaten you this time," he murmured. "There won't be anything left for you to find, no papers, no drugs, no records."

"They've destroyed a building," she said between her teeth. She hadn't wanted to be kissed, she told herself. She'd been shaken up, dazed, a victim of temporary insanity. "But someone owns it, and I'll find out who that is."

"This was meant as a warning, Miss O'Roarke. One you might want to consider."

"I won't be frightened off. Not by exploding buildings or by you." She turned to face him, but wasn't surprised that he was gone.

Chapter 3

It was after one in the morning when Deborah dragged herself down the hallway toward her apartment. She'd spent the best part of two hours answering questions, giving her statement to the police and avoiding reporters. Even through the fatigue was a nagging annoyance for the man called Nemesis.

Technically he'd saved her life again. If she'd been standing within ten feet of the antique shop when the bomb had gone off, she would certainly have met a nasty death. But then he'd left her holding the bag, a very large, complicated bag she'd been forced to sort through, assistant D.A. or not, for the police.

Added to that was the fact he had shown in the short, pithy conversation they'd had, that he held no respect for her profession or her judgment. She had studied and worked toward the goal of prosecutor since she'd been eighteen. Now with a shrug, he was dismissing those years of her life as wasted.

No, she thought as she dug in her purse for her keys, he preferred to skulk around the streets, meting out his own personal sense of justice. Well, it didn't wash. And before it was over, she was going to prove to him that the system worked.

And she would prove to herself that she hadn't been the least bit attracted to him.

"You look like you had a rough night."

Keys in hand, Deborah turned. Her across-the-hall neighbor, Mrs. Greenbaum, was standing in her open doorway, peering out through a pair of cherry-red framed glasses.

"Mrs. Greenbaum, what are you doing up?"

"Just finished watching David Letterman. That boy cracks me up." At seventy, with a comfortable pension to buffer her against life's storms, Lil Greenbaum kept her own hours and did as she pleased. At the moment she was wearing a tatty terry-cloth robe, Charles and Di bedroom slippers and a bright pink bow in the middle of her hennaed hair. "You look like you could use a drink. How about a nice hot toddy?"

Deborah was about to refuse, when she realized a hot toddy was exactly what she wanted. She smiled, dropped the keys into her jacket pocket and crossed the hall. "Make it a double."

"Already got the hot water on. You just sit down and kick off your shoes." Mrs. Greenbaum patted her hand then scurried off to the kitchen.

Grateful, Deborah sank into the deep cushions of the couch. The television was still on, with an old black-and-white movie flickering on the screen. Deborah recognized a young Cary Grant, but not the film. Mrs. Greenbaum would know, she mused. Lil Greenbaum knew everything.

The two-bedroom apartment—Mrs. Greenbaum kept a second bedroom ready for any of her numerous grandchildren—was both cluttered and tidy. Tables were packed with photographs and trinkets. There was a lava lamp atop the television, with a huge brass peace symbol attached to its base. Lil was proud of the fact that she'd marched against the establishment in the sixties. Just as she had protested nuclear reactors, Star Wars, the burning of rain forests and the increased cost of Medicare.

She liked to protest, she'd often told Deborah. When you could argue against the system, it meant you were still alive and kicking.

"Here we are." She brought out two slightly warped ceramic mugs—the product of one of her younger children's creativity. She flicked a glance at the television. "*Penny Serenade,* 1941, and oh, wasn't that Cary Grant something?" After setting down the mugs, she picked up her remote and shut the TV off. "Now, what trouble have you been getting yourself into?"

"It shows?"

Mrs. Greenbaum took a comfortable sip of whiskey-laced tea. "Your suit's a mess." She leaned closer and took a sniff. "Smells like smoke. Got a smudge on your cheek, a run in your stocking and fire in your eyes. From the look in them, there's got to be a man involved."

"The UPD could use you, Mrs. Greenbaum." Deborah sipped at the tea and absorbed the hot jolt. "I was doing a little legwork. The building I was checking out blew up."

The lively interest in Mrs. Greenbaum's eyes turned instantly to concern. "You're not hurt?"

"No. Few bruises." They would match the ones she'd gotten the week before. "I guess my ego suffered a little. I ran into Nemesis.'' Deborah hadn't mentioned her first encounter, because she was painfully aware of her neighbor's passionate admiration for the man in black.

Behind the thick frames, Mrs. Greenbaum's eyes bulged. ''You actually saw him?''

''I saw him, spoke to him and ended up being tossed to the concrete by him just before the building blew up.''

''God.'' Lil pressed a hand to her heart. ''That's even more romantic than when I met Mr. Greenbaum at the Pentagon rally.''

''It had nothing to do with romance. The man is impossible, very likely a maniac and certainly dangerous.''

''He's a hero.'' Mrs. Greenbaum shook a scarlet-tipped finger at Deborah. ''You haven't learned to recognize heroes yet. That's because we don't have enough of them today.'' She crossed her feet so that Princess Di grinned up at Deborah. ''So, what does he look like? The reports have all been mixed. One day he's an eight-foot black man, another he's a pale-faced vampire complete with fangs. Just the other day I read he was a small green woman with red eyes.''

''He's not a woman,'' Deborah muttered. She could remember, a bit too clearly, the feel of his body over hers. ''And I can't really say what he looks like. It was dark and most of his face was masked.''

''Like Zorro?'' Mrs. Greenbaum said hopefully.

''No. Well, I don't know. Maybe.'' She gave a little sigh and decided to indulge her neighbor. ''He's six-one or six-two, I suppose, lean but well built.''

''What color is his hair?''

''It was covered. I could see his jawline.'' Strong, tensed. ''And his mouth.'' It had hovered for one long, exciting moment over hers. "Nothing special," she said quickly, and gulped more tea.

"Hmm." Mrs. Greenbaum had her own ideas. She'd been married and widowed twice, and in between had enjoyed what she considered her fair share of affairs and romantic entanglements. She recognized the signs. "His eyes? You can always tell the make of a man by his eyes. Though I'd rather look at his tush."

Deborah chuckled. "Dark."

"Dark what?"

"Just dark. He keeps to the shadows."

"Slipping through the shadows to root out evil and protect the innocent. What's more romantic than that?"

"He's bucking the system."

"My point exactly. It doesn't get bucked enough."

"I'm not saying he hasn't helped a few people, but we have trained law enforcement officers to do that." She frowned into her mug. There hadn't been any cops around either time she had needed help. They couldn't be everywhere. And she probably could have handled both situations herself. Probably. She used her last and ultimate argument. "He doesn't have any respect for the law."

"I think you're wrong. I think he has great respect for it. He just interprets it differently than you do." Again she patted Deborah's hand. "You're a good girl, Deborah, a smart girl, but you've trained yourself to walk down a very narrow path. You should remember that this country was founded on rebellion. We often forget, then we become fat and lazy until someone comes along and questions the status quo. We need rebels, just as we need heroes. It would be a dull, sad world without them."

"Maybe." Though she was far from convinced. "But we also need rules."

"Oh, yes." Mrs. Greenbaum grinned. "We need rules. How else could we break them?"

Gage kept his eyes closed as his driver guided the limo across town. Through the night after the explosion and the day that followed, he had thought of a dozen reasons why he should cancel his date with Deborah O'Roarke.

They were all very practical, very logical, very sane reasons. To offset them had been only one impractical, illogical and potentially insane reason.

He needed her.

She was interfering with his work, both day and night. Since the moment he'd seen her, he hadn't been able to think of anyone else. He'd used his vast network of computers to dig out every scrap of available information on her. He knew she'd been born in Atlanta, twenty-five years before. He knew she had lost her parents, tragically and brutally, at the age of eight. Her sister had raised her, and together they had hopscotched across the country. The sister worked in radio and was now station manager at KHIP in Denver where Deborah had gone to college.

Deborah had passed the bar the first time and had applied for a position in the D.A.'s office in Urbana, where she had earned a reputation for being thorough, meticulous and ambitious.

He knew she had had one serious love affair in college, but he didn't know what had ended it. She dated a variety of men, none seriously.

He hated the fact that that one last piece of information had given him tremendous relief.

She was a danger to him. He knew it, understood it
and seemed unable to avoid it. Even after their encounter the night before when she had come within a hair's
breadth of making him lose control—of his temper and
his desire—he wasn't able to shove her out of his mind.

To go on seeing her was to go on deceiving her. And
himself.

But when the car pulled to the curb in front of her
building, he got out, walked into the lobby and took the
elevator up to her floor.

When Deborah heard the knock, she stopped pacing
the living room. For the past twenty minutes she'd been
asking herself why she had agreed to go out with a man
she barely knew. And one with a reputation of being a
connoisseur of women but married to his business.

She'd fallen for the charm, she admitted, that smooth,
careless charm with the hint of underlying danger.
Maybe she'd even been intrigued, and challenged, by his
tendency to dominate. She stood for a moment, hand on
the knob. It didn't matter, she assured herself. It was
only one evening, a simple dinner date. She wasn't naïve
and wide-eyed, and expected no more than good food
and intelligent conversation.

She wore blue. Somehow he'd known she would. The
deep midnight-blue silk of her dinner suit matched her
eyes. The skirt was snug and short, celebrating the length
of long, smooth legs. The tailored, almost mannish
jacket made him wonder if she wore more silk, or simply her skin, beneath it. The lamp she had left on beside
the door caught the gleam of the waterfall of blue and
white stones she wore at her ears.

The easy flattery he was so used to dispensing lodged
in his throat. "You're prompt," he managed.

"Always." She smiled at him. "It's like a vice." She closed the door behind her without inviting him in. It seemed safer that way.

A few moments later, she settled back in the limo and vowed to enjoy herself. "Do you always travel this way?"

"No. Just when it seems more convenient."

Unable to resist, she slipped off her shoes and let her feet sink into the deep pewter carpet. "I would. No hassling for cabs or scurrying to the subway."

"But you miss a lot of life on, and under, the streets."

She turned to him. In his dark suit and subtly striped tie he looked elegant and successful. There were burnished gold links at the cuffs of his white shirt. "You're not going to tell me you ride the subway."

He only smiled. "When it seems most convenient. You don't believe that money should be used as an insulator against reality?"

"No. No, I don't." But she was surprised he didn't. "Actually, I've never had enough to be tempted to try it."

"You wouldn't be." He contented himself, or tried, by toying with the ends of her hair. "You could have gone into private practice with a dozen top firms at a salary that would have made your paycheck at the D.A.'s office look like pin money. You didn't."

She shrugged it off. "Don't think there aren't moments when I question my own sanity." Thinking it would be safer to move to more impersonal ground, she glanced out the window. "Where are we going?"

"To dinner."

"I'm relieved to hear that since I missed lunch. I meant where."

"Here." He took her hand as the limo stopped. They had driven to the very edge of the city, to the world of old money and prestige. Here the sound of traffic was only a distant echo, and there was the light, delicate scent of roses in bloom.

Deborah stifled a gasp as she stepped onto the curb. She had seen pictures of his home. But it was entirely different to be faced with it. It loomed over the street, spreading for half a block.

It was Gothic in style, having been built by a philanthropist at the turn of the century. She'd read somewhere that Gage had purchased it before he'd been released from the hospital.

Towers and turrets rose up into the sky. High mullioned windows gleamed with the sun that was lowering slowly in the west. Terraces jutted out, then danced around corners. The top story was dominated by a huge curving glass where one could stand and look out over the entire city.

"I see you take the notion that a man's home is his castle literally."

"I like space, and privacy. But I decided to postpone the moat."

With a laugh, she walked up to the carved doors at the entrance.

"Would you like a tour before we eat?"

"Are you kidding?" She hooked her arm through his. "Where do we start?"

He led her through winding corridors, under lofty ceilings, into rooms both enormous and cramped. And he couldn't remember enjoying his home more than now, seeing it through her eyes.

There was a two-level library packed with books— from first editions to dog-eared paperbacks. Parlors with curvy old couches and delicate porcelain. Ming vases, Tang horses, Lalique crystal and Mayan pottery. Walls were done in rich, deep colors, offset by gleaming wood and Impressionist paintings.

The east wing held a tropical greenery, an indoor pool and a fully equipped gymnasium with a separate whirlpool and sauna. Through another corridor, up a curving staircase, there were bedrooms furnished with fourposters or heavy carved headboards.

She stopped counting rooms.

More stairs, then a huge office with a black marble desk and a wide sheer window that was growing rosy with sundown. Computers silent and waiting.

A music room, complete with a white grand piano and an old Wurlitzer jukebox. Almost dizzy, she stepped into a mirrored ballroom and stared at her own multiplied reflection. Above, a trio of magnificent chandeliers blazed with sumptuous light.

"It's like something out of a movie," she murmured. "I feel as though I should be wearing a hooped skirt and a powdered wig."

"No." He touched her hair again. "I think it suits you just fine as it is."

With a shake of her head, she stepped further inside, then went with impulse and turned three quick circles. "It's incredible, really. Don't you ever get the urge to just come into this room and dance?"

"Not until now." Surprising himself as much as her, he caught her around the waist and swung her into a waltz.

She should have laughed—have shot him an amused and flirtatious look and have taken the impulsive gesture for what it was. But she couldn't. All she could do was stare up at him, stare into his eyes as he spun her around and around the mirrored room.

Her hand lay on his shoulder, her other caught firmly in his. Their steps matched, though she gave no thought to them. She wondered, foolishly, if he heard the same music in his head that she did.

He heard nothing but the steady give and take of her breathing. Never in his life could he remember being so totally, so exclusively aware of one person. The way her long, dark lashes framed her eyes. The subtle trace of bronze she had smudged on the lids. The pale, moist gloss of rose on her lips.

Where his hand gripped her waist, the silk was warm from her body. And that body seemed to flow with his, anticipating each step, each turn. Her hair fanned out, making him ache to let his hands dive into it. Her scent floated around him, not quite sweet and utterly tempting. He wondered if he would taste it if he pressed his lips to the long, white column of her throat.

She saw the change in his eyes, the deepening, the darkening of them as desire grew. As her steps matched his, so did her need. She felt it build and spread, like a living thing, until her body thrummed with it. She leaned toward him, wondering.

He stopped. For a moment they stood, reflected dozens and dozens of times. A man and a woman caught in a tentative embrace, on the brink of something neither of them understood.

She moved first, a cautious half step in retreat. It was her nature to think carefully before making any decision. His hand tightened on hers. For some reason she thought it was a warning.

"I . . . my head's spinning."

Very slowly his hand slipped away from her waist and the embrace was broken. "Then I'd better feed you."

"Yes." She nearly managed to smile. "You'd better."

They dined on sautéed shrimp flavored with orange and rosemary. Though he'd shown her the enormous dining room with its heavy mahogany servers and sideboards, they took their meal in a small salon at a table by a curved window. Between sips of champagne, they could watch the sunset over the city. On the table, between them, were two slender white candles and a single red rose.

"It's beautiful here," she commented. "The city. You can see all its possibilities, and none of its problems."

"Sometimes it helps to take a step back." He stared out at the city himself, then turned away as if dismissing it. "Or else those problems can eat you alive."

"But you're still aware of them. I know you donate a lot of money to the homeless and rehabilitation centers, and other charities."

"It's easy to give money away when you have more than you need."

"That sounds cynical."

"Realistic." His smile was cool and easy. "I'm a businessman, Deborah. Donations are tax deductible."

She frowned, studying him. "It would be a great pity, I think, if people were only generous when it benefited them."

"Now you sound like an idealist."

Riled, she tapped a finger against the champagne goblet. "That's the second time in a matter of days you've accused me of that. I don't think I like it."

"It wasn't meant as an insult, just an observation." He glanced up when Frank came in with individual

chocolate soufflés. "We won't need anything else tonight."

The big man shrugged. "Okay."

Deborah noted that Frank moved with a dancer's
grace, an odd talent in a man who was big and bulky.
Thoughtful, she dipped a spoon into the dessert. "Is he
your driver or your butler?" she asked.

"Both. And neither." He topped off her wine. "You
might say he's an associate from a former life."

Intrigued, she lifted a brow. "Which means?"

"He was a pickpocket I collared a time or two when I
was a cop. Then he was my snitch. Now . . . he drives my
car and answers my door, among other things."

She noted that Gage's fingers fit easily around the
slender stem of the crystal glass. "It's hard to imagine
you working the streets."

He grinned at her. "Yes, I suppose it is." He watched
the way the candlelight flickered in her eyes. Last night,
he had seen the reflection of fire there, from the burning building and her own smothered desires.

"How long were you a cop?"

"One night too long," he said flatly, then reached for
her hand. "Would you like to see the view from the
roof?"

"Yes, I would." She pushed back from the table, understanding that the subject of his past was a closed
book.

Rather than the stairs, he took her up in a small
smoked-glass elevator. "All the comforts," she said as
they started their ascent. "I'm surprised the place
doesn't come equipped with a dungeon and secret pas-
sageways."

"Oh, but it does. Perhaps I'll show you . . . another
time."

Another time, she thought. Did she want there to be another time? It had certainly been a fascinating evening, and with the exception of that moment of tension in the ballroom, a cordial one. Yet despite his polished manners, she sensed something restless and dangerous beneath the tailored suit.

That was what attracted her, she admitted. Just as that was what made her uneasy.

"What are you thinking?"

She decided it was best to be perfectly honest. "I was wondering who you were, and if I wanted to stick around long enough to find out."

The doors to the elevator whispered open, but he stayed where he was. "And do you?"

"I'm not sure." She stepped out and into the topmost turret of the building. With a sound of surprise and pleasure, she moved toward the wide curve of glass. Beyond it, the sun had set and the city was all shadow and light. "It's spectacular." She turned to him, smiling. "Just spectacular."

"It gets better." He pushed a button on the wall. Silently, magically, the curved glass parted. Taking her hand, he led her onto the stone terrace beyond.

Setting her palms on the stone railing, she leaned out into the hot wind that stirred the air. "You can see the trees in City Park, and the river." Impatiently she brushed her blowing hair out of her eyes. "The buildings look so pretty with their lights on." In the distance, she could see the twinkling lights of the Dover Heights suspension bridge. They draped like a necklace of diamonds against the dark.

"At dawn, when it's clear, the buildings are pearly gray and rose. And the sun turns all the glass into fire."

She looked at him and the city he faced. "Is that why you bought the house, for the view?"

"I grew up a few blocks from here. Whenever we walked in the park, my aunt would always point it out to me. She loved this house. She'd been to parties here as a child—she and my mother. They had been friends since childhood. I was the only child, for my parents, and then for my aunt and uncle. When I came back and learned they were gone...well, I couldn't think of much of anything at first. Then I began to think about this house. It seemed right that I take it, live in it."

She laid a hand over his on the rail. "There's nothing more difficult, is there, than to lose people you love and need?"

"No." When he looked at her, he saw that her eyes were dark and glowing with her own memories and with empathy for his. He brought a hand to her face, skimming back her hair with his fingers, molding her jawline with his palm. Her hand fluttered up to light on his wrist and trembled. Her voice was just as unsteady.

"I should go."

"Yes, you should." But he kept his hand on her face, his eyes on hers as he shifted to trap her body between his and the stone parapet. His free hand slid gently up her throat until her face was framed. "Have you ever been compelled to take a step that you knew was a mistake? You knew, but you couldn't stop."

A haze was drifting over her mind, and she shook her head to clear it. "I—no. No, I don't like to make mistakes." But she already knew she was about to make one. His palms were rough and warm against her skin. His eyes were so dark, so intense. For a moment she blinked, assaulted by a powerful sense of déjà vu.

But she'd never been here before, she assured herself as he skimmed his thumbs over the sensitive skin under her jawline.

"Neither do I."

She moaned and shut her eyes, but he only brushed his lips over her brow. The light whisper of contact shot a spear of reaction through her. In the hot night she shuddered while his mouth moved gently over her temple.

"I want you." His voice was rough and tense as his fingers tightened in her hair. Her eyes were open again, wide and aware. In his she could see edgy desire. "I can barely breathe from wanting you. You're my mistake, Deborah. The one I never thought I would make."

His mouth came down on hers, hard and hungry, with none of the teasing seduction she had expected and told herself she would have resisted. There was nothing of the smooth and sophisticated man she had dined with here. This was the reckless and dangerous man she had caught only glimpses of.

He frightened her. He fascinated her. He seduced her.

With no hesitation, no caution, no thought, she responded, meeting power for power and need for need.

She didn't feel the rough stone against her back, only the hard long length of him as his body pressed to hers. She could taste the zing of wine on his tongue and something darker, the potent flavor of passion barely in check. With a groan of pleasure, she pulled him closer until she could feel his heart thudding against hers. Beat for beat.

She was more than he had dreamed. All silk and scent and long limbs. Her mouth was heated, yielding against his, then demanding. Her hands slid under his jacket, fingers flexing even as her head fell back in a taunting surrender that drove him mad.

A pulse hammered in her throat, enticing him to press his lips there and explore the new texture, the new flavor, before he brought his mouth back to hers. With teeth he nipped, with tongue he soothed, pushing them closer and closer to the edge of reason. He swallowed her gasp as he stroked his hands down her, seeking, cupping, molding.

He felt her shudder, then his own before he forced himself to grip tight to a last thin line of control. Very cautiously, like a man backing away from a sheer drop, he stepped away from her.

Dazed, Deborah brought a hand to her head. Fighting to catch her breath, she stared at him. What kind of power did he have, she wondered, that he could turn her from a sensible woman into a trembling puddle of need?

She turned, learning over the rail and gulping air as though it were water and she dying of thirst. "I don't think I'm ready for you," she managed at length.

"No. I don't think I'm ready for you, either. But there won't be any going back."

She shook her head. Her palms were pressed so hard into the rail that the stone was biting her skin. "I'll have to think about that."

"Once you've turned certain corners, there's no place to go but forward."

Calmer, she turned back to him. It was time, past time, to set the ground rules. For both of them. "Gage, however it might appear after what just happened, I don't have affairs with men I hardly know."

"Good." He, too, was calmer. His decision was made. "When we have ours, I want it to be exclusive."

Her voice chilled. "Obviously I'm not making myself clear. I haven't decided if I want to be involved with you, and I'm a long way from sure if I'd want that involvement to end up in bed."

"You are involved with me." Reaching out, he cupped the back of her neck before she could evade. "And we both want that involvement to end up in bed."

Very deliberately, she reached up and removed his hand. "I realize you're used to women falling obligingly at your feet. I have no intention of joining the horde. And I make up my own mind."

"Should I kiss you again?"

"No." She threw a hand up and planted it solidly against his chest. In an instant she was reminded of how she had stood, just like this, with the man called Nemesis. The comparison left her shaken. "No. It was a lovely evening, Gage." She took a long steadying breath. "I mean that. I enjoyed the company, the dinner and...and the view. I'd hate to see you spoil it completely by being arrogant and argumentative."

"It's not being either to accept the inevitable. I don't have to like it to accept it." Something flickered in his eyes. "There is such a thing as destiny, Deborah. I had a long time to consider, and to come to terms with that." His brows drew together in a frown as he looked at her. "God help both of us, but you're part of mine." He looked back, then offered a hand. "I'll take you home."

Chapter 4

Groaning, her eyes firmly shut, Deborah groped for the shrilling phone on her nightstand. She knocked over a book, a brass candlestick and a notepad before she managed to snag the receiver and drag it under the pillow.

"Hello?"

"O'Roarke?"

She cleared her throat. "Yes."

"Mitchell here. We've got a problem."

"Problem?" She shoved the pillow off her head and squinted at her alarm clock. The only problem she could see was that her boss was calling her at 6:15 a.m. "Has the Slagerman trial been postponed? I'm scheduled for court at nine."

"No. It's Parino."

"Parino?" Scrubbing a hand over her face, she struggled to sit up. "What about him?"

"He's dead."

"Dead." She shook her head to clear her groggy brain. "What do you mean he's dead?"

"As in doornail," Mitchell said tersely. "Guard found him about half an hour ago."

She wasn't groggy now, but was sitting ramrod straight, brain racing. "But—but how?"

"Knifed. Looks like he went up to the bars to talk to someone, and they shoved a stiletto through his heart."

"Oh, God."

"Nobody heard anything. Nobody saw anything," Mitchell said in disgust. "There was a note taped to the bars. It said, 'Dead birds don't sing.'"

"Somebody leaked that he was feeding us information."

"And you can bet that I'm going to find out who. Listen, O'Roarke, we're not going to be able to muzzle the press on this one. I figured you'd want to hear it from me instead of on the news during your morning coffee."

"Yeah." She pressed a hand to her queasy stomach. "Yeah, thanks. What about Santiago?"

"No show yet. We've got feelers out, but if he's gone to ground, it might be a while before we dig him up."

"They'll be after him, too," she said quietly. "Whoever arranged for Parino to be murdered will be after Ray Santiago."

"Then we'll just have to find him first. You're going to have to shake this off," he told her. "I know it's a tough break all around, but the Slagerman case is your priority now. The guy's got himself a real slick lawyer."

"I can handle it."

"Never figured otherwise. Give him hell, kid."

"Yeah. Yeah, I will." Deborah hung up and stared blankly into space until her alarm went off at 6:30.

* * *

"Hey! Hey, beautiful." Jerry Bower charged up the courthouse steps after Deborah. "Boy, that's concentration," he panted when he finally snagged her arm and stopped her. "I've been calling you for half a block."

"Sorry. I'm due in court in fifteen minutes."

He gave her a quick, smiling going-over. She'd pinned her hair back into a simple twist and wore pearl buttons at her ears. Her red linen suit was severely tailored and still managed to show off each subtle curve. The result was competent, professional and completely feminine.

"If I was on the jury, I'd give you a guilty verdict before you finished your opening statement. You look incredible."

"I'm a lawyer," she said tightly. "Not Miss November."

"Hey." He had to race up three more steps to catch her. "Hey, look, I'm sorry. That was a poorly phrased compliment."

She found a slippery hold on her temper. "No, I'm sorry. I'm a little touchy this morning."

"I heard about Parino."

With a grim nod, Deborah continued up the steps to the high carved doors of city courthouse. "News travels fast."

"He was a walking statistic, Deb. You can't let it get to you."

"He deserved his day in court," she said as she crossed the marble floor of the lobby and started toward a bank of elevators. "Even he deserved that. I knew he was afraid, but I didn't take it seriously enough."

"Do you think it would have mattered?"

"I don't know." It was that single question she would have to live with. "I just don't know."

"Look, the mayor's got a tough schedule today. There's this dinner tonight, but I can probably slip out before the brandy and cigar stage. How about a late movie?"

"I'm lousy company, Jerry."

"You know that doesn't matter."

"It matters to me." A ghost of a smile touched her lips. "I'd bite your head off again and hate myself." She stepped into the elevator.

"Counselor." Jerry grinned and gave her a thumbs-up before the doors slid shut.

The press was waiting for her on the fourth floor. Deborah had expected no less. Moving quickly, she waded through them, dispensing curt answers and no comments.

"Do you really expect to get a jury to convict a pimp for knocking around a couple of his girls?"

"I always expect to win when I go into court."

"Are you going to put the prostitutes on the stand?"

"Former prostitutes," she corrected, and let the question go unanswered.

"Is it true Mitchell assigned you to this case because you're a woman?"

"The D.A. doesn't choose his prosecutors by their sex."

"Do you feel responsible for the death of Carl Parino?"

That stopped her on the threshold of the courtroom. She looked around and saw the reporter with curly brown hair, hungry brown eyes and a sarcastic smirk. Chuck Wisner. She'd run foul of him before and would again. In his daily column in the *World,* he preferred the sensational to the factual.

"The D.A.'s office regrets that Carl Parino was murdered and not allowed his day in court."

In a quick, practiced move, he blocked her way. "But do you feel responsible? After all, you're the one who turned the deal."

She choked back the urge to defend herself and met his eyes levelly. "We're all responsible, Mr. Wisner. Excuse me."

He simply shifted, crowding her back from the door. "Any more encounters with Nemesis? What can you tell us about your personal experiences with the city's newest hero?"

She could feel her temper begin to fray, strand by strand. Worse, she knew that was exactly what he was hoping for. "Nothing that could compete with your fabrications. Now if you'll move aside, I'm busy."

"Not too busy to socialize with Gage Guthrie. Are you and he romantically involved? It makes a wild kind of triangle, doesn't it? Nemesis, you, Guthrie."

"Get a life, Chuck," she suggested, then elbowed him aside.

She barely had enough time to settle behind the prosecutor's table and open her briefcase when the jury filed in. She and the defense counsel had taken two days to select them, and she was satisfied with the mix of genders and races and walks of life. Still, she would have to convince those twelve men and women that a couple of prostitutes deserved justice.

Turning slightly, she studied the two women in the first row. They had both followed her instructions and dressed simply, with a minimum of makeup and hair spray. She knew they were on trial today, as much as the man charged with assault and battery. They huddled together, two young, pretty women who might have been mistaken for college students. Deborah sent them a reassuring smile before she shifted again.

James P. Slagerman sat at the defense table. He was thirty-two, dashingly blond and handsome in a dark suit and tie. He looked precisely like what he claimed he was, a young executive. His escort service was perfectly legitimate. He paid his taxes, contributed to charity and belonged to the Jaycees.

It would be Deborah's primary job to convince the jury that he was no different than a street pimp, taking his cut from the sale of a woman's body. Until she did that, she had no hope of convicting him on assault.

As the bailiff announced the judge, the courtroom rose.

Deborah kept her opening statement brief, working the jury, dispensing facts. She didn't attempt to dazzle them. She was already aware that this was the defense counsel's style. Instead, she would underplay, drawing their attention with the contrast of simplicity.

She began her direct examination by calling the doctor who had attended Marjorie Lovitz. With a few brief questions she established the extent of Marjorie's injuries on the night she and Suzanne McRoy had been brought into Emergency. She wanted the jury to hear of the broken jaw, the blackened eyes, the cracked ribs, even before she entered the photographs taken of the women that night into evidence.

She picked her way slowly, carefully through the technicalities, doctors, ambulance attendants, uniformed cops, social workers. She weathered her opponent's parries. By the noon recess, she had laid her groundwork.

She hustled Marjorie and Suzanne into a cab and took them across town for lunch and a last briefing.

"Do I have to go on the stand today, Miss O'Roarke?" Marjorie fidgeted in her seat and ate nothing. Though her bruises had faded over the weeks since the beating, her jaw still tended to ache. "Maybe what the doctors and all said was enough, and Suzanne and I won't have to testify."

"Marjorie." She laid a hand over the girl's and found it ice-cold and trembly. "They'll listen to the doctors, and they'll look at the pictures. They'll believe you and Suzanne were beaten. But it's you, both of you, who will convince them that Slagerman was the one who did it, that he is not the nice young businessman he pretends to be. Without you, he'll walk away and do it again."

Suzanne bit her lip. "Jimmy says he's going to get off anyway. That people will know we're whores, even though you helped us get regular jobs. He says when it's over he's going to find us, and hurt us real bad."

"When did he say that?"

"He called last night." Marjorie's eyes filled with tears. "He found out where we're living and he called. He said he was going to mess us up." She wiped at a tear with the heel of her hand. "He said he was going to make us wish we'd never started this. I don't want him to hurt me again."

"He won't. I can't help you unless you help me. Unless you trust me."

For the next hour, she talked, soothing, bullying, cajoling and promising. At two o'clock, both frightened women were back in court.

"The State calls Marjorie Lovitz," Deborah announced, and flicked a cool glance at Slagerman.

Gage slipped into the courtroom just as she called her first witness for the afternoon session. He'd had to cancel two meetings in order to be there. The need to see her had been a great deal stronger than the need to hear quarterly reports. It had been, Gage admitted, stronger than any need he had ever experienced.

For three days he'd kept his distance. Three very long days.

Life was often a chess match, he thought. And you took what time you needed to work out your next move. He chose a seat in the rear of the courtroom and settled back to watch her work.

"How old are you, Marjorie?" Deborah asked.

"Twenty-one."

"Have you always lived in Urbana?"

"No, I grew up in Pennsylvania."

With a few casual questions, she helped Marjorie paint a picture of her background, the poverty, the unhappiness, the parental abuse.

"When did you come to the city?"

"About four years ago."

"When you were seventeen. Why did you come?"

"I wanted to be an actress. That sounds pretty dumb, but I used to be in plays in school. I thought it would be easy."

"Was it?"

"No. No, it was hard. Real hard. Most of the time I didn't even get to audition, you know? And I ran out of money. I got a job waiting tables part-time, but it wasn't enough. They turned off the heat, and the lights."

"Did you ever think of going home?"

"I couldn't. My mother said if I took off then she was done with me. And I guess I thought, I still thought I could do okay, if I just got a break."

"Did you get one?"

"I thought I did. This guy came into the grill where I worked. We got kind of friendly, talking, you know. I told him how I was an actress. He said he'd known it as soon as he'd seen me, and what was I doing working in a dump like that when I was so pretty, and so talented. He told me he knew lots of people, and that if I came to work for him, he'd introduce me. He gave me a business card and everything."

"Is the man you met that night in the courtroom, Marjorie?"

"Sure, it was Jimmy." She looked down quickly at her twisting fingers. "Jimmy Slagerman."

"Did you go to work for him?"

"Yeah. I went the next day to his offices. He had a whole suite, all these desks and phones and leather chairs. A real nice place, uptown. He called it Elegant Escorts. He said I could make a hundred dollars a night just by going to dinner and parties with these businessmen. He even bought me clothes, pretty clothes and had my hair done and everything."

"And for this hundred dollars a night, all you had to do was go to dinner or parties?"

"That's what he told me, at first."

"And did that change?"

"After a while . . . he took me out to nice restaurants and places. Dress rehearsals, he called them. He bought me flowers and . . ."

"Did you have sex with him?"

"Objection. Irrelevant."

"Your Honor, the witness's relationship, her physical relationship with the defendant is very relevant."

"Overruled. You'll answer the question, Miss Lovitz."

"Yes. I went to bed with him. He treated me so nice. After, he gave me money—for the bills, he said."

"And you accepted it?"

"Yes. I guess I knew what was going on. I knew, but I pretended I didn't. A few days later, he told me he had a customer for me. He said I was to dress up real nice, and go out to dinner with this man from D.C."

"What instructions were you given by Mr. Slagerman?"

"He said, 'Marjorie, you're going to have to earn that hundred dollars.' I said I knew that, and he told me I was going to have to be real nice to this guy. I said I would."

"Did Mr. Slagerman define 'nice' for you, Marjorie?"

She hesitated, then looked down at her hands again. "He said I was to do whatever I was told. That if the guy wanted me to go back to his hotel after, I had to go or I wouldn't get my money. It was all acting, he said. I acted like I enjoyed the guy's company, like I was attracted to him, and I acted like I had a great time in bed with him."

"Did Mr. Slagerman specifically tell you that you would be required to have sex with this customer?"

"He said it was part of the job, the same as smiling at bad jokes. And if I was good at it, he'd introduce me to this director he knew."

"And you agreed?"

"He made it sound okay. Yes."

"And were there other occasions when you agreed to exchange sex for money in your capacity as an escort for Mr. Slagerman's firm?"

"Objection."

"I'll rephrase." She flicked a glance at the jury. "Did you continue in Mr. Slagerman's employ?"

"Yes, ma'am."

"For how long?"

"Three years."

"And were you satisfied with the arrangement?"

"I don't know."

"You don't know if you were satisfied?"

"I got used to the money," Marjorie said, painfully honest. "And after a while you get so you can forget what you're doing, if you think about something else when it's going on."

"And was Mr. Slagerman happy with you?"

"Sometimes." Fearful, she looked up at the judge. "Sometimes he'd get real mad, at me or one of the other girls."

"There were other girls?"

"About a dozen, sometimes more."

"And what did he do when he got mad?"

"He'd smack you around."

"You mean he'd hit you?"

"He'd just go crazy and—"

"Objection."

"Sustained."

"Did he ever strike you, Marjorie?"

"Yes."

Deborah let the simplicity of the answer hang over the jury. "Will you tell me the events that took place on the night of February 25 of this year?"

As she'd been instructed, Marjorie kept her eyes on Deborah and didn't let them waver back to Slagerman. "I had a job, but I got sick. The flu or something. I had a fever and my stomach was really upset. I couldn't keep anything down. Suzanne came over to take care of me."

"Suzanne?"

"Suzanne McRoy. She worked for Jimmy, too, and we got to be friends. I just couldn't get up and go to work,

so Suzanne called Jimmy to tell him." Her hands began
to twist in her lap. "I could hear her arguing with him
over the phone, telling him I was sick. Suzanne said he
could come over and see for himself if he didn't believe
her."

"And did he come over?"

"Yes." The tears started, big silent drops that cruised
down her cheeks. "He was really mad. He was yelling at
Suzanne, and she was yelling back, telling him I was
really sick, that I had a fever line a hundred and two. He
said—" She licked her lips. "He said we were both lazy,
lying sluts. I heard something crash and she was crying.
I got up, but I was dizzy." She rubbed the heel of her
hands under her eyes, smearing mascara. "He came into
the bedroom. He knocked me down."

"You mean he bumped into you?"

"No, he knocked me down. Backhanded me, you
know?"

"Yes. Go on."

"Then he told me to get my butt up and get dressed.
He said the customer had asked for me, I was going to
do it. He said all I had to do was lie on my back and
close my eyes anyway." She fumbled for a tissue, blew
her nose. "I told him I was sick, that I couldn't do it. He
was yelling and throwing things. Then he said he'd show
me how it felt to be sick. And he started hitting me."

"Where did he hit you?"

"Everywhere. In the face, in the stomach. Mostly my
face. He just wouldn't stop."

"Did you call for help?"

"I couldn't. I couldn't hardly breathe."

"Did you try to defend yourself?"

"I tried to crawl away, but he kept coming after me,
kept hitting me. I passed out. When I woke up, Suz-

anne was there, and her face was all bloody. She called an ambulance."

Gently Deborah continued to question. When she took her seat at the prosecutor's table, she prayed that Marjorie would hold up under cross-examination.

After almost three hours on the witness stand, Marjorie was pale and shaky. Despite the defense counselor's attempt to destroy her character, she stepped down looking young and vulnerable.

And it was that picture, Deborah thought with satisfaction, that would remain in the jury's mind.

"Excellent job, Counselor."

Deborah turned her head and, with twin pricks of annoyance and pleasure, glanced up at Gage. "What are you doing here?"

"Watching you work. If I ever need a lawyer..."

"I'm a prosecutor, remember?"

He smiled. "Then I'll just have to make sure I don't get caught breaking the law." When she stood, he took her hand. A casual gesture, even a friendly one. She couldn't have said why it seemed so possessive. "Can I offer you a lift? Dinner, dessert? A quiet evening?"

And she'd said he wouldn't tempt her again. Fat chance. "I'm sorry, I have something to do."

Tilting his head, he studied her. "I think you mean it."

"I do have work."

"No, I mean that you're sorry."

His eyes were so deep, so warm, she nearly sighed. "Against my better judgment, I am." She started out of the courtroom into the hall.

"Just the lift then."

She sent him a quick, exasperated look over her shoulder. "Didn't I tell you once how I felt about persistent men?"

"Yes, but you had dinner with me anyway."

She had to laugh. After all the tense hours in court, it was a relief. "Well, since my car's in the shop, I could use a lift."

He stepped into the elevator with her. "It's a tough case you've taken on here. And a reputation maker."

Her eyes cooled. "Really?"

"You're getting national press."

"I don't take cases for clippings." Her voice was as frigid as her eyes.

"If you're going to be in for the long haul, you'll have to develop a thicker skin."

"My skin's just fine, thanks."

"I noticed." Relaxed, he leaned back against the wall. "I think anyone who knows you realizes the press is a by-product, not the purpose. You're making a point here, that no one, no matter who or what they are, should be victimized. I hope you win."

She wondered why it should have unnerved her that he understood precisely what she was reaching for. "I will win."

She stepped out of the elevator into the marble lobby.

"I like your hair that way," he commented, pleased to see he'd thrown her off. "Very cool, very competent. How many pins would I have to pull out to have it fall loose?"

"I don't think that's—"

"Relevant?" he supplied. "It is to me. Everything about you is, since I don't seem to be able to stop thinking about you."

She kept walking quickly. It was typical, she imagined, that he would say such things to a woman in a lobby swarming with people—and make her feel as though they were completely alone. "I'm sure you've managed to keep busy. I noticed a picture of you in this morning's paper—there was a blonde attached to your arm. Candidate Tarrington's dinner party." She set her teeth when he kept smiling. "You switch your allegiances quickly, politically speaking."

"I have no allegiances, politically speaking. I was interested to hear what Fields's opposition had to say. I was impressed."

She remembered the lush blonde in the skinny black dress. "I bet."

This time he grinned. "I'm sorry you weren't there."

"I told you before I don't intend to be part of a horde." At the wide glass doors, she stopped, braced. "Speaking of hordes." Head up, she walked into the crowd of reporters waiting on the courthouse steps.

They fired questions. She fired answers. Still, as annoyed as she was with him, she was grateful to see Gage's big black limo with its hulk of a driver waiting at the curb.

"Mr. Guthrie, what's your interest in this case?"

"I enjoy watching justice at work."

"You enjoy watching gorgeous D.A.s at work." Wisner pushed his way through his associates to shove a recorder into Gage's face. "Come on, Guthrie, what's happening between you and Darling Deb?"

Hearing her low snarl, Gage put a warning hand on Deborah's arm and turned to the reporter. "I know you, don't I?"

Wisner smirked. "Sure. We ran into each other plenty in those bad old days when you worked for the city instead of owning it."

"Yeah. Wisner." He summed the man up with one quick, careless look. "Maybe my memory's faulty, but I don't recall you being as big a jerk then as you are now." He bundled a chuckling Deborah into the limo.

"Nicely done," she said.

"I'll have to consider buying *The World,* just to have the pleasure of firing him."

"I have to admire the way you think." With a sigh, she slipped out of her shoes and shut her tired eyes. She could get used to traveling this way, she thought. Big cushy seats and Mozart playing softly in the speakers. A pity it wasn't reality. "My feet are killing me. I'm going to have to buy a pedometer to see how many miles I put in during an average day in court."

"Will you come home with me if I promise you a foot massage?"

She opened one eye. He'd be good at it, she thought. At massaging a woman's foot—or anything else that happened to ache. "No." She shut her eye again. "I have to get back to my office. And I'm sure there are plenty of other feet you can rub."

Gage opened the glass long enough to give Frank their destination. "Is that what concerns you? The other . . . feet in my life?"

She hated the fact that it did. "They're your business."

"I like yours. Your feet, your legs, your face. And everything in between."

She ignored, tried to ignore, the quick frisson of response. "Do you always try to seduce women in the back of limos?"

"Would you prefer someplace else?"

She opened both eyes. Some things, she thought, were better handled face-to-face. "Gage, I've done some thinking about this situation."

His mouth curved charmingly. "Situation?"

"Yes." She didn't chose to call it a relationship. "I'm not going to pretend I'm not attracted to you, or that I'm not flattered you seem to be attracted to me. But—"

"But?" He picked up her hand, rubbed his lips over her knuckles. The skin there smelled as fresh and clear as rainwater.

"Don't." Her breath caught when he turned her hand over to press a slow, warm kiss in the palm. "Don't do that."

"I love it when you're cool and logical, Deborah. It makes me crazy to see how quickly I can make you heat up." He brushed his lips over her wrist and felt the fast thud of her pulse. "You were saying?"

Was she? What woman could be cool and logical when he was looking at her? Touching her. She snatched her hand away, reminding herself that was precisely the problem. "I don't want this—situation to go any further, for several good reasons."

"Mmm-hmm."

She knocked his hand away when he began to toy with the pearl at her ear. "I mean it. I realize you're used to picking and discarding women like poker chips, but I'm not interested. So ante up with someone else."

Yes, she was heating up nicely. "That's a very interesting metaphor. I could say that there are some winnings I prefer to hold on to rather than gamble with."

Firing up, she turned to him. "Let's get this straight. I'm not this week's prize. I have no intention of being Wednesday's brunette following Tuesday's blonde."

"So, we're back to those feet again."

"You might consider it a joke, but I take my life, personally and professionally, very seriously."

"Maybe too seriously."

She stiffened. "That's my business. The bottom line here is that I'm not interested in becoming one of your conquests. I'm not interested in becoming tangled up with you in any way, shape or form." She glanced over when the limo glided to the curb. "And this is my stop."

He moved quickly, surprising them both, dragging her across the seat so that she lay across his lap. "I'm going to see to it that you're so tangled up you'll never pull free." Hard and sure, his mouth met hers.

She didn't struggle. She didn't hesitate. Every emotion she had felt along the drive had been honed down to one: desire. Irrevocable. Instantaneous. Irresistible. Her fingers dived into his hair as her mouth moved restless and hungry under his.

She wanted, as she had never wanted before. Never dreamed of wanting. The ache of it was so huge it left no room for reason. The rightness of it was so clear it left no room for doubt. There was only the moment—and the taking.

He wasn't patient as he once had been. Instead, his mouth was fevered as it raced over her face, streaked down her throat. With an urgent murmur, she pulled his lips back to hers.

Never before had he known anyone who had matched his needs so exactly. There was a fire burning in her, and he had only to touch to make it leap and spark. He'd known desire before, but not this gnawing, tearing desperation.

He wanted to drag her down on the seat, pull and tug at that slim, tidy suit until she was naked and burning beneath him.

But he also wanted to give her comfort and compassion and love. He would have to wait until she was ready to accept it.

With real regret, he gentled his hands and drew her away. "You're everything I want," he told her. "And I've learned to take what I want."

Her eyes were wide. As the passion faded from them, it was replaced by a dazed fear that disturbed him. "It's not right," she whispered. "It's not right that you should be able to do this to me."

"No, it's not right for either of us. But it's real."

"I won't be controlled by my emotions."

"We all are."

"Not me." Shaky, she reached down for her shoes. "I've got to go."

He reached across her to unlatch the door. "You will belong to me."

She shook her head. "I have to belong to myself first." Climbing out, she bolted.

Gage watched her retreat before he opened his fisted hand. He counted six hairpins and smiled.

Deborah spent the evening with Suzanne and Marjorie in their tiny apartment. Over the Chinese takeout she'd supplied, she discussed the case with them. It helped, pouring herself into her work helped. It left little time to brood about Gage and her response to him. A response that worried her all the more since she had felt much the same stunning sexual pull toward another man.

Because she wanted to turn to both, she couldn't turn to either. It was a matter of ethics. To Deborah, when a woman began to doubt her ethics, she had to doubt everything.

It helped to remind herself that there were things she could control. Her work, her life-style, her ambitions. Tonight she hoped to do something to control the outcome of the case she was trying.

Each time the phone rang, she answered it herself while Marjorie and Suzanne sat on the sofa, hands clutched. On the fifth call, she hit pay dirt.

"Marjorie?"

She took a chance. "No."

"Suzanne, you bitch."

Though a grim smile touched her lips, she made her voice shake. "Who is this?"

"You know damn well who it is. It's Jimmy."

"I'm not supposed to talk to you."

"Fine. Just listen. If you think I messed you up before, it's nothing to what I'm going to do to you if you testify tomorrow. You little slut, I picked you up off the street where you were earning twenty a trick and set you up with high rolling johns. I own you, and don't you forget it. Do yourself a favor, Suze, tell that tight-assed D.A. that you've changed your mind, that you and Marjorie lied about everything. Otherwise, I'll hurt you, real bad. Understand?"

"Yes." She hung up and stared at the phone. "Oh, yeah. I understand." Deborah turned to Marjorie and Suzanne. "Keep your door locked tonight and don't go out. He doesn't know it yet, but he just hanged himself."

Pleased with herself, she left them. It had taken a great deal of fast talking to get a tap on Marjorie and Suzanne's line. And it would take more to subpoena Slagerman's phone records. But she would do it. When Slagerman took the stand in a few days, both he and his defense counsel were in for a surprise.

She decided to walk a few blocks before trying to hunt up a cab. The night was steamy. Even the buildings were sweating. Across town there was a cool room, a cool shower, a cool drink waiting. But she didn't want to go home, alone, yet. Alone it would be too easy to think about her life. About Gage.

She had lost control in his arms in the afternoon. That was becoming a habit she didn't care for. It wasn't possible to deny that she was attracted to him. More, pulled toward him in a basic, almost primitive way that was all but impossible to resist.

Yet, she also felt something, a very strong something, for a man who wore a mask.

How could she, who had always prized loyalty, fidelity, above all else, have such deep and dramatic feelings for two different men?

She hoped she could blame her own physicality. To want a man wasn't the same as to need one. She wasn't ready to need one, much less two.

What she needed was control, over her emotions, her life, her career. For too much of her life she had been a victim of circumstance. Her parents' tragic deaths, and the depthless well of fear and grief that had followed it. The demands of her sister's job that had taken them both from city to city to city.

Now she was making her own mark, in her own way, in her own time. For the past eighteen months she had worked hard, with a single-minded determination to earn and deserve the reputation as a strong and honest representative of the justice system. All she had to do was keep moving forward on the same straight path.

As she stepped into the shadows of the World Building, she heard someone whisper her name. She knew that voice, had heard it in her dreams—dreams she'd refused to acknowledge.

He seemed to flow out of the dark, a shadow, a silhouette, then a man. She could see his eyes, the gleam of them behind the mask. The longing came so quickly, so strongly, she nearly moaned aloud.

And when he took her hand to draw her into the shadows, she didn't resist.

"You seem to be making it a habit to walk the streets at night alone."

"I had work." Automatically she pitched her voice low to match his. "Are you following me?"

He didn't answer, but his fingers curled around hers in a way that spoke of possession.

"What do you want?"

"It's dangerous for you." She'd left her hair down, he saw, so that it flowed around her shoulders. "Those who murdered Parino will be watching you." He felt her pulse jump, but not with fear. He recognized the difference between fear and excitement.

"What do you know about Parino?"

"They won't be bothered by the fact you're a woman, not if you're in their way. I don't want to see you hurt."

Unable to help herself, she leaned toward him. "Why?"

As helpless as she, he lifted both of her hands to his lips. He clutched them there, his grip painfully tight. His eyes met hers over them. "You know why."

"It isn't possible." But she didn't, couldn't step away when he brushed a hand over her hair. "I don't know who you are. I don't understand what you do."

"Sometimes neither do I."

She wanted badly to step into his arms, to learn what it was like to be held by him, to have his mouth hot on hers. But there were reasons, she told herself as she held back. Too many reasons. She had to be strong, strong enough not only to resist him, but to use him.

"Tell me what you know. About Parino, about his murder. Let me do my job."

"Leave it alone. That's all I have to tell you."

"You know something. I can see it." With a disgusted breath, she stepped back. She needed the distance, enough of it so that she could hear her brain and remember that she was an officer of the court and he a wrench in the system in which she believed fervently. "It's your duty to tell me."

"I know my duty."

She tossed back her hair. Attracted to him? Hell, no, she was infuriated by him. "Sure, skulking around shadows, dispensing your own personal sense of justice when and where the whim strikes. That's not duty, Captain Bonehead, it's ego." When he didn't respond, she let out a hiss of breath and stepped toward him again. "I could bring you up on charges for withholding information. This is police business, D.A.'s business, not a game."

"No, it isn't a game." His voice remained low, but she thought she caught hints of both amusement and annoyance. "But it has pawns. I wouldn't like to see you used as one."

"I can take care of myself."

"So you continue to say. You're out of your league this time, Counselor. Leave it alone." He stepped back.

"Just hold on." She rushed forward, but he was gone. "Damn it, I wasn't finished arguing with you." Frustrated, she kicked the side of the building, missing his shin by inches. "Leave it alone," she muttered. "Not on your life."

Chapter 5

Dripping, swearing, Deborah rushed toward the door. Knocks at 6:45 a.m. were the same as phone calls at three in the morning. They spelled trouble. When she opened the door and found Gage, she knew her instincts had been on target.

"Get you out of the shower?" he asked her.

She pushed an impatient hand through her wet hair. "Yes. What do you want?"

"Breakfast." Without waiting for an invitation, he strolled inside. "Very nice," he decided.

She'd used the soft cream of ivory with slashes of color—emerald, crimson, sapphire—in the upholstery of the low sofa, in the scatter of rugs on the buffed wood floor. He noted, too, that she had left a damp trail on that same floor.

"Looks like I'm about five minutes early."

Realizing the belt of her robe was loose, she snapped it tight. "No, you're not, because you shouldn't be here at all. Now—"

But he cut her off with a long, hard kiss. "Mmm, you're still wet."

She was surprised the water wasn't steaming off her. Surprised with the sudden urge that poured through her just to lay her head against his shoulder. "Look, I don't have time for this. I have to be in court—"

"In two hours," he said with a nod. "Plenty of time for breakfast."

"If you think I'm going to fix you breakfast, you're doomed to disappointment."

"I wouldn't dream of it." He skimmed a glance down her short silky robe. The single embrace had made him achingly aware that she wore nothing else. "I like you in blue. You should always wear blue."

"I appreciate the fashion advice, but—" She broke off when another knock sounded.

"I'll get it," he offered.

"I can answer my own door." She stomped over to it, her temper fraying. She was never at her best in the morning, even when she only had herself to deal with. "I'd like to know who hung out the sign that said I was having an open house this morning." Wrenching the door open, she was confronted by a white-jacketed waiter pushing an enormous tray.

"Ah, that would be breakfast. Over by the window, I think," Gage said, gesturing the waiter in. "The lady likes a view."

"Yes, sir, Mr. Guthrie."

Deborah set her hands on her hips. It was difficult to take a stand before seven in the morning, but it had to be done. "Gage, I don't know what you're up to, but it isn't going to work. I've tried to make my position clear, and at the moment, I don't have the time or the inclination . . . is that coffee?''

"Yes." Smiling, Gage lifted the big silver pot and poured a cup. The scent of it seduced her. "Would you like some?"

Her mouth moved into a pout. "Maybe."

"You should like this blend." Crossing to her, he held the cup under her nose. "It's one of my personal favorites."

She sipped, shut her eyes. "You don't play fair."

"No."

She opened her eyes to study the waiter, who moved briskly about his business. "What else is there?"

"Shirred eggs, grilled ham, croissants, orange juice— fresh, of course."

"Of course." She hoped she wasn't drooling.

"Raspberries and cream."

"Oh." She folded her tongue inside her mouth to keep it from hanging out.

"Would you like to sit?"

She wasn't a weak woman, Deborah assured herself of that. But there were rich and wonderful smells filling her living room. "I guess." Giving up, she took one of the ladder-back chairs the waiter had pulled up to the table.

Gage passed the waiter a bill and gave him instructions to pick up the dishes in an hour. She couldn't bring herself to complain when Gage topped off her cup.

"I suppose I should ask what brought all this on."

"I wanted to see what you looked like in the morning." He poured juice out of a crystal pitcher. "This seemed like the best way. For now." He toasted her with his cup, his eyes lingering on her face, free of makeup and unframed by her slicked-back hair. "You're beautiful."

"And you're charming." She touched the petals of the red rose beside her plate. "But that doesn't change anything." Thoughtful, she tapped a finger on the peach-colored cloth. "Still, I don't see any reason to let all this food go to waste."

"You're a practical woman." He'd counted on it. "It's one of the things I find most attractive about you."

"I don't see what's attractive about being practical." She cut a small slice of ham and slipped it between her lips. His stomach muscles tightened.

"It can be . . . very attractive."

She did her best to ignore the tingles sprinting through her system and concentrate on a safer kind of hunger. "Tell me, do you always breakfast this extravagantly?"

"When it seems appropriate." He laid a hand over hers. "Your eyes are shadowed. Didn't you sleep well?"

She thought of the long and restless night behind her. "No, I didn't."

"The case?"

She only shrugged. Her insomnia had had nothing to do with the case and everything to do with the man she had met in the shadows. Yet now she was here, just as fascinated with, just as frustrated by the man she sat with in the sunlight.

"Would you like to talk about it?"

She glanced up. In his eyes she saw patience, understanding and something beneath it all she knew would burn to the touch. "No." Cautious, she drew her hand away again.

He found himself enjoying the not-so-subtle pursuit and retreat. "You work too hard."

"I do what I have to do. What about you? I don't even know what you do, not really."

"Buy and sell, attend meetings, read reports."

"I'm sure it's more complicated than that."

"And often more boring."

"That's hard to believe."

Steam and fragrance erupted when he broke open a flaky croissant. "I build things, buy things."

She wouldn't be put off that easily. "Such as?"

He smiled at her. "I own this building."

"Trojan Enterprises owns this building."

"Right. I own Trojan."

"Oh."

Her reaction delighted him. "Most of the Guthrie money came from real estate, and that's still the basis. We've diversified quite a bit over the past ten years. So, one branch handles the shipping, another the mining, another the manufacturing."

"I see." He wasn't an ordinary man, she thought. Then again she didn't seem to be attracted to ordinary men lately. "You're a long way from the twenty-fifth."

"Yeah." A shadow flickered into his eyes. "Looks that way." He lifted a spoonful of berries and cream and offered it.

Deborah let the fruit lie on her tongue a moment. "Do you miss it?"

He knew if he kissed her now she would taste sharp, fresh, alive. "I don't let myself miss it. There's a difference."

"Yes." She understood. It was the same way she didn't let herself miss her family, those who were gone and those who were so many miles away.

"You're very appealing when you're sad, Deborah."
He trailed a finger over the back of her hand. "In fact,
irresistible."

"I'm not sad."

"You are irresistible."

"Don't start." She made a production out of pouring more coffee. "Can I ask you a business question?"

"Sure."

"If the owner, or owners, of a particular piece of
property didn't want that ownership publicized, could
they hide it?"

"Easily. Bury it in paper corporations, in different tax
numbers. One corporation owns another, another owns
that, and so on. Why?"

But she leaned forward, waving his question aside.
"How difficult would it be to track down the actual
owners?"

"That would depend on how much trouble they'd
gone to, and how much reason they had to keep their
names off the books."

"If someone was determined enough, and patient
enough, those names could be found?"

"Eventually. If you found the common thread."

"Common thread?"

"A name, a number, a place. Something that would
pop up over and over." He would have been concerned
by her line of questioning if he hadn't been one step
ahead of her. Still, it was best to be cautious. "What are
you up to, Deborah?"

"My job."

Very carefully, he set his cup back in its saucer. "Does
this have anything to do with Parino?"

Her eyes sharpened. "What do you know about Parino?"

"I still have contacts at the twenty-fifth. Don't you have enough to do with the Slagerman trial?"

"I don't have the luxury of working on one case at a time."

"This is one you shouldn't be working on at all."

"Excuse me?" Her tone had dropped twenty degrees.

"It's dangerous. The men who had Parino murdered are dangerous. You don't have any idea what you're playing with."

"I'm not playing."

"No, and neither are they. They're well protected, and well-informed. They'll know what your next move is before you do." His eyes darkened, seemed to turn inward. "If they see you as an obstacle, they'll remove you, very quickly, very finally."

"How do you know so much about the men who killed Parino?"

He brought himself back. "I was a cop, remember? This isn't something you should be involved in. I want you to turn it over to someone else."

"That's ridiculous."

He gripped her hand before she could spring up. "I don't want you hurt."

"I wish people would stop saying that to me." Pulling her hand away, she rose. "This is my case, and it's going to stay mine."

His eyes darkened, but he remained seated. "Ambition is another attractive trait, Deborah. Until you let it blind you."

She turned back to him slowly, fury shimmering around her. "All right, part of it is ambition. But that's not all of it, not nearly. I believe in what I do, Gage, and in my ability to do it well. It started out with a kid named

Rico Mendez. He wasn't a pillar of the community. In fact, he was a petty thief who had already done time, and would have done more. But he was gunned down while standing on a street corner. Because he belonged to the wrong gang, wore the wrong colors.''

She began to pace, her hands gesturing and emphasizing. ''Then his killer is killed, because he talked to me. Because I made a deal with him. So when does it stop, when do we stop and say this is not acceptable, I'll take the responsibility and change it?''

He stood then and came toward her. ''I'm not questioning your integrity, Deborah.''

''Just my judgment?''

''Yes, and my own.'' His hands slid up, inside the sleeves of her robe. ''I care about you.''

''I don't think—''

''No, don't. Don't think.'' He covered her mouth with his, his fingers tightening on her arms as he pulled her against him.

Instant heat, instant need. How was she to fight it? His body was so solid against hers, his lips were so skilled. And she could feel the waves, not just of desire, but of something deeper and truer, pouring out of him and into her. As if he were already inside her.

She was everything. When he held her he didn't question the power she had to both empty his mind and fill it, to sate his hunger even as she incited it. She made him strong; she left him weak. With her, he began, almost, to believe in miracles again.

When he stepped away, his hands were still on her arms. She struggled for balance. How could he do this to her each time, every time, with only a touch?

''I'm not ready for this,'' she managed.

"Neither am I. I don't think it matters." He brought her close again. "I want to see you tonight." He crushed his mouth to hers. "I want to be with you tonight."

"No, I can't." She could hardly breathe. "The trial."

He bit back an oath. "All right. After the trial is over. Neither one of us can keep walking away from this."

"No." He was right. It was time to resolve it. "No, we can't. But I need time. Please don't push me."

"I may have to." He turned for the door, but paused with his hand on the knob. "Deborah, is there someone else?"

She started to deny it, but found she could only be honest with him. "I don't know."

Nodding, he closed the door at his back. With a bitter kind of irony, he realized he was competing with himself.

She worked late that night, poring over papers and law books at the desk in her bedroom. After court she had spent hours cleaning her already clean apartment. It was one of the best ways she knew to relieve tension. Or to ignore it. The other was work, and she had dived into it, knowing sleep was impossible.

As she reached for her mug of coffee, the phone rang.

"Hello."

"O'Roarke? Deborah O'Roarke?"

"Yes, who is this?"

"Santiago."

Instantly alert, she grabbed a pencil. "Mr. Santiago, we've been looking for you."

"Yeah. Right."

"I'd like very much to talk to you. The D.A.'s office is prepared to offer you cooperation and protection."

"Like Parino got?"

She smothered the quick pang of guilt. "You'll be safer with us than on your own."

"Maybe." There was fear in his voice, tight and nervy.

"I'm willing to set up an interview any time you agree to come in."

"No way. I'm not going nowhere. They'd hit me before I got two blocks." He began to talk quickly, words tumbling over each other. "You come to me. Listen, I got more than Parino had. Lots more. I got names, I got papers. You want to hear about it, sister, you come to me."

"All right. I'll have the police—"

"No cops!" His voice turned vicious with terror. "No cops or no deal. You come, and you come alone. That's it."

"We'll do it your way then. When?"

"Now, right now. I'm at the Darcy Hotel, 38 East 167th. Room 27."

"Give me twenty minutes."

"You're sure this is where you want to go, lady?" Though his fare was wearing worn jeans and a T-shirt, the cabbie could see she had too much class for an armpit like the Darcy.

Deborah looked through the hard mean rain that was falling. She could see the dark windows, the scarred surface of the building and the deserted street. "Yes. I don't suppose I could convince you to wait."

"No, ma'am."

"I didn't think so." She pushed a bill through the slot in the thick security glass. "Keep it." Taking a breath, holding it, she plunged into the rain and up the broken steps to the entrance.

In the lobby she stood, dripping. The check-in desk was behind rusty iron bars and was deserted. There was a light, shooting its yellow beam over the sticky linoleum floor. The air smelled of sweat and garbage and something worse. Turning, she started up the stairs.

A baby was crying in long, steady wails. The sound of misery rolled down the graffiti-washed stairwell. Deborah watched something small and quick scuttle past her foot and into a crack. With a shudder, she continued up.

She could hear a man and woman, voices raised in a vicious argument. As she turned into the hallway of the second floor, a door creaked open. She saw a pair of small, frightened eyes before it creaked shut again and a chain rattled into place.

Her feet crunched over broken glass that had once been the ceiling light. Down the dim hall, she heard the bad-tempered squeal of brakes from a television car chase. Lightning flashed outside the windows as the storm broke directly overhead.

At Room 27, she stopped. The raucous television boomed on the other side of the door. Lifting a hand, she knocked hard.

"Mr. Santiago."

When she received no response, she knocked and called again. Cautious, she tried the knob. The door opened easily.

In the gray, flickering light of the television, she saw a cramped room with one dingy window. There were heaps of clothes and garbage. The single dresser had a drawer missing. There was the stench of beer gone hot and food gone bad.

She saw the figure stretched across the bed and swore. Not only would she have the pleasure of conducting an interview in this hellhole, she would have to sober up her witness first.

Annoyed, she switched off the television so that there was only the sound of drumming rain and the shouts of the argument down the hall. She spotted a stained sink bolted to the wall, a chunk of its porcelain missing. It would come in handy, she thought, if she could manage to hold Santiago's head in it.

"Mr. Santiago." She raised her voice as she picked her way across the room, trying to avoid greasy take-out bags and spilled beer. "Ray." Reaching him, she started to shake him by the shoulder, then noted his eyes were open. "I'm Deborah O'Roarke," she began. Then she realized he wasn't looking at her. He wasn't looking at all. Lifting her trembling hand, she saw it was wet with blood.

"Oh, God." She took one stumbling step back, fighting down the hot nausea that churned in her stomach. Another drunken step, then another. She turned and all but ran into a small well-built man with a mustache.

"*Señorita,*" he said quietly.

"The police," she managed. "We have to call the police. He's dead."

"I know." He smiled. She saw the glint of gold in his mouth. And the glint of silver when he lifted the stiletto. "Miss O'Roarke. I've been waiting for you."

He grabbed her by the hair when she lunged toward the door. She cried out in pain, then was silent, deathly still as she felt the prick of the knife at the base of her throat.

"No one listens to screams in a place such as this," he said, and the gentleness in his voice made her shudder as he turned her to face him. "You are very beautiful,

señorita. What a pity it would be to damage that cheek."
Watching her, he laid the shaft of the knife against it.
"You will tell me, *por favor,* what Parino discussed with
you before his . . . accident. All names, all details. And
with whom you shared this information."

Struggling to think through her terror, she looked into
his eyes. And saw her fate. "You'll kill me anyway."

He smiled again. "Wise and beautiful. But there are
ways, and ways. Some are very slow, very painful." He
glided the blade lightly down her cheek. "You will tell
me what I need to know."

She had no names, nothing to bargain with. She had
only her wits. "I wrote them down, I wrote all of it down
and locked it away."

"And told?"

"No one." She swallowed. "I told no one."

He studied her for a moment, twirling the stiletto. "I
think you lie. Perhaps after I show you what I can do
with this, you'll be willing to cooperate. Ah, that cheek.
Like satin. What a pity I must tear it."

Even as she braced, there was another flash of light-
ing and the sound of the window glass crashing.

He was there, all in black, illuminated by a new spear
of lightning. This time the thunder shook the room. Before she could so much as breathe, the knife was at her
throat and a beefy arm banded her waist.

"Come closer," her captor warned, "and I will slit her
throat from ear to ear."

Nemesis stood where he was. He didn't look at her.
Didn't dare. But in his mind's eye he could see her, face
pale with fear. Eyes glazed with it. Was it her fear, or his
own that had made him unable to concentrate, unable to
come into the room as a shadow instead of a man? If he
was able to do so now, to divorce himself from his fear

for her and vanish, would it be a weapon, or would it cause the stiletto to strike home before he could act? He hadn't been quick enough to save her. Now he had to be clever enough.

"If you kill her, you lose your shield."

"A risk we both take. No closer." He slid the blade more truly against her throat until she whimpered.

There was fear now, and fury. "If you hurt her, I will do things to you that even in your own nightmares you have never imagined."

Then he saw the face, the full looping mustache, the gleam of gold. He was back, back on the docks with the smell of fish and garbage, the sound of water lapping. He felt the hot explosion in his chest and nearly staggered.

"I know you, Montega." His voice was low, harsh. "I've been looking for you for a long time."

"So, you have found me." Though his tone was arrogant, Deborah could smell his sweat. It gave her hope. "Put down your weapon."

"I don't have a weapon," Nemesis said, his hands held out from his sides. "I don't need one."

"Then you are a fool." Montega eased his arm from around Deborah's waist and slipped a hand into his pocket. Just as the shot rang out, Nemesis lunged to the side.

It happened so fast. Afterward, Deborah couldn't be sure who had moved first. She saw the bullet smash into the stained wallpaper and plaster of the wall, saw Nemesis fall. With a strength fueled by rage and terror, she slammed her elbow into Montega's stomach.

More concerned with his new quarry than her, he shoved her away. Her head struck the edge of the sink. There was another flash of lightning. Then the dark.

* * *

"Deborah. Deborah, I need you to open your eyes. Please."

She didn't want to. Small vicious explosions were going off behind them. But the voice was so desperate, so pleading. She forced her eyelids to lift. Nemesis swam into focus.

He was holding her, cradling her head, rocking her. For a moment, she could only see his eyes. Beautiful eyes, she thought dizzily. She had fallen in love with them the first time she'd seen them. She had looked through the crowd of people through the dazzle of lights and had seen him, seen them.

With a little groan, she lifted a hand to the knot already forming on her temple. She must be concussed, she thought. The first time she had seen Nemesis she had been in a dark alley. And there had been a knife. Like tonight.

"A knife," she murmured. "He had a knife."

Stunned by relief, he lowered his brow to hers. "It's all right. He didn't get a chance to use it."

"I thought he'd killed you." She lifted a hand to his face, found it warm.

"No."

"Did you kill him?"

His eyes changed. Concern rushed out as fury rushed in. "No." He had seen Deborah crumpled on the floor and had known such blank terror, the kind he thought he'd forgotten how to feel. It had been easy for Montega to get away. But there would be another time. He promised himself that. And he would have his justice. And his revenge.

"He got away?"

"For now."

"You knew him." Over the pounding in her head, she tried to think. "You called him by name."

"Yes, I knew him."

"He had a gun." She squeezed her eyes tight, but the pain continued to roll. "Where did he have a gun?"

"In his pocket. He makes it a habit to ruin his suits."

That was something she would have to consider later. "We have to call the police." She put a hand on his arm for balance and felt the warm stickiness on her fingers. "You're bleeding."

He glanced down to where the bullet had grazed him. "Some."

"How badly?" Ignoring the throbbing in her temple, she pushed away. Before he could answer, she was ripping his sleeve to expose the wound. The long, ugly graze had her stomach doing flip-flops. "We need to stop the bleeding."

She couldn't see his lifted brow, but heard it in his voice. "You could tear your T-shirt into a tourniquet."

"You should be so lucky." She glanced around the room, scrupulously avoiding looking at the form sprawled over the bed. "There's nothing in here that wouldn't give you blood poisoning."

"Try this." He offered her a square of black cloth.

She fumbled with the bandage. "It's my first gunshot wound, but I think this should be cleaned."

"I'll see to it later." He enjoyed having her tend to him. Her fingers were gentle on his skin, her brows drawn together in concentration. She had found a murdered man, had nearly been murdered herself. But she had bounced back and was doing competently what needed to be done.

Practicality. His lips curved slightly. Yes, it could be very attractive. Added to that, he could smell her hair as she bent close, feel the softness of it as it brushed against his cheek. He heard her breathing, slow, steady, under the sound of the quieting rain.

Having done her best, Deborah sat back on her heels. "Well, so much for invulnerability."

He smiled and stopped her heart. "There goes my reputation."

She could only stare, spellbound as they knelt on the floor of the filthy little room. She forgot where she was, who she was. Unable to stop herself, she lowered her gaze to his mouth. What tastes would she find there? What wonders would he show her?

He could barely breathe when she lifted her eyes to his again. In hers he saw passion smoldering, and an acceptance that was terrifying. Her fingers were still on his skin, gently stroking. He could see each quick beat of her heart in the pulse that hammered at her throat.

"I dream of you." He reached out to bring her unresistingly against him. "Even when I'm awake I dream of you. Of touching you." His hands slid up to cup, to caress her breasts. "Of tasting you." Compelled, he buried his mouth at her throat where the flavor and the scent were hot.

She leaned toward him, into him, stunned and shattered by the wildly primitive urges beating in her blood. His lips were like a brand on her skin. And his hands . . . Oh, Lord, his hands. With a deep, throaty moan, she arched back, eager and willing.

And Gage's face swam in front of her eyes.

"No." She jerked away, shocked and shamed. "No, this isn't right."

He cursed himself. Her. Circumstance. How could he have touched her now, here? "No, it isn't." He rose, stepped away. "You don't belong here."

Because she was on the verge of tears, her voice was sharp. "And you do?"

"More than you," he murmured. "Much more than you."

"I was doing my job. Santiago called me."

"Santiago's dead."

"He wasn't." She pressed her fingers to her eyes and prayed for composure. "He called, asked me to come."

"Montega got here first."

"Yes." Telling herself she was strong, she lowered her hands and looked at him. "But how? How did he know where to find Santiago? How did he know I was coming here tonight? He was waiting for me. He called me by name."

Interested, Nemesis studied her. "Did you tell anyone you were coming here tonight?"

"No."

"I'm beginning to believe you are a fool." He swung away from her. "You come here, to a place like this, alone, to see a man who would as soon put a bullet in your brain as speak to you."

"He wouldn't have hurt me. He was terrified, ready to talk. And I know what I'm doing."

He turned back. "You don't begin to know."

"But you do, of course." She pushed at her tousled hair and had fresh pain shooting through her head. "Oh, why the hell don't you go away? Stay away? I don't need this kind of grief from you. I've got work to do."

"You need to go home, leave this to others."

"Santiago didn't call others," she snapped. "He called me, talked to me. And if I had gotten to him first I would know everything I need to know. I don't..." She trailed off as a thought struck. "My phone. Damn it, they've got a tap on my phone. They knew I was coming here tonight. My office phone, too. That's how they knew I was about to get a court order to deal with the antique shop." Her eyes blazed. "Well, we can fix that in a hurry."

She sprang up. The room spun. He caught her before she slid to the floor again.

"You're not going to be doing anything in a hurry for a day or two." Smoothly he hooked an arm under her knees and lifted her.

She liked the feeling of being carried by him, a bit too much. "I walked into this room, Zorro, I'll walk out."

He carried her into the hall. "Are you always so thickheaded?"

"Yes. I don't need your help."

"I can see you're doing just dandy on your own."

"I may have had some trouble before," she said as he started down the stairs. "But now I have a name. Montega. Five-eight, a hundred and sixty. Brown hair, brown eyes, brown mustache. Two gold incisors. It shouldn't be too hard to run a make on him."

He stopped and his eyes were ice. "Montega's mine."

"The law doesn't make room for personal vendettas."

"You're right. The law doesn't." He shifted her slightly as he came to the base of the stairs.

There was something in his tone—disillusionment?— that had her lifting a hand to his cheek. "Was it very bad?"

"Yes." God, how he wished he could turn to her, bury his face in her hair and let her soothe him. "It was very bad."

"Let me help you. Tell me what you know and I swear I'll do everything I can do to see that Montega and whoever is behind him pays for what they've done to you."

She would try. Realizing it moved something in him, even as it frightened him. "I pay my own debts, my own way."

"Damn it, talk about thickheaded." She squirmed as he carried her into the rain. "I'm willing to bend my principles and work with you, to form a partnership, and you—"

"I don't want a partner."

She could feel him stiffen with the words, all but feel the pain rush through him. But she wouldn't soften. Not again. "Fine, just great. Oh, put me down, you can hardly carry me a hundred blocks."

"I don't intend to." But he could have. He could imagine carrying her through the rain to her apartment, inside, to the bed. Instead, he walked to the end of the block, toward the lights and the traffic. At the curb he stopped. "Hail a cab."

"Hail a cab? Like this?"

He wondered why she could make him burn and want to laugh at the same time. He turned his head and watched the heat flare in her eyes as their lips hovered an inch apart. "You can still lift your arm, can't you?"

"Yes, I can lift my arm." She did so, stewing as they stood and waited. After five soaking minutes, a cab cruised up the curb. Miffed as she was, she had to bite back a smile at the way the driver's mouth fell open when he got a load of her companion.

"Jeez, you're him, ain't ya? You're Nemesis. Hey, buddy, want a ride?"

"No, but the lady does." Effortlessly he slid Deborah into the back seat. His gloved hand brushed once over her cheek, like a memory. "I'd try an ice pack and some aspirin."

"Thanks. Thanks a lot. Listen, I'm not finished—"

But he stepped back, disappearing into the dark, thin rain.

"That was really him, wasn't it?" The cabbie craned his neck around to Deborah, ignoring the bad-tempered honks around him. "What'd he do, save your life or something?"

"Or something," she muttered.

"Jeez. Wait till I tell the wife." Grinning, he switched off the meter. "This ride's on me."

Chapter 6

Grunting, his body running with sweat, Gage lifted the weights again. He was on his back on the bench press, stripped down to a pair of jogging shorts. His muscles were singing, but he was determined to reach his quota of a hundred presses. Perspiration soaked his sweatband and ran into his eyes as he concentrated on one small spot on the ceiling. There was a satisfaction even in pain.

He remembered, too well, when he'd been so weak he'd barely been able to lift a magazine. There had been a time when his legs had turned to rubber and his breath had been ragged at trying to walk the length of the hospital corridor. He remembered the frustration of it, and more, the helplessness.

He'd resisted therapy at first, preferring to sit alone and brood. Then he'd used it, like a punishment because he'd been alive and Jack had been dead. The pain had been excruciating.

And one day, weak, sick, darkly depressed, he'd stood weaving in his hospital room, braced against the wall. He'd wished with all of his strength, with all of his will, that he could simply vanish.

And he had.

He'd thought he'd been hallucinating. Going mad. Then, terrified and fascinated, he'd tried it again and again, going so far as to tilt a mirror across the room so that he could watch himself fade back, fade into the pastel wall beside his bed.

He would never forget the morning a nurse came in with his breakfast tray, walked right past him without seeing him, grumbling about patients who didn't stay in bed where they belonged.

And he'd known what he'd brought out of the coma with him. He'd known it had come with him for a purpose.

So therapy had become like a religion, something he'd dedicated every ounce of strength to, every particle of will. He'd pushed himself harder, harder still, until his muscles had toned and firmed. He had thrown himself into lessons in the martial arts, spent hours with weight lifting, the treadmills, the punishing laps in the pool every day.

He had exercised his mind, as well, reading everything, pushing himself to understand the myriad businesses he had inherited, spending hours day after day until he was skilled with complex computer systems.

Now he was stronger, faster, sharper than he had been during his years on the force. But he would never wear a badge again. He would never take another partner.

He would never be helpless.

His breath hissed out, and he continued to lift when Frank strolled in with a tall glass of iced juice.

Setting the glass on the table beside the bench press, Frank watched in silence for a moment. "Pushing it a bit today," he commented. "Course you pushed it a bit yesterday, too, and the day before." Frank grinned. "What is it about some women that makes guys go out and lift heavy objects?"

"Go to hell, Frank."

"She's a looker, all right," he said, unoffended. "Smart, too, I guess, being a lawyer and all. Must be hard to think about her mind though when she looks at you with those big, blue eyes."

With a last grunt, Gage set the bar in the safety. "Go lift a wallet."

"Now, you know I don't do that anymore." His wide face split with a new grin. "Nemesis might get me." He plucked up a towel from the neatly folded pile beside the bench.

Saying nothing, Gage took it and swiped at the sweat on his face and chest.

"How's the arm?"

"Fine." Gage didn't bother to glance at the neat white bandage Frank had used to replace Deborah's effort.

"Must be getting slow. Never known you to catch one before."

"Do you want to be fired?"

"Again? Nah." He waited, patient, while Gage switched to leg presses. "I'm looking for job security. If you go out and get yourself killed, I'll have to go back to fleecing tourists."

"Then I'll have to stay alive. The tourists have enough trouble in Urbana."

"Wouldn't have happened if I'd been with you."

Gage flashed him a look and continued to push. "I work alone. You know the deal."

"She was there."

"And that was the problem. She doesn't belong on the streets, she belongs in a courtroom."

"You don't want her in a courtroom, you want her in the bedroom."

The weights came down with a crash. "Drop it."

He'd known Gage too long to be intimidated. "Look, you're crazy about her, and it's throwing you off, messing up your concentration. It isn't good for you."

"I'm not good for her." He stood and grabbed the glass of juice. "She has feelings for me, and she has feelings for Nemesis. It's making her unhappy."

"So, tell her she's only got feelings for one guy, and make her happy."

"What the hell am I supposed to do?" He drained the glass and barely prevented himself from heaving it against the wall. "Take her out to dinner, and over cocktails I could say, oh, by the way, Deborah, besides being a businessman and a pillar of the damn community, I have this sideline. An alter ego. The press likes to call him Nemesis. And we're both nuts about you. So, when I take you to bed, do you want it with the mask or without?"

Frank considered a moment. "Something like that."

With a half laugh, Gage set down the glass. "She's a straight arrow, Frank. I know, because I used to be one myself. She sees things in black and white—the law and the crime." Suddenly tired, he looked out over the sparkling water of the pool. "She'd never understand what I do or why I do it. And she'd hate me for lying to her, because every time I'm with her, I'm deceiving her."

"I don't think you're giving her enough credit. You've got reasons for what you do."

"Yeah." Absently he touched the jagged scar on his chest. "I've got reasons."

"You could make her understand. If she really does have feelings for you, she'd have to understand."

"Maybe, just maybe she'd listen, even accept without agreeing. She might even forgive the lies. But what about the rest?" He set his hand down on the bench, waited, watched it disappear into the damp leather. "How do I ask her to share her life with a freak?"

Frank swore once, violently. "You're not a freak. You've got a gift."

"Yeah." Gage lifted his hand, flexed his fingers. "But I'm the one who has to live with it."

At twelve-fifteen sharp, Deborah walked into City Hall. She made her way to the mayor's office, walking under the stern-faced portraits of former mayors, governors, presidents. She moved past marble busts of the country's founding fathers. The current mayor of Urbana liked having his walls lined with tradition, his floor carpeted in red.

She didn't begrudge him. In fact, Deborah appreciated the hushed, reverential feel of tradition. She enjoyed walking past the doors and hearing the quiet hum of keyboards, the click of copiers, the muted phone conversations as people worked for the city.

She paused in the reception area. Tucker Fields's secretary glanced up and, recognizing her, smiled. "Miss O'Roarke. He's expecting you. Just let me buzz him."

Within an efficient twenty seconds, she was escorted into the mayor's office. Fields sat behind his desk, a trim and tidy man with a fringe of snowy hair and the ruddy outdoor complexion of his farmer forebears. Beside him, Jerry looked like a preppy executive.

Fields had earned a reputation during his six years in office as a man not afraid to get his hands dirty to keep his city clean.

At the moment, his jacket was off, his white shirt-sleeves rolled up his sinewy forearms. His tie was askew and he reached up to straighten it as Deborah entered.

"Deborah, always a pleasure to see you."

"Good to see you, Mayor. Hello, Jerry."

"Have a seat, have a seat." Fields gestured her to a chair as he settled back against the cushy leather of his own. "So, how's the Slagerman trial going?"

"Very well. I think he'll take the stand after the noon recess."

"And you're ready for him."

"More than."

"Good, good." He waved in his secretary as she came to the door with a tray. "I thought since I'm making you miss lunch, I could at least offer you some coffee and a Danish."

"Thank you." She took the cup, exchanged idle conversation, though she knew she hadn't been sent for to drink coffee and chat.

"Heard you had some excitement last night."

"Yes." It was no more than she'd expected. "We lost Ray Santiago."

"Yes, I heard. It's unfortunate. And this Nemesis character, he was there, as well?"

"Yes, he was."

"He was also there the night the antique store on Seventh blew up." Steepling his fingers, Fields sat back. "One might begin to think he was involved."

"No, not in the way you mean. If he hadn't been there last night, I wouldn't be sitting here now." Though it annoyed her, she was compelled to defend him. "He's not a criminal—at least not in the standard sense."

The mayor merely lifted a brow. "In whatever sense, I prefer to have the police enforce the law in my city."

"Yes, I agree."

Satisfied, he nodded. "And this man . . ." He pushed through the papers on his desk. "Montega?"

"Enrico Montega," Deborah supplied. "Also known as Ricardo Sanchez and Enrico Toya. A Colombian national who entered the U.S. about six years ago. He's suspected of the murder of two drug merchants in Columbia. He was based in Miami for a while, and Vice there has a fat file on him. As does Interpol. Allegedly, he is the top enforcer on the East Coast. Four years ago, he murdered a police officer, and seriously wounded another." She paused, thinking of Gage.

"You've been doing your homework," Fields commented.

"I always like a firm foundation when I go after someone."

"Hmm. You know, Deborah, Mitchell considers you his top prosecutor." Fields grinned. "Not that he'd admit it. Mitch doesn't like to hand out compliments."

"I'm aware of that."

"We're all very pleased with your record, and particularly with the way the Slagerman case seems to be going. Both Mitch and I agree that we want you to concentrate more fully on your litigation. So, we've decided to take you off this particular case."

She blinked, stunned. "I beg your pardon?"

"We've decided you should turn your notes, your files over to another D.A."

"You're pulling me?"

He held up a hand. "We're simply beefing up the police investigation. With your caseload, we prefer to have you turn over your files on this to someone else."

She set her cup down with a snap. "Parino was mine."

"Parino is dead."

She shot a glance at Jerry, but he only lifted his hands. She rose, fighting to hold her temper. "This sprang out of that. All of it. This is my case, it has been all along."

"And you've endangered yourself, and the case, twice already."

"I've been doing my job."

"Someone else will be doing it, this part of it, after today." He spread his hands. "Deborah, this isn't a punishment, merely a shifting of responsibilities."

She shook her head and snatched up her briefcase. "Not good enough, not nearly. I'm going to speak with Mitchell myself." Turning, she stormed out. She had to struggle to maintain her dignity and not give in to the urge to slam the door behind her.

Jerry caught up with her at the elevators. "Deb, wait."

"Don't even try it."

"What?"

"To soothe and placate." After jamming the Down button, she whirled on him. "What the hell is this, Jerry?"

"Like the mayor said—"

"Don't hand me that. You knew, you knew what was going on, why I was being called in, and you didn't tell me. Not even a warning so I could prepare myself."

"Deb—" He laid a hand on her shoulder, but she shrugged it off. "Look, not that I don't agree with everything the mayor said—"

"You always do."

"I didn't know. I didn't know, damn it," he repeated when she only stared at him. "Not until ten o'clock this morning. And whatever I think, I would have told you."

She stopped pounding her fist against the Down button. "Okay, I'm sorry I jumped all over you. But it's not right. Something's not right about all this."

"You nearly got yourself killed," he reminded her. "When Guthrie came in this morning—"

"Gage?" she interrupted. "Gage was here?"

"The ten-o'clock appointment."

"I see." Hands fisted, she whirled back to the elevator. "So he's behind it."

"He was concerned, that's all. He suggested—"

"I get the picture." She cut him off again and stepped into the elevator. "This isn't finished. And you can tell your boss I said so."

She had to bank her temper when she walked into court. Personal feelings, personal problems had no place here. There were two frightened young women and the justice system depending on her.

She sat, taking careful notes as the defense counsel questioned Slagerman. She blanked Gage and his handiwork out of her mind.

When it came time for cross-examination, she was ready. She remained seated a moment, studying Slagerman.

"You consider yourself a businessman, Mr. Slagerman?"

"Yes."

"And your business consists of hiring escorts, both male and female, for clients?"

"That's right. Elegant Escorts provides a service, finding suitable companions for other businessmen and women, often from out of town."

She let him ramble a few moments, describing his profession. "I see." Rising, she strolled past the jury. "And is it in—let's say the job description—of any of your employees to exchange sex for money with these clients?"

"Absolutely not." Attractive and earnest, he leaned forward. "My staff is well screened and well trained. It's a firm policy that if anyone on staff develops this kind of a relationship with a client, it would result in termination."

"Are you aware that any of your employees have indeed exchanged sex for money?"

"I am now." He aimed a pained look at Suzanne and Marjorie.

"Did you request that Marjorie Lovitz or Suzanne McRoy entertain a client on a sexual level?"

"No."

"But you're aware that they did so?"

If he was surprised by her train of questioning, he didn't bat an eye. "Yes, of course. They admitted to it under oath."

"Yes, they were under oath, Mr. Slagerman. Just as you are. Have you ever struck an employee?"

"Certainly not."

"Yet both Miss Lovitz and Miss McRoy claim, under oath, that you did."

"They're lying." And he smiled at her.

"Mr. Slagerman, didn't you go to Miss Lovitz's apartment on the night of February 25th, angry that she was unable to work, and in your anger, beat her?"

"That's ridiculous."

"You swear that, under oath?"

"Objection. Asked and answered."

"Withdrawn. Mr. Slagerman, have you contacted either Miss Lovitz or Miss McRoy since this trial began?"

"No."

"You have not telephoned either of them?"

"No."

Nodding, she walked back to her table and picked up a stack of papers. "Is the number 555-2520 familiar to you?"

He hesitated. "No."

"That's odd. It's your private line, Mr. Slagerman. Shouldn't you recognize your own private telephone number?"

Though he smiled, she saw the icy hate in his eyes. "I call from it, not to it, so I don't have to remember it."

"I see. And did you, on the night of June 18, use that private line to call the apartment where both Miss Lovitz and Miss McRoy now live?"

"No."

"Objection, Your Honor. This is leading nowhere."

Deborah shifted again, facing the judge and leaving the jury's view of Slagerman unobstructed. "Your Honor. I'll show you where it leads in just a moment."

"Overruled."

"Mr. Slagerman, perhaps you could explain why, according to your phone records, a call was placed from your private line to the number at Miss Lovitz and Miss McRoy's apartment at 10:47 p.m. on June 18?"

"Anybody could have used my phone."

"Your private line?" She lifted a brow. "It's hardly worth having a private line if anyone can use it. The caller identified himself as Jimmy. You are known as Jimmy, aren't you?"

"Me and a lot of other people."

"Did you speak to me on the phone on the night of June 18?"

"I've never spoken with you on the phone."

She smiled coolly and moved closer to the chair. "Have you ever noticed, Mr. Slagerman, how to some men all women's voices sound alike? How, to some men, all women look alike? How to some men, women's bodies are for one purpose?"

"Your Honor." Defense counsel leaped to his feet.

"Withdrawn." Deborah kept her eyes level with Slagerman's. "Can you explain, Mr. Slagerman, how someone using your private line, using your name, called Miss McRoy on the night of June 18? And how when I answered the phone, this person, using your line and your name, mistook my voice for hers, and threatened Miss McRoy?" She waited a beat. "Would you like to know what that person said?"

Sweat was beading on his upper lip. "You can make up whatever you want."

"That's true. Fortunately we had a tap on Miss McRoy's phone. I have the transcript." She turned over a sheet of paper. "Should I refresh your memory?"

She had won. Though there were still closing arguments to take place, she knew she had won. Now, as she stormed through the Justice Building, she had other business to tend to.

She found Mitchell in his office, a phone to his ear. He was a big bull-chested man who had played linebacker in college. Pictures of him in his jersey were scattered on the wall among his degrees. He had short red hair and a sprinkling of freckles that did nothing to soften his leathered looks.

When he spotted Deborah, he waved her in, gestured toward a chair. But she remained standing until he'd completed his call.

"Slagerman?"

"I've got him nailed." She took a step closer to the desk. "You sold me out."

"That's bull."

"What the hell do you call it? I get pulled into the mayor's office and get the brush-off. Damn it, Mitch, this is my case."

"It's the state's case," he corrected, chomping on the end of his unlit cigar. "You're not the only one who can handle it."

"I made Parino, I made the deal." She slapped her palms down on his desk so they were eye to eye. "I'm the one who's been busting my tail over this."

"And you've been overstepping your bounds."

"You're the one who taught me that trying a case takes more than putting on a pin-striped suit and dancing in front of a jury. I know my job, damn it."

"Going to see Santiago alone was an error in judgment."

"Now, that *is* bull. He called me. He asked for me. You tell me what you'd have done if he'd called you."

He scowled at her. "That's entirely different."

"That's entirely the same," she snapped back, certain from the look in his eyes that he knew it. "If I'd screwed things up I'd expect to get bumped, but I haven't. I'm the one who's been sweating and frying my brains over this case. Now when I get a lead, I find out Guthrie chirps up and you and the mayor keel over. Still the old boy's network, is it, Mitch?"

He stabbed the cigar toward her face. "Don't pull that feminist crap on me. I don't care what way you button your shirt."

"I'm telling you, Mitch, if you pull me off this without good cause, I'm gone. I can't work for you if I can't depend on you, so I might as well go out on my own and take on divorce cases for three hundred an hour."

"I don't like ultimatums."

"Neither do I."

He leaned back, measuring her. "Sit down."

"I don't want—"

"Damn it, O'Roarke, sit."

Tight-lipped and fuming, she did. "So?"

He rolled the cigar between his fingers. "If Santiago had called me, I would have gone, just like you. But," he continued before she could speak, "your handling of this case isn't the only reason I've considered pulling you."

"Considered" took her position back several notches. Calming a bit, she nodded. "Well, then?"

"You've been getting a lot of press on this."

"I hardly see what that has to do with it."

"Did you see this morning's paper?" He snatched it up from his desk and waved it in her face. "Read the headline?" Because she had, and had winced over it already, she simply shrugged. Darling Deb Swept Through City In Arms of Nemesis.

"So, some cab driver wanted his name in the paper, what does that have to do with the case?"

"When my prosecutors start having their names linked with the masked marauder, it has everything to do with everything." He popped the cigar back in his mouth, gnashing it. "I don't like the way you keep running into him."

Neither did she. "Look, if the police can't stop him, I can hardly be responsible for his popping up all over the place. And I'd hate to think you'd take me off a case because some jerk had to fill his column."

Personally Mitch hated the weasely reporter. And he hadn't cared for the strong-arm tactics the mayor had used. "You've got two weeks."

"That's hardly enough time to—"

"Two weeks, take it or leave it. You bring me something we can take to a jury, or I pass the ball. Got it?"

"Yeah." She rose. "I got it."

She stormed out, past snickering associates. A paper was tacked on the door of her office. Someone had used magic markers and highlighter pens to draw a caricature of Deborah being carried in the arms of a lantern-jawed, muscle-bound masked man. Under it was a caption. The Continuing Adventures Of Darling Deb.

On a snarl, she ripped it down, balling it into her pocket as she stomped out. She had another stop to make.

She kept her finger pressed to the button of Gage's doorbell until Frank pulled the door open.

"Is he in?"

"Yes, ma'am." He stepped back as she pushed past him. He'd seen furious women before. Frank would have preferred to have faced a pack of hungry wolves.

"Where?"

"He's up in his office. I'll be glad to tell him you're here."

"I'll announce myself," she said as she started up the steps.

Frank looked after her, lips pursed. He considered buzzing Gage on the intercom and giving him fair warning. But he only grinned. Surprises were good for you.

Deborah didn't bother to knock, but pushed open the door and strode in. Gage was behind his desk, a phone in one hand, a pen in the other. Computer screens blinked. Across from him sat a trim, middle-aged woman with a steno pad. At Deborah's unannounced entrance she rose and glanced curiously at Gage.

"I'll get back to you," he said into the receiver before lowering it to the cradle. "Hello, Deborah."

She tossed her briefcase onto a chair. "I think you might prefer to have this conversation in private."

He nodded. "You can transcribe those notes tomorrow, Mrs. Brickman. It's late. Why don't you go home?"

"Yes, sir." She gathered her things and made a fast, discreet exit.

Deborah hooked her thumbs in the pockets of her skirt. Like a gunfighter hooking thumbs in a holster. He'd seen her take that pose in court. "It must be nice," she began, "sitting up here in your lofty tower and dispensing orders. I bet it feels just dandy. Not all of us are so fortunate. We don't have enough money to buy castles, or private planes or thousand-dollar suits. We work on the streets. But most of us are pretty good at our jobs, and happy enough." As she spoke, she walked slowly toward him. "But you know what makes us mad, Gage? You know what really ticks us off? That's when someone in one of those lofty towers sticks his rich, influential nose in our business. It makes us so mad that we think real hard about taking a punch at that interfering nose."

"Should we break out the boxing gloves?"

"I prefer my bare hands." As she had in Mitchell's office, she slapped them down on his desk. "Who the hell do you think you are, going to the mayor, pressuring him to take me off this case?"

"I went to the mayor," he said slowly, "and gave him my opinion."

"Your opinion." She blew a breath between her teeth and snatched up an onyx paperweight from the desk. Though she gave careful consideration to heaving it through the plate glass at his back, she contented herself with passing it from hand to hand. "And I bet he just fell all over himself to accommodate you and your thirty million."

Gage watched her pace and waited until he was sure he could speak rationally. "He agreed with me that you're more suitable to a courtroom than a murder scene."

"Who are you to say what's more suitable for me?" She whirled back, her voice rich with fury. "I say it, not you. All my life I've prepared myself for this job and I'm not having anyone come along and tell me I'm not suitable for any case I take on." She snapped the paperweight back on the desk, a hard crack of stone against stone. "You stay out of my business, and out of my life."

No, he realized, he wasn't going to be able to be rational. "Are you finished?"

"No. Before I leave I want you to know that it didn't work. I'm still on this case, and I'm staying on. So you wasted your time, and mine. And lastly, I think you're arrogant, officious and overbearing."

His hands were fisted beneath the desk. "Is that all?"

"You bet it is." She snatched up her briefcase, turned on her heel and headed for the door.

Gage pushed a button under the desk and had the locks snap into place. "I'm not," he said quietly.

She hadn't known she could be more furious. But as she spun back to him, a red haze formed in front of her eyes. "Unlock that door immediately, or I'll have you up on charges."

"You've had your say, Counselor." He rose. "Now I'll have mine."

"Not interested."

He came around the desk, but only leaned back against it. He didn't trust himself to approach her, not yet. "You've got all the evidence, don't you, Counselor? All your neat little facts. So, I'll save time and plead guilty as charged."

"Then we have nothing more to say."

"Isn't the prosecution interested in motive?"

She tossed back her head, bracing as he crossed to her. Something about the way he moved just then, slowly, soundlessly, set off a flash of memory. But it was gone, overwhelmed by her own temper.

"Motive isn't relevant in this case, results are."

"You're wrong. I went to the mayor, I asked him to use his influence to have you taken off the case. But I'm guilty of more than that—I'm guilty of being in love with you."

Her tensed hands went limp at her side so that the briefcase fell to the floor. Though she opened her mouth to speak, she could say nothing.

"Amazing." His eyes were dark and furious as he took that final step toward her. "A sharp woman like you being surprised by that. You should have seen it every time I looked at you. You should have seen it every time I touched you." He put his hands on her shoulders. "You should have tasted it, every time I kissed you."

Pushing her back against the door, he brushed his mouth over hers, once, twice. Then he devoured her lips.

Her knees were weak. She hadn't thought it was possible, but they were shaking so she had to hold on to him or slide bonelessly to the floor. Even clinging, she was afraid. For she had seen it, had felt it, had tasted it. But that was nothing compared to hearing him say it, or to hearing the echo of her own voice repeating the words inside her mind.

He was lost in her. And the more she opened to him, the deeper he fell. He took his hands over her face, through her hair, down her body, wanting to touch all of her. And to know as he did, that she trembled in response.

When he lifted his head, she saw the love, and she saw the desire. With them was a kind of war she didn't understand.

"There were nights," he said quietly, "hundreds of nights when I lay awake sweating and waiting for morning. I'd wonder if I'd ever find someone I could love, that I could need. No matter how I drew the fantasy, it's nothing compared to what I feel for you."

"Gage." She lifted her hands to his face, wishing with all her heart. Knowing well that heart was already lost to him. But she remembered that she had swayed close to another man only the night before. "I don't know what I'm feeling."

"Yes, you do."

"All right, I do, but I'm afraid to feel it. It's not fair. I'm not being fair, but I have to ask you to let me think this through."

"I'm not sure I can."

"A little while longer, please. Unlock the door, and let me go."

"It is unlocked." He stepped back to open it for her. But he blocked her exit for one last moment. "Deborah. I won't let you go the next time."

She looked up again and saw the truth of his words in his eyes. "I know."

Chapter 7

The jury was out. Deborah spent their deliberating time in her office, using both her telephone and computer to try to track down what Gage had referred to as the common thread. The antique shop, Timeless, had been owned by Imports Incorporated, whose address was a vacant lot downtown. The company had filed no insurance claim on the loss, and the manager of the shop had vanished. The police had yet to locate the man Parino had referred to as Mouse.

More digging turned up the Triad Corporation, based in Philadelphia. A phone call to Triad put Deborah in touch with a recording telling her that the number had been disconnected. As she placed a call to the D.A.'s office in Philadelphia, she inputted all of her known data into the computer.

Two hours later, she had a list of names, social security numbers and the beginnings of a headache.

Before she could make her next call, the receiver rang under her hand. "Deborah O'Roarke."

"Is this the same Deborah O'Roarke who can't keep her name out of the paper?"

"Cilla." At the sound of her sister's voice, the headache faded a bit. "How are you?"

"Worried about you."

"What else is new?" Deborah rolled her shoulders to relieve the stiff muscles, then leaned back in the chair. Coming tinnily through the earpiece was the music Deborah imagined was pulsing in Cilla's office at the radio station. "How's Boyd?"

"That's Captain Fletcher to you."

"Captain?" She sat straight again. "When did that happen?"

"Yesterday." The pride and pleasure came through clearly. "I guess I'll really have to watch myself now, sleeping with a police captain."

"Tell him I'm proud of him."

"I will. We all are. Now—"

"How are the kids?" Deborah had learned to stall and evade long before taking the bar exam.

"It's dangerous to ask a mother how her kids are during summer vacation, no elementary school, no kindergarten, so they outnumber me and the cop three to two." Cilla gave a rich, warm laugh. "All three members of the demon brigade are fine. Allison pitched a shutout in a Little League game last week—then got into a wrestling match with the opposing pitcher."

"Sounds like he was a rotten loser."

"Yeah. And Allison's always been a rotten winner. I practically had to sit on her to make her give over. Let's see . . . Bryant knocked out a tooth roller-skating then, being a clever little capitalist, sold it to the boy next door for fifty cents. Keenan swallowed it.''

"Swallowed what?''

"The fifty cents. Five dimes. My youngest son eats anything. I'm thinking about putting in a hot line to the Emergency room. Now let's talk about you.''

"I'm fine. How are things at KHIP?''

"About as chaotic as they are around the house. All in all, I'd rather be in Maui.'' Cilla recognized the delaying tactics well and pushed a little harder. "Deborah, I want to know what you're up to.''

"Work. In fact, I'm about to win a case.'' She glanced at the clock and calculated how long the jury had been out. "I hope.''

Sometimes, Cilla mused, you just had to be direct. "Since when have you started dating guys in masks?''

Stalling couldn't last forever, she thought with regret. "Come on, Cilla, you don't believe everything you read in the paper.''

"Right. Or everything that comes over the wire, even though we ran your latest adventure at the top of every hour yesterday. Even if I didn't go to the trouble to get the Urbana papers, I'd have heard all the noise. You're making national news out there, kid, and I want to know what's going on. That's why I'm asking you.''

It was usually easier to evade if you added a couple of dashes of truth. "This Nemesis character is a nuisance. The press is glorifying him—and worse. Just this morning at a shop two blocks from the courthouse, I saw a display of Nemesis T-shirts.''

"Isn't merchandising wonderful?'' But Cilla wasn't about to be distracted again. "Deborah, I've been in radio too long not to be able to read voices—especially my baby sister's. What's between you?''

"Nothing," she insisted, wanting it to be true. "I've simply run into him a couple of times during this investigation I'm doing. The press plays it up."

"I've noticed, Darling Deb."

"Oh, please."

"I do want to know what's going on, but it's more to the point right now why you're involved in something so dangerous. And why I had to read in the paper that some maniac had a knife to my sister's throat."

"It's exaggerated."

"Oh, so no one held a knife to your throat?"

No matter how well she lied, Deborah thought, Cilla would know. "It wasn't as dramatic as it sounds. And I wasn't hurt."

"Knives at your throat," Cilla muttered. "Buildings blowing up in your face. Damn it, Deb, don't you have a police force out there?"

"I was just doing some legwork. Don't start," she said quickly. "Cilla, do you know how frustrating it is to have to keep repeating that you know what you're doing, that you can take care of yourself and do your job?"

Cilla let out a long breath. "Yeah. I can't stop worrying about you, Deborah, just because you're a couple thousand miles away. It's taken me years to finally accept what happened to Mom and Dad. If I lost you, I couldn't handle it."

"You're not going to lose me. Right now, the most dangerous thing I'm facing is my computer."

"Okay. Okay." Arguing with her sister wouldn't change a thing, Cilla knew. And whatever answers Deborah gave her, she would keep right on worrying. "Listen, I also saw a picture of my little sister with some millionaire. I'm going to have to start a scrapbook. Anything you want to tell me?"

The automatic no caught in her throat. "I don't know. Things are pretty complicated right now and I haven't had time to think it through."

"Is there something to think through?"

"Yes." The headache was coming back. She reached into her drawer for a bottle of aspirin. "A couple of things," she murmured, thinking of Gage and of Nemesis. That was something not even Cilla could help her with. But there were other matters. "Cilla, since you're married to a police captain, how about using your influence to have him do me a favor?"

"I'll threaten to cook. He'll do anything I want."

With a laugh, Deborah picked up one of her printouts. "I'd like him to check out a couple of names for me. George P. Drummond and a Charles R. Meyers, both with Denver addresses." She spelled out both names, then added social security numbers. "Got it?"

"Mmm-hmm," Cilla murmured as she scribbled the information.

"And there's a Solar Corporation, also based in Denver. Drummond and Meyers are on the board of directors. If Boyd could run these through the police computer, it would save me several steps through the bureaucracy."

"I'll threaten him with my pot roast."

"That should do the trick."

"Deb, you will be careful, won't you?"

"Absolutely. Give everyone a hug for me. I miss you. All of you." Mitchell came to the door and signaled. "I've got to go, Cilla. The jury's coming back."

Deep in the recesses of his home, in an echoing cavern of a room, Gage studied a bank of computers. There was some work he couldn't do in his office. Some work he preferred to do in secret. With his hands hooked in the pockets of his jeans, he watched the monitors. Names and numbers flashed by.

He could see on one of the monitors just what Deborah had inputted in her computer across town. She was making progress, he thought. Slow, it was true, but it still worried him. If he could follow the steps she was taking, so could others.

Eyes intent, face sober, he took his fingers flying over one keyboard, then another and still another. He had to find the link. Once he did, he would carefully, systematically locate the name of the man responsible for Jack's death. As long as he found it before Deborah, she was safe.

The computers offered him one way. Or he could take another. Leaving the machines to their work, he turned, pressed a button. On the wall on the far side of the high-ceilinged, curving room a huge map slid into place. Crossing to it, he studied a very large scaled detail of the city of Urbana.

Using yet another keyboard, he had colored lights blinking at various parts of the city. Each represented a major drug exchange, many of which were as yet unknown to the UPD.

They flashed in the East End, and the West, in the exclusive neighborhoods uptown, in the barrios, in the financial district. There seemed to be no pattern. Yet there was always a pattern. He had only to find it.

As he studied the map, his gaze lit and lingered on one building. Deborah's apartment. Was she home yet? he wondered. Was she safe inside? Was she wearing her blue robe and studying files, the television news murmuring in the background?

Was she thinking of him?

Gage rubbed his hands over his face. Frank was right, she was interfering with his concentration. But what could he do about it? Every attempt he made to see that she withdrew from the case had failed. She was too stubborn to listen.

He smiled a bit. He hadn't believed he would ever fall in love. How inconvenient, he thought wryly, that when he did, it was with a dedicated public servant. She wouldn't budge. He knew it. And neither would he. But however much discipline he had over his body and his mind, he seemed to have none over his heart.

It wasn't just her beauty. Though he had always loved beautiful things and had grown up learning to appreciate them for no more than their existence. After he'd come out of the coma, he had found a certain comfort in surrounding himself with beauty. All that color, all that texture after so much flat gray.

It wasn't just her mind. Though he respected intelligence. As a cop and as a businessman, he had learned that a sharp mind was the most powerful and the most dangerous weapon.

There was something, some indefinable something beyond her looks and her mind that had captured him. Because he was just as much her prisoner as he was of his own fate. And he had no idea how to resolve the two.

He was only sure that the first step would be to find the key himself, to find the name and to find the justice. When this was behind him, and her, there might be a chance for a future.

Clearing his mind, he studied the lights then, bending over a computer, went to work.

Balancing a pizza box, a bottle of Lambrusco and a briefcase full of paperwork, Deborah stepped off the elevator. As she wondered how she would manage to dig for her keys, she glanced up at the door of her apartment. Colorful draping letters crossed the door. CON-GRATULATIONS, DEBORAH.

Mrs. Greenbaum, she thought with a grin. Even as she turned toward her neighbor's apartment, Mrs. Greenbaum's door opened.

"I heard it on the six-o'clock news. You put that little weasel away." Mrs. Greenbaum adjusted the hem of her tie-dyed T-shirt. "How do you feel?"

"Good. I feel good. How about some celebratory pizza?"

"You twisted my arm." Mrs. Greenbaum let her door slam, then crossed the hall in her bare feet. "I guess you noticed the air-conditioning's on the fritz again."

"I got the picture during my steam bath in the elevator."

"This time I think we should mobilize the rest of the tenants." She gave Deborah a shrewd look. "Especially if we had some sharp, fast-talking lawyer lead the way."

"You're already leading the way," Deborah said as she shifted the wine. "But if it's not on within twenty-four hours, I'll contact the landlord and put on the pressure." She fumbled around in her pocket. "Now if I could just get my keys."

"I've got the copy you gave me." Reaching into the pocket of her baggy jeans, Mrs. Greenbaum produced a key ring crowded with keys. "Here we go."

"Thanks." Inside, Deborah set the pizza box on a table. "I'll get some glasses and plates."

Lil lifted the lid and saw with approval that the pizza was loaded with everything. "You know, a pretty young girl like you should be celebrating with some pretty young boy on a Friday night instead of with an old woman.''

"What old woman?" Deborah called from the kitchen and made Lil laugh.

"With a slightly above-middle-aged woman then. What about that mouth-watering Gage Guthrie?"

"I can't imagine him eating pizza and drinking cheap wine." She walked back in, carrying the bottle and two glasses, paper plates and napkins tucked under her arm. "He's more the caviar type."

"Something wrong with that?"

"No." She frowned. "No, but I'm in the mood for pizza. And after I gorge myself, I have work."

"Honey, don't you ever let up?"

"I've got a deadline," Deborah said, and found she still resented it. She poured two glasses, handed one to her friend. "To justice," she said. "The most beautiful lady I know."

Just as they sat, gooey slices of pizza split between them, there was a knock on the door. Licking sauce from her fingers, Deborah went to answer. She saw a huge basket of red roses that appeared to have legs.

"Delivery for Deborah O'Roarke. Got someplace I can put this thing, lady?"

"Oh . . . yes, ah. Here." She stood on tiptoe and got a glimpse of the deliveryman's head under the blossoms. "On the coffee table."

They not only sat on the coffee table, Deborah noted as she signed the clipboard, they covered it from end to end. "Thanks." She dug into her wallet for a bill.

"Well?" Lil demanded when they were alone again. "Who are they from?"

Though she already knew, Deborah picked up the card.

Nice work, Counselor.
Gage

She couldn't prevent the softening, or the smile that bloomed on her lips. "They're from Gage."

"The man knows how to make a statement." Behind her lenses, Lil's eyes sparkled. There was nothing she liked better than romance—unless it was a good protest rally. "Must be five dozen in there."

"They're beautiful." She slipped the card into her pocket. "I suppose I'll have to call him and thank him."

"At least." Lil bit into the pizza. "Why don't you do it now, while it's on your mind?" And while she could eavesdrop.

Deborah hesitated, the scent of the flowers surrounding her. No, she thought with a shake of her head. If she called him now, while his gesture weakened her, she might do or say something rash. "Later," she decided. "I'll call him later."

"Stalling," Lil said over a mouthful of pizza.

"Yeah." Not ashamed to admit it, Deborah sat again. She ate for a moment in silence, then picked up her wine. "Mrs. Greenbaum," she began, frowning into her glass. "You were married twice."

"So far," Lil answered with a grin.

"You loved both of them?"

"Absolutely. They were good men." Her sharp little eyes became young and dreamy. "Both times I thought it was going to be forever. I was about your age when I lost my first husband in the war. We only had a few years together. Mr. Greenbaum and I were a bit luckier. I miss both of them."

"Have you ever wondered . . . I guess it's an odd sort of question, but have you ever wondered what would have happened if you'd met both of them at the same time?''

Lil arched her eyebrows, intrigued with the notion. "That would have been a problem."

"You see what I mean. You loved both of them, but if they had come into your life at the same time, you couldn't have loved both of them."

"There's no telling what tricks the heart will play."

"But you can't love two men the same way at the same time." She leaned forward, her own conflict showing clearly on her face. "And if somehow you did, or thought you did, you couldn't make a commitment to either one, without being unfaithful to the other."

Taking her time, Lil topped off both glasses. "Are you in love with Gage Guthrie?"

"I might be." Deborah glanced back at the basket bursting with roses. "Yes, I think I am."

"And with someone else?"

With her glass cupped in her hand, Deborah pushed away from the table and rose to pace. "Yes. But that's crazy, isn't it?"

Not crazy, Lil thought. Nothing to do with love was ever crazy. And for some, such a situation would be delightful and exciting. Not for Deborah. For Deborah, she understood it would only be painful.

"Are you sure it's love on either side, and not just sex?"

After letting out a long breath, Deborah sat again. "I thought it was just physical. I wanted it to be. But I've thought about it, tried to be honest with myself, and I know it's not. I even get them mixed up in my mind. Not just comparisons, but well, as if I'm trying to make them one man, so it would be simpler." She drank again.

"Gage told me he loves me, and I believe him. I don't know what to do."

"Follow your heart," Lil told her. "I know that sounds trite, the truest things often do. Let your mind take a back seat and listen to your heart. It usually makes the right choice."

At eleven, Deborah switched on the late news. She wasn't displeased to see her victory in the Slagerman case as the top story. She watched her own image give a brief statement on the courthouse steps, frowning a bit when Wisner pushed through to ask his usual nonsense about Nemesis.

The news team segued from that into Nemesis's latest exploits—the liquor store robbery he had scotched, the mugger he had captured, the murder he had prevented.

"Busy man," Deborah muttered, and drained the last of the wine. If Mrs. Greenbaum hadn't spent most of the evening with her, Deborah thought, she would have contented herself with one glass of wine rather than half the bottle.

Well, tomorrow was Saturday, she thought with a shrug, as the anchorman reported on the upcoming mayoral debates. She could sleep a little late before she went into the office. Or, if she was lucky, she would uncover something that evening. But she wouldn't get anything done if she continued to sit in front of the television.

She waited long enough to hear the weather report, which promised continuing heat, raging humidity and chances of thunderstorms. Switching off the set, she went to the bedroom to settle at her desk.

She'd left the window open in the vain hope of catching a breeze. The traffic noise was a steady din from five stories down. The heat rose from the street, intensifying on its upward journey. She could all but see it.

Hot nights. Hot needs.

She walked to the window, hoping for a breath of air to ease the aching even the wine hadn't dulled. But it remained, a deep, slow throb. Was he out there? she wondered, then put a hand to her temple. She wasn't even sure which man she was thinking of. And it would be best, she knew, if she thought of neither.

Turning on her desk lamp, she opened a file, then glanced at the phone.

She'd called Gage an hour before, only to be told by the taciturn Frank that Mr. Guthrie was out for the evening. She could hardly call him again, she thought. It would look as though she were checking up on him. Something she had no right to do—especially since she was the one who had asked for the time and space.

That was what she wanted, she assured herself. What she had to have. And thinking of him wouldn't help her find the answers that were buried somewhere in the papers on her desk.

She began to read through them again, making notations on a legal pad. As she worked, time slipped past and thunder muttered in the distance.

He shouldn't have come. He knew it wasn't right. But as he had walked the streets, his steps had taken him closer and closer to her apartment. Draped in shadows, he looked up and saw the light in her window. In the heat-drenched night he waited, telling himself if the light switched off, he would leave. He would go.

But it remained, a pale yet steady beacon.

He wondered if he could convince himself he wanted only to see her, to speak with her. It was true that he needed to find out how much she knew, how close she was. Facts on her computer didn't take in her intuition or her suspicions. The closer she came to answers, the more jeopardy she was in.

Even more than he wanted to love her, he needed to protect her.

But that wasn't why he crossed the street, why he swung himself onto the fire escape and began to climb. What he did he did because he couldn't stop himself.

Through the open window, he saw her. She was seated at a desk, the slant of light directed onto the papers she read through. A pencil moved quickly in her hand.

He could smell her. The tauntingly sexy scent she wore reached out to him like an invitation. Or a dare.

He could see only her profile, the curve of her cheek and jaw, the shape of her mouth. Her short blue robe was loosely tied, and he could see the long white column of her throat. As he watched, she lifted a hand to rub at the back of her neck. The robe shifted, sliding up her thighs, parting gently as she crossed her legs and bent over her work again.

Deborah read the same paragraph three times before she realized her concentration had been broken. She rubbed her eyes, intending to begin again. And her whole body stiffened. Heat rushed over her skin. Slowly she turned and saw him.

He was standing inside the window, away from the light. Her heart was hammering—not in shock, she realized. In anticipation.

"Taking a break from crime fighting?" she asked, hoping the sharp tone of her voice would cover her trembling. "According to the eleven-o'clock news, you've been busy."

He hadn't bothered to concentrate. This time, at least this time, he'd needed to come to her whole. "So have you."

"And I still am." She pushed at her hair and discovered her hand wasn't quite steady. "How did you get in?" When he glanced toward the window, she nodded. "I'll have to remember to keep that locked."

"It wouldn't have mattered. Not after I saw you."

Every nerve in her body was on edge. Telling herself it would add more authority, she rose. "I'm not going to let this go on."

"You can't stop it." He stepped toward her. "Neither can I." His gaze shifted to the papers on her desk. "You haven't listened."

"No. I don't intend to. I'll wade through all the lies, navigate all the dead ends until I find the truth. Then I'll finish it." Her stance was tense and watchful. Her eyes challenged him. "If you want to help me, then tell me what you know."

"I know I want you." He hooked a hand in the belt of her robe to hold her still. At that moment, she was his only need, his only quest, his only hunger. "Now. Tonight."

"You have to go." She could do nothing to prevent the shudder of response or the flare of desire. Integrity warred with passion. "You have to leave."

"Do you know how I ache for you?" His voice was harsh as he jerked her against him. "There is no law I wouldn't break, no value I wouldn't sacrifice to have you. Do you understand that kind of need?"

"Yes." It was clawing her. "Yes. It's wrong."

"Right or wrong, it's tonight." With one sweep of his hand, he sent the lamp crashing to the floor. As the room was plunged into darkness, he lifted her into his arms.

"We can't." But her fingers dug hard into his shoulder, negating the denial.

"We will."

Even as she shook her head, his mouth came down on hers, fast and fevered, strong and seductive. The power of it slammed into her, leaving her reeling and rocky— and helpless, helpless to resist her own answering need. Her lips softened without yielding, parted without surrendering. As she tumbled deaf and blind into the kiss, her mind heard what her heart had been trying to tell her.

He pressed her into the mattress, his mouth frantic and impatient as it roamed her face, his hands already tearing at the thin robe that covered her. Beneath it she was just as he'd dreamed. Hot and smooth and fragrant. Stripping off his gloves he let himself feel what he had craved.

Like a river she flowed under his hands. He could have drowned in her. Though he burned to see what he was making his, he contented himself with texture, with taste, with scent. In the hot storm-haunted night, he was relentless.

He was still a shadow, but she knew him. And wanted him. With all reason, all rationality aside, she clung to him, mouth seeking mouth as they rolled over the bed. Desperate to feel him against her, to feel the wild beat of his heart match the wild beat of hers, she pulled at his shirt. There were harshly whispered words against her lips, against her throat, her breast, as she frantically undressed him.

Then he was as vulnerable as she, his skin as slick, his hands as greedy. Thunder rumbled, lightning flickered in the moonless night. The scent of roses and passion hung heavy in the air. She shuddered, mindless with the pleasures he so recklessly showed her.

It was all heat, all ache, all glory. Even as she wept with it, she strained against him, demanding more. Before she could demand, he gave, sending her soaring again. Dark, secret delights. Moans and whispers. Bruising caresses. Insatiable hungers.

When she thought she would surely go mad, he plunged inside her. And it was madness. She gave herself to it, to him, with all her strength, all her eagerness.

"I love you." She wrapped tight around him as the words poured out.

They filled him, even as he filled her. They moved him even as their bodies moved together. He buried his face in her hair. Her nails dug into his back. He felt his own shattering release, then hers as she cried out his name.

He lay in the dark. The roaring in his head gradually subsided until all he heard was the sound of traffic on the street below and Deborah's deep, unsteady breaths. Her arms were no longer tight around him, but had slid off. She was still now, and quiet.

Slowly, unnerved by his own weakness, he shifted from her. She didn't move, didn't speak. In the dark, he touched a hand to her face and found it damp. And he hated that part of him that had caused her grief.

"How long have you known?"

"Not until tonight." Before he could touch her again, she turned away and groped for her robe. "Did you think I wouldn't know when you kissed me? Didn't you realize that no matter how dark it was, no matter how confused you made me, once this happened I would know?"

It wasn't just anger in her voice, but pain. He could have withstood the anger. "No, I didn't think of it."

"Didn't you?" She switched on the bedside lamp and stared at him. "But you're so clever, Gage, so damn clever to have made such a mistake."

He looked at her. Her hair was tumbled, her pale skin still flushed and warm from his hands. There were tears in her eyes, and behind them a bright anger. "Maybe I did know. Maybe I just didn't want to let it matter." He rose and reached for her. "Deborah—"

She slapped him once, then twice. "Damn you, you lied to me. You made me doubt myself, my values. You knew, you had to know I was falling in love with you." With a half laugh she turned away. "With both of you."

"Please listen." When he touched her on the shoulder, she jerked away.

"It wouldn't be wise to touch me just now."

"All right." He curled his hand into a fist. "I fell in love with you so fast, I couldn't think. All I knew was that I needed you, and that I wanted you to be safe."

"So, you put on your mask and looked out for me. I won't thank you for it. For any of it."

The finality in her voice had panic racing through him. "Deborah, what happened here tonight—"

"Yes, what happened here. You trusted me enough for this." She gestured to the bed. "But not for the rest. Not for the truth."

"No, I didn't. I couldn't because I know how you feel about what I'm doing."

"That's a whole different story, isn't it?" She swiped away tears. The anger was dying away to misery. "If you knew you had to lie to me, why didn't you just stay away from me?"

He forced himself not to reach for her again. He had lied and, by lying, hurt her. Now he could only offer the truth and hope it would begin to heal. "You're the only thing in four years I haven't been able to overcome. You're the only thing in four years I've needed as much as I've needed to live. I don't expect you to understand or even accept, but I need you to believe me."

"I don't know what to believe. Gage, since I met you I've been torn in two different directions, believing I was falling in love with two different men. But it's just you. I don't know what to do." On a sigh, she shut her eyes. "I don't know what's right."

"I love you, Deborah. Nothing's righter than that. Give me a chance to show you, time to explain the rest."

"I don't seem to have much choice. Gage, I can't condone—" She opened her eyes and for the first time focused on the long, jagged scars on his chest. Pain slammed into her, all but bringing her to her knees. Dulled with horror, her eyes lifted to his. "They did that to you?" she whispered.

His body stiffened. "I don't want pity, Deborah."

"Be quiet." She moved quickly, going to him, wrapping her arms around him. "Hold me." She shook her head. "No, tighter. I might have lost you all those years ago before I ever had the chance to have you." There were tears in her eyes again as she lifted her head. "I don't know what to do, or what's right. But tonight it's enough that you're here. You'll stay?"

He touched his lips to hers. "As long as you want."

Chapter 8

Deborah always awakened reluctantly. She snuggled into sleep, easily blocking out the honks and gunning engines from the street. A jackhammer was machine-gunning the concrete, but she only yawned and shifted. If she put her mind to it, she could sleep through an atomic bomb.

It wasn't the noise that had her opening her groggy eyes. It was the faint and glorious scent of brewing coffee.

Ten-thirty, she noted, peering at the clock. *Ten-thirty!* Deborah struggled to sit up and discovered she was alone in bed.

Gage, she thought, pressing the heels of her hands to her eyes. Had he ordered breakfast again? Eggs Benedict? Belgian waffles? Strawberries and champagne? God, what she would have given for a simple cup of black coffee and a stale doughnut.

Pushing herself from the bed, she reached down for her robe, which was lying in a heap on the floor. Beneath it was a swatch of black cloth. She picked it up, then lowered herself to the bed again.

A mask. She balled the material in her hand. So, it hadn't been a dream. It was real, all of it. He had come to her in the night, loved her in the night. Both of her fantasies. The charming businessman, the arrogant stranger in black. They were one man, one lover.

On a low groan, she buried her face in her hands. What was she going to do? How the hell was she going to handle this? As a woman? As a D.A.?

God, she loved him. And by loving him, she betrayed her principles. If she revealed his secret, she betrayed her heart.

And how could she love him without understanding him?

Yet she did, and there was no way she could take back her heart.

They had to talk, she decided. Calmly and sensibly. She could only pray she would find the strength and the right words. It wouldn't be enough to tell him she disapproved. He already knew it. It wouldn't be enough to tell him she was afraid. That would only prompt him to reassure. Somehow, she had to find the words to convince him that the path he had taken was not only dangerous, but wrong.

Deborah braced herself, prepared.

When the phone rang, she muttered an oath. Struggling into her robe, she climbed across the bed to snatch up the receiver.

"...Deborah's sister." Cilla's voice held both amusement and curiosity. "And how are you?"

"Fine, thanks," Gage said. "Deborah's still sleeping. Would you like me to—"

"I'm right here." Sighing, Deborah pushed at her tousled hair. "Hello, Cilla."

"Hi."

"Goodbye, Cilla." Deborah heard Gage set the phone on the hook. There was a moment of humming silence.

"Ah . . . I guess I called at a bad time."

"No. I was just getting up. Isn't it a bit early in Denver?"

"With three kids, this is the middle of the day. Bryant, take that basketball outside. *Out!* No dribbling in the kitchen. Deb?"

"Yes?"

"Sorry. Anyway, Boyd checked out those names, and I thought you'd like the information right away."

"That's great." She picked up a pen.

"I'll let Boyd fill you in." The phone rattled. "No, I'll take him. Keenan, don't put that in your mouth. Good grief, Boyd, what's all over his face?" There was some giggling, a crash as the receiver hit the kitchen floor and the sound of running feet.

"Deb?"

"Congratulations, Captain Fletcher."

"Thanks. I guess Cilla's been bragging again. How's it going?"

She looked down at the mask she still held in her hand. "I'm not at all sure." Shaking off the mood, she smiled into the phone. "Things sound normal out there."

"Nothing's ever normal out here. Hey, Allison, don't let that dog—" There was another crash and a flurry of barking. "Too late."

Yes, it sounded perfectly normal. "Boyd, I appreciate you moving so fast on this."

"No problem. It sounded important."

"It is."

"Well, it isn't much. George P. Drummond was a plumber, owned his own business—"

"Was?" Deborah interrupted.

"Yeah. He died three years ago. Natural causes. He was eighty-two and had no connection with a Solar Corporation or any other."

She shut her eyes. "And the other?"

"Charles R. Meyers. High school science teacher and football coach. Deceased five years. They were both clean as a whistle."

"And the Solar Corporation?"

"We can't find much so far. The address you gave Cilla was nonexistent."

"I should have guessed. Every time I turn a corner on this, I run into a dead end."

"I know the feeling. I'll do some more digging. Sorry I can't be more helpful."

"But you have been."

"Two dead guys and a phony address? Not much. Deborah, we've been following the papers out here. Can you tell me if this business has anything to do with your masked phantom?"

She balled the black cloth in her hand again. "Off the record, yes."

"I imagine Cilla's already said it, but be careful, okay?"

"I will."

"She wants to talk to you again." There was some muttering, a chuckle. "Something about a man answering your phone." Boyd laughed again, and Deborah could almost see them wrestling over the receiver.

"I just want to know—" Cilla was breathless. "Boyd, cut it out. Go feed the dog or something. I just want to know," she repeated into the receiver, "who owns the terrific, sexy voice."

"A man."

"I figured that out. Does he have a name?"

"Yes."

"Well, do you want me to guess? Phil, Tony, Maximillion?"

"Gage," Deborah muttered, giving up.

"The millionaire? Nice going."

"Cilla—"

"I know, I know. You're a grown woman. A sensible woman with a life of her own. I won't say another word. But is he—"

"Before you take this any further, I should warn you I haven't had coffee yet."

"Okay. But I want you to call me, and soon. I need details."

"I'll let you know when I have them. I'll be in touch."

"You'd better."

She hung up and sat a moment. It seemed she was back to square one, all around. But first things first, she reminded herself, and followed the scent of coffee into the kitchen.

Gage was at the stove, in jeans and bare feet, his shirt unbuttoned. She wasn't surprised to see him there, but she was surprised at what he was doing.

"You're cooking?" she said from the doorway.

He turned. The impact of seeing her there in the strong sunlight, her eyes sleepy and cautious, nearly bowled him over. "Hi. Sorry about the phone, I thought I could get it before it woke you up."

"It's all right. I was...awake." Feeling awkward, she took a mug from a hook over the sink and poured coffee. "It was my sister."

"Right." He put his hands on her shoulders, running his hands gently down to her elbows and back. When she stiffened, he felt the pain knife into him. "Would you rather I wasn't here?"

"I don't know." She drank without turning around. "I guess we have to talk." But she couldn't bring herself to face it yet. "What are you making?"

"French toast. You didn't have much in the fridge, so I went down to the corner and picked some things up."

So normal, she thought as her stomach clenched. So easy. "How long have you been up?"

"Two or three hours."

When he walked back to the stove, she turned around. "You didn't get much sleep."

His eyes met hers. She was holding back, he thought, on both the hurt and the anger. But they were there. "I don't need much—not anymore." He added two eggs to the milk he already had in a bowl. "I spent the better part of a year doing nothing but sleeping. After I came back I didn't seem to need more than four hours a night."

"I guess that's how you manage to run your businesses, and . . . the other."

"Yeah." He continued to mix ingredients, then dunked bread into the bowl. "You could say my metabolism changed—among other things." Coated bread sizzled when he placed it in the skillet. "Do you want me to apologize for what happened last night?"

She didn't speak for a moment, then opened a cupboard. "I'll get some plates."

He bit off an oath. "Fine. This only takes a few minutes."

He waited until they were seated by the window. Deborah said nothing while she toyed with her breakfast. Her silence and the miserable look in her eyes were more disturbing to him than a hundred shouted accusations.

"It's your call," he said quietly.

Her eyes lifted to his. "I know."

"I won't apologize for being in love with you. Or for making love with you. Being with you last night was the most important thing that's ever happened to me."

He waited, watching her. "You don't believe that, do you?"

"I'm not sure what I believe. What I can believe." She cupped her hands around her mug, her fingers tense. "You've lied to me, Gage, from the very beginning."

"Yes, I have." He banked down on the need to reach out for her, just to touch her. "Apologies for that really don't matter much. It was deliberate, and if it had been possible, I would have continued to lie to you."

She pushed away from the table to wrap her arms around herself. "Do you know how that makes me feel?"

"I think I do."

Hurting, she shook her head. "You couldn't possibly know. You made me doubt myself on the most basic of levels. I was falling in love with you—with both of you, and I was ashamed. Oh, I can see now that I was a fool not to have realized it sooner. My feelings were exactly the same for what I thought were two different men. I would look at you, and think of him. Look at him, and think of you." She pressed her fingers to her lips. The words were pouring out too quickly.

"That night, in Santiago's room, after I came to and you were holding me. I looked up into your eyes and remembered the first time I had seen you in the ballroom at the Stuart Palace. I thought I was going crazy."

"It wasn't done to hurt you, only to protect you."

"From what?" she demanded. "From myself, from you? Every time you touched me, I . . ." Her breath hitched as she fought for composure. That was her problem, after all. Her emotions. "I don't know if I can forgive you, Gage, or trust you. Even loving you, I don't know."

He sat where he was, knowing she would resist if he tried to approach her. "I can't make up for what was done. I didn't want you, Deborah. I didn't want anyone who could make me vulnerable enough to make a mistake." He thought of his gift. His curse. "I don't even have the right to ask you to take me as I am."

"With this?" She pulled the mask from the pocket of her robe. "No, you don't have the right to ask me to accept this. But that's just what you're doing. You're asking me to love you. And you're asking me to close my eyes to what you're doing. I dedicated my life to the law. Am I supposed to say nothing while you ignore it?"

His eyes darkened. "I nearly lost my life to the law. My partner died for it. I've never ignored it."

"Gage, this can't be personal."

"The hell it can't. It's all personal. Whatever you read in your law books, whatever precedents or procedures you find, it all comes down to people. You know that. You feel that. I've seen you work."

"Within the law," she insisted. "Gage, you must see what you're doing is wrong, not even to mention dangerous. You have to stop."

His eyes were very dark, very clear. "Not even for you."

"And if I go to Mitchell, to the police commissioner, to Fields?"

"Then I'll do whatever I have to do. But I won't stop."

"Why?" She crossed to him, the mask fisted in her hand. "Damn it, why?"

"Because I don't have a choice." He rose, his hands gripping her shoulders hard before he let go and turned away. "There's nothing I can do to change it. Nothing I would do."

"I know about Montega." When he turned back, she saw the pain. "I'm sorry, Gage, so sorry for what happened to you. For what happened to your partner. We'll bring Montega in, I swear it. But revenge isn't the answer for you. It can't be."

"What happened to me four years ago changed my life. That's not trite. That's reality." He laid his hand against the wall, stared at it, then pulled it back to stick it into his pocket. "You read the reports of what happened the night Jack was killed?"

"Yes, I read them."

"All the facts," he murmured. "But not all the truth. Was it in the report that I loved him? That he had a pretty wife and a little boy who liked to ride a red tricycle?"

"Oh, Gage." She couldn't prevent her eyes from filling, or her arms from reaching out. But he shook his head and moved away.

"Was it in the report that we had given nearly two years of our lives to break that case? Two years of dealing with the kind of slime who have big yachts, big houses, fat portfolios all from the money they earn selling drugs to smaller dealers, who pay the rent by putting it out on the streets, and the playgrounds and the projects. Two years working our way in, our way up. Because we were cops and we believed we could make a difference."

He put his hands on the back of the chair, fingers curling, uncurling. She could only stand and watch in silence as he remembered.

"Jack was going to take a vacation when it was over. Not to go anywhere, just to sit around the house, mow the grass, fix a leaky sink, spend time with Jenny and his kid. That's what he said. I was thinking about going to Aruba for a couple of weeks, but Jack, he didn't have big dreams. Just ordinary ones."

He looked up, out the window, but he didn't see the sunlight or the traffic crowding the streets. Effortlessly he slid into the past. "We got out of the car. We had a case full of marked bills, plenty of backup and a solid cover. What could go wrong? We were both ready, really ready. We were going to meet the man in charge. It was hot. You could smell the water, hear it lapping against the docks. I was sweating, not just because of the heat, but because it didn't feel right. But I didn't listen to my instincts. And then Montega..."

Gage could see him, standing in the shadows of the docks, gold glinting in his grin.

Stinking cops.

"He killed Jack before I could even reach for my weapon. And I froze. Just for an instant, just for a heartbeat, but I froze. And he had me."

She thought of the scars on his chest and could hardly breathe. To have watched his partner murdered. To have had that moment, that instant of time to see his own death coming. The sharp, shuddering pain that ripped through her was all for him.

"Don't. What good does it do to go back and remember? You couldn't have saved Jack. No matter how quick you had been, no matter what you had done, you couldn't have saved him."

He looked back at her. "Not then. I died that night."

The way he said it, so flat, so passionlessly, had her blood going cold. "You're alive."

"Death's almost a technical term these days. Technically, I died. And part of me slipped right out of my body." Her face grew only paler as he spoke, but she had to know. He had to tell her. "I watched them working on me, there on the docks. And again in the operating room. I almost—almost floated free. And then . . . I was trapped."

"I don't understand."

"Back in my body, but not *back*." He lifted his hands, spread them. He'd never tried to explain it to anyone before, and wasn't certain he could. "Sometimes I could hear—voices, the classical music the nurse left playing by the bed, crying. Or I'd smell flowers. I couldn't speak, I couldn't see. But more than that I couldn't feel anything." He let his hands drop again. "I didn't want to. Then I came back—and I felt too much."

It was impossible to imagine, but she felt the pain and the despair in her own heart. "I won't say I understand what you went through. No one could. But it hurts me to think of it, of what you're still going through."

He looked at her, watched a tear slide down her cheek. "When I saw you that night, in the alley, my life changed again. I was just as helpless to stop it as I had been the first time." His gaze shifted down to the mask she held tight. "Now, my life's in your hands."

"I wish I knew what was right."

He came to her again, lifting his hands to her face. "Give me some time. A few more days."

"You don't know what you're asking me."

"I do," he said, holding her still when she would have turned away. "But I don't have a choice. Deborah, if I don't finish what I've started I might as well have died four years ago."

Her mouth opened to argue, to protest, but she saw the truth of his words in his eyes. "Isn't there another way?"

"Not for me. A few more days," he repeated. "After that, if you feel you have to take what you know to your superiors, I'll accept it. And take the consequences."

She shut her eyes. She knew what he could not. That she would have given him anything. "Mitchell gave me two weeks," she said dully. "I can't promise you any longer."

He knew what it cost her and prayed he would find the time and the place to balance the scales. "I love you."

She opened her eyes, looked into his. "I know," she murmured, then laid her head against his chest. The mask dangled from her fingers. "I know you do."

She felt his arms around her, the solid reality of them. She lifted her head again to meet his lips with hers, to let the kiss linger, warm and promising, even while her conscience waged a silent battle.

What was going to happen to them? Afraid, she tightened her grip and held on. "Why can't it be simple?" she whispered. "Why can't it be ordinary?"

He couldn't count the times he had asked himself the same questions. "I'm sorry."

"No." Shaking her head, she drew away. "I'm sorry. It doesn't do any good to stand here whining about it." With a sniffle, she brushed away tears. "I may not know what's going to happen, but I know what has to be done. I have to go to work. Maybe I can find a way out of this thing." She lifted a brow. "Why are you smiling?"

"Because you're perfect. Absolutely perfect." As he had the night before, he hooked a hand in the belt of her robe. "Come to bed with me. I'll show you what I mean."

"It's nearly noon," she said as he lowered his head to nibble at her ear. "I have work."

"Are you sure?"

Her eyes drifted closed. Her body swayed toward his. "Ah . . . yes." She pulled away, holding both palms out. "Yes, really. I don't have much time. Neither of us do."

"All right." He smiled again when her lips moved into a pout at his easy acquiescence. Perhaps, with luck, he could give her something ordinary. "On one condition."

"Which is?"

"I have a charity function tonight. A dinner, a couple of performers, dancing. At the Parkside."

"The Parkside." She thought of the old, exclusive and elegant hotel overlooking City Park. "Are you talking about the summer ball?"

"Yeah, that's it. I'd considered skipping it, but I've changed my mind. Will you go with me?"

She lifted a brow. "You're asking me at noon, if I'll go with you to the biggest, glitziest event in the city—which begins eight hours from now. And you're asking me when I've got to go to work, have absolutely no hope of getting an appointment at a hairdresser, no time to shop for the right dress.''

"That about covers it," he said after a moment.

She blew out a breath. "What time are you going to pick me up?''

At seven, Deborah stepped under a steaming hot shower. She didn't believe it could possibly ease all the aches, and she was over her quota of aspirin for the day. Six hours in front of a computer terminal, a phone receiver at her ear, had brought her minimal results.

Each name she had checked had turned out to belong to someone long dead. Each address was a blind alley, and each corporation she investigated led only to a maze of others.

The common thread, as Gage had termed it, seemed to be frustration.

More than ever she needed to find the truth. It wasn't only a matter of justice now. It was personal. Though she knew that warped her objectivity, it couldn't be helped. Until this was resolved, she couldn't begin to know where her future, and Gage's, lay.

Perhaps nowhere, she thought as she bundled into a towel. They had come together like lightning and thunder. But storms passed. She knew that an enduring relationship required more than passion. Her parents had had passion—and no understanding. It required even more than love. Her parents had loved, but they had been unhappy.

Trust. Without trust, love and passion faded, paled and vanished.

She wanted to trust him. And to believe in him. Yet he didn't trust her. There were things he knew that could bring her closer to the truth in the case they were both so involved in. Instead, he kept them to himself, determined that his way and only his way was the right one.

With a sigh, she began to dry her hair. Wasn't she just as determined that her way, only her way, was the right one?

If they were so opposed on this one fundamental belief, how could love be enough?

But she had agreed to see him that night. Not because she wanted to go to a fancy ball, she thought. If he had asked her for hot dogs and bowling, she would have gone. Because she couldn't stay away. If she was honest, she would admit she didn't want to stay away.

She would give herself tonight, Deborah thought, carefully applying blusher. But like Cinderella, when the ball was over, she would have to face reality.

Moving briskly, she walked into the bedroom. Spread over the bed was the dress she had bought less than an hour before. Fate, she mused, running a hand over its shimmering sequins. He'd said he liked her in blue. When she'd rushed into the dress shop, frantic, it had been there, waiting. A liquid column of rich, royal blue, studded with silvery sequins. And it fit like a glove from its high-banded collar to its ankle-skimming hem.

Deborah had winced at the price tag, then had gritted her teeth. She'd thrown caution and a month's pay to the winds.

Now, looking in the mirror, she couldn't regret it. The rhinestone swirls at her ears were the perfect match. With her hair swept up and back, her shoulders were bare. She shifted. So was most of her back.

She was just slipping on her shoes when Gage knocked.

His smile faded when she opened the door. Her own lips curved at the sudden and intense desire she saw in his eyes. Very slowly she turned a full circle.

"What do you think?"

He discovered, if he did so very slowly, he could breathe. "I'm glad I didn't give you more time to prepare."

"Why?"

"I couldn't have handled it if you were any more beautiful."

She tilted her chin. "Show me."

He was almost afraid to touch her. Very gently he laid his hands on her shoulders, lowered his mouth to hers. But the taste of her punched into his system, making his fingers tighten, his mouth greedy. With a murmur, he shifted, reaching out to shut the door.

"Oh, no." She was breathless, and unsteady enough to have to lean back against the door. But she was also determined. "For what I paid for this dress, I want to take it out in public."

"Always practical." He gave her one last, lingering kiss. "We could be late."

She smiled at him. "We'll leave early."

When they arrived, the ballroom was already crowded with the glamorous, the influential, the wealthy. Over champagne and appetizers, Deborah scanned the tables and the table-hoppers.

She saw the governor glad-handing a well-known actress, a publishing tycoon cheek-bussing an opera star, the mayor exchanging grins and guffaws with a best-selling author.

"Your usual crowd?" Deborah murmured, smiling at Gage.

"A few acquaintances." He touched his glass to hers.

"Mmm. That's Tarrington, isn't it?" She nodded her head toward a young, earnest-looking man. "What do you think his chances are in the debates?"

"He has a lot to say," Gage commented. "Sometimes a bit tactlessly, but he has a point. Still, he'll have a hard time swaying the over-forty vote."

"Gage." Arlo Stuart stopped at their table, patting his hand on Gage's shoulder. "Good to see you."

"Glad you could make it."

"Wouldn't have missed it." A tall, tanned man with a wavy mane of snowy hair and clear green eyes, he gestured with his glass of Scotch. "You've done nice things in here. I haven't been in since you finished the renovations."

"We like it."

It took Deborah only a minute to realize they were talking about the hotel. And that the hotel belonged to Gage. She glanced up at the opulent crystal chandeliers. She should have known.

"I like knowing my competition has class." His gaze flicked to Deborah. "Speaking of class. Your face is very familiar. And I'm too old for you to consider that a line."

"Arlo Stuart, Deborah O'Roarke."

He took Deborah's hand, holding it in a hearty squeeze. "O'Roarke—O'Roarke." His eyes were both friendly and crafty. "You're the hot lawyer, aren't you? The D.A. who knocked that little creep Slagerman down a peg. The newspaper pictures aren't even close."

"Mr. Stuart."

"The mayor has good things to say about you. Very good things. We'll have to have a dance later so you can tell me all you know about our friend, Nemesis."

Her hand jerked in his, but she managed to keep her eyes level. "It would be a short conversation."

"Not according to our favorite journalist. Of course Wisner's an ass." He had yet to release her hand. "Where did you meet our up-and-coming D.A., Gage? I must be frequenting the wrong places."

"At your hotel," he said easily. "The mayor's fund-raiser."

Stuart gave a hearty laugh. "Well, that will teach me to run around drumming up votes for Fields, won't it? Don't forget that dance."

"I won't," she said, grateful to have her hand, sore fingers and all, back in her lap.

When he walked away, Deborah wiggled her fingers. "Is he always so...exuberant?"

"Yes." Gage picked up her hand and kissed it. "Anything broken?"

"I don't think so." Content to have her hand in his, she glanced around the room. Lush palms, a musical fountain, mirrored ceilings. "This is your hotel?"

"Yeah. Do you like it?"

"It's okay." She gave a little shrug when he grinned. "Shouldn't you be socializing?"

"I am." He touched his lips to hers.

"If you keep looking at me like that—"

"Go on. Please."

She let out one long, unsteady breath. "I think I'll take a trip to the powder room."

Halfway across the ballroom, she was waylaid by the mayor. "I'd like a moment, Deborah."

"Of course."

With an arm around her waist, flashing a broad political smile, he steered her expertly through the crowd and through the high ballroom doors.

"I thought we could use a little privacy."

Glancing back, she noted that Jerry was moving their way. At a signal from the mayor, he stopped, sent Deborah an apologetic look and merged back with the crowd.

"It's quite an elaborate event," Deborah began, schooled enough to know the mayor preferred to launch a topic himself.

"I was surprised to see you here." He nudged her away from the doors toward an alcove that held potted plants and pay phones. "Then again, perhaps I shouldn't have been, since your and Guthrie's names have been linked so often lately."

"I'm seeing Gage," she said coolly. "If that's what you mean. On a personal level." She was already weary of playing politics. "Is that what you wanted to talk to me about, Mayor? My social life?"

"Only as it affects your professional one. I was disturbed and disappointed to learn that against my wishes you're remaining on this investigation."

"Your wishes?" she countered. "Or Mr. Guthrie's?"

"I respected and agreed with his viewpoint." There was a flash of anger in his eyes he rarely showed outside of the privacy of his own offices. "Frankly, I'm displeased with your performance on this matter. Your excellent record in the courtroom does not override your reckless mistakes outside of it."

"Reckless? Believe me, Mayor Fields, I haven't begun to be reckless. I'm following my superior's orders in pursuing this matter. I began it, and I intend to finish it. Since we're supposed to be on the same side, I'd think you'd be pleased with the dedication of the D.A.'s office in this case, not only with our persistence in tracking down and prosecuting the men trafficking drugs, but in finding Montega, a known cop killer, and bringing him to justice."

"Don't tell me whose side I'm on." Clearly on the edge of losing control, he wagged a finger in her face. "I've worked for this city since before you could tie your own shoes. You don't want to make an enemy of me, young lady. I run Urbana, and I intend to keep right on running it. Young, overeager prosecutors are a dime a dozen."

"Are you threatening to have me fired?"

"I'm warning you." With an obvious effort of will, he brought himself under control. "You either work with the system, or you work against it."

"I know that." Her fingers tightened on her evening bag.

"I admire you, Deborah," he said more calmly. "But while you have enthusiasm, you lack experience, and a case like this requires more experienced hands and minds."

She stood her ground. "Mitchell gave me two weeks."

"I'm aware of that. Make sure you play by the book for the time you have left." Though his eyes were still hot, he laid an avuncular hand on her arm. "Enjoy yourself this evening. The menu's excellent."

When he left her, she stood there for a moment, quietly shaking with rage. Grappling for control, she strode toward the ladies' room. Inside, she stormed through two arching ficus trees and into the adjoining room with its rose-colored chairs and mint-green counters. Still seething, she tossed her bag onto the counter and plopped down into a chair in front of one of the oval lighted mirrors.

So the mayor was displeased, she thought. He was disappointed. He was disturbed. She grabbed a lipstick out of her purse and concentrated on painting her lips. What he was, she thought, was spitting mad because she had bucked him.

Did he think there was only one way to do things, only one route to take? What the hell was wrong with taking a few detours, as long as they led to the same destination? Especially if they got you there quicker.

She tossed the lipstick back into her purse and reached for her compact. In the glass, she met her own eyes.

What was she thinking? Only twenty-four hours before, she had been sure there was only one way, only one route. And though she wouldn't have appreciated the mayor's tactics, she would have applauded his sentiments.

And now? She dropped her chin on her hand. And now she just wasn't sure. Wasn't she, even at this moment, veering outside of the system that she believed in? Wasn't she allowing her feelings, her personal feelings for Gage, to interfere with her professional ethics?

Or did it all come down to a matter of right and wrong, with her not knowing which was which? How could she continue, how could she function as a lawyer, if she couldn't see clearly what was right?

Maybe it was time to examine the facts, along with her own conscience, and ask herself if it wouldn't be better for everyone if she did withdraw.

As she sat studying her own face and her own values, the lights went out.

Chapter 9

Deborah clutched her evening bag and set one hand on the counter to orient herself. Big, fancy hotel like this, she thought, and it blows a fuse. Though she tried to see the humor of it as she stood, her heart was pounding. She swore when her hip bumped the chair as she groped through the dark.

Though it was foolish, she was afraid, and felt both trapped and smothered by the dark.

The door creaked open. There was a shaft of light, then blackness.

"Hey, pretty lady."

She froze, holding her breath.

"I got a message for you." The voice was high and piping with a giggle at the end of each sentence. "Don't worry. I'm not going to hurt you. Montega wants you all for himself, and he'd get real mad if I messed you up any first."

Her skin iced over. He couldn't see her, Deborah reminded herself as she fought the paralyzing fear. That evened the odds. "Who are you?"

"Me?" Another giggle. "You've been looking for me, but I'm hard to find. That's why they call me Mouse. I can get in and out of anyplace."

He was moving toward her soundlessly. Deborah could only guess at the direction of his voice. "You must be very clever." After she spoke, she too moved, shifting a careful foot to the left.

"I'm good. I'm the best. Ain't nobody better than old Mouse. Montega wanted me to tell you he's real sorry you didn't get to talk more before. He wants you to know he's keeping an eye on you. All the time. And on your family."

For an instant her blood stopped flowing. Her thoughts of outmaneuvering him, of slipping past him to the door vanished. "My family?"

"He knows people in Denver, too. Real slick people." He was closer now, so close she could smell him. But she didn't move away. "If you cooperate, he'll make sure your sister and the rest stay safe and snug in their beds tonight. Get the picture?"

She reached into her bag, felt the cool metal in her hand. "Yes, I get the picture." Pulling it out, she aimed in the direction of his voice and fired.

Screaming, he crashed into the chairs. Deborah sprinted around him, ramming her shoulder against one wall, then another until she located the door. Mouse was weeping and cursing as she tugged and found the door jammed.

"Oh, God. Oh, God." Panicked, she continued to pull.

"Deborah!" She heard her name shouted. "Get away from the door. Step back from the door."

She took one stumbling step backward and heard the heavy thud. Another, and the door crashed open. She ran into the light and Gage's arms.

"You're all right?" His hands were running over her, checking for hurts.

"Yes. Yes." She buried her face in his shoulder, ignoring the gathering crowd. "He's inside." When he started to push away, Deborah held on tighter. "No, please."

His face grim, Gage nodded to a pair of security guards. "Come and sit down."

"No, I'm okay." Though her breath was still shuddering, she drew away to look at his face. She saw murder there and tightened her hold on him. "Really. He didn't even touch me. He was trying to frighten me, Gage. He didn't hurt me."

His voice was low as he studied her pale face. "Is that supposed to make me want to kill him less?"

With a burly guard on each arm, the weeping Mouse stumbled out, his hands covering his face. Deborah noted he was wearing a waiter's uniform.

Alarmed by the look in Gage's eyes, she pulled his attention back to her. "He's in a lot worse shape than I am. I used this." With an unsteady hand, Deborah held up a can of Mace. "I've been carrying it with me since that night in the alley."

Gage wasn't sure if he should laugh or swear. Instead, he pulled her against him and kissed her. "It looks as though I can't let you out of my sight."

"Deborah." Jerry elbowed through the onlookers. "Are you all right?"

"I am now. The police?"

"I called them myself." Jerry glanced up at Gage. "You should get her out of here."

"I'm fine," Deborah insisted, glad the full-length dress concealed her knocking knees. "I'll have to go down to the police station and make a statement. But I need to make a phone call first."

"I'll call whomever you like." Jerry gave her hand a quick squeeze.

"Thanks, but I need to do this." Behind him, she spotted the mayor. "You could do me a favor and hold Fields off my back for a while."

"Done." He looked at Gage again. "Take care of her."

"I intend to." Keeping Deborah tight at his side, Gage led her away from the crowd. He moved quickly across the lobby and toward a bank of elevators.

"Where are we going?"

"I keep an office here, you can make the call from there." Inside the elevator, he turned her to him again and held tight. "What happened?"

"Well, I didn't get to powder my nose." She turned her face into his collar, breathing deeply. "First, Fields waylaid me and read me the riot act. He's not pleased with my performance." When the elevator doors opened, she loosened her hold so they could walk into the hallway. "When we parted ways, I was seeing red. I sat down in the powder room to repair my makeup and my composure." She was calming, and grateful the shaking had stopped. "Very elegant, by the way."

He shot her a look as he slid a key into a lock. "I'm glad you approve."

"I liked it a lot." She stepped into the parlor of a suite and crossed the thick oatmeal-colored carpet. "Until the lights went out. I was just orienting myself when the door opened, and he came in. The elusive Mouse,'' she said as her stomach began to churn again. "He had a message for me from Montega.''

The name, just the name, had Gage's muscles tensing. "Sit down. I'll get you a brandy."

"The phone?"

"Right there. Go ahead."

Gage was fighting his own demons as he moved to the bar for the decanter and two snifters. She'd been alone, and however resourceful she was, she'd been vulnerable. When he'd heard the screaming... His fingers went white on the decanter. If it had been Montega instead of his messenger boy, she could have been dead. And he would have been too late.

Nothing that had happened to him before, nothing that could happen to him in the future would be more devastating than losing her.

She was sitting now, very straight, very tense, her face too pale, her eyes too dark. In one hand she held the receiver while the other vised around the cord. She was talking fast, to her brother-in-law, Gage realized after a moment.

They had threatened her family. He could see the possibility they would be harmed was more terrifying to her than any attempt on her own life.

"I need you to call me every day," she insisted. "You'll make sure Cilla has guards at the radio station. The children..." She covered her face with her hand. "God, Boyd." She listened a moment, nodding, trying to smile. "Yes, I know, I know. You didn't make captain for nothing. I'll be fine. Yes, and careful. I love you. All of you." She paused again, inhaling deeply. "Yes, I know. Bye."

She replaced the receiver. Saying nothing, Gage pushed the snifter into her hands. She cupped it a moment, staring down at the amber liquid. On another deep breath, she tipped the glass to her lips and drank deeply. She shuddered, drank again.

"Thanks."

"Your brother-in-law's a good cop. He won't let anything happen to them."

"He saved Cilla's life years ago. That's when they fell in love." Abruptly she looked up, her eyes wet and eloquent. "I hate this, Gage. They're my family, all I have left of family. The idea that something I've done, something I'm doing could—" She broke off, pulling herself back from the unthinkable. "When I lost my parents, I didn't think anything would ever be as bad. But this…" With a shake of her head, she looked down at the brandy again. "My mother was a cop."

He knew. He knew it all, but he only covered her hand with his and let her talk.

"She was a good one, or so I was told. I was only eight when it happened. I didn't know her very well, not really. She wasn't cut out to be a mother."

She shrugged it off, but even in that casual, dismissive gesture, he saw the scars.

"And my father," she continued. "He was a lawyer. A public defender. He tried hard to keep it all together, the family—the illusion of family. But he and my mother just couldn't pull it off." She sipped the brandy again, grateful for its numbing smoothness. "Two uniforms came to school that day, picked me up, took me back to the house. I guess I knew. I knew my mother was dead. They told me, as gently as possible, that it was both of them. Both of them. Some creep my father was defending managed to smuggle in a gun. When they were in the conference room, he cut loose.''

''I'm sorry, Deborah. I know how hard it is to lose family.''

She nodded, setting the empty snifter aside. ''I guess that's why I was determined to be a lawyer, a prosecutor. Both of my parents dedicated their lives, and lost them defending the law. I didn't want it to have been for nothing. Do you understand?''

''Yes.'' He brought her hands to his lips. ''For whatever reason you chose to be a lawyer, it was the right decision. You're a good one.''

''Thanks.''

''Deborah.'' He hesitated, wanting to phrase his thoughts carefully. ''I respect both your integrity and your abilities.''

''I feel a *but* coming on.''

''I want to ask you again to back off from this. To leave the rest to me. You'll have your chance to do what you do best, and that's prosecute Montega and the rest of them.''

She gave herself a moment, wanting, as he had, to make her thoughts clear. ''Gage, tonight, after the mayor came down on me, I sat in the powder room. Once I got over being mad, I started to think, to examine my position, and my motives. I began to think maybe the mayor was right, maybe it would be better if I turned this over to someone with more experience and less personal involvement.'' Then she shook her head. ''And I can't, especially now. They threatened my family. If I stepped back, I'd never be able to trust myself again, to believe in myself. I have to finish this.'' Before he could speak, she put her hands on his shoulders. ''I don't agree with you. I don't know if I ever can, but I understand, in my heart, what you're doing and why you have to do it. That's all I'm asking from you."

How could he refuse? "Then I guess we have a stalemate, for now."

"I have to go down and make my statement." She rose, held out a hand. "Will you come with me?"

They wouldn't let her talk to Mouse. Deborah figured she could work around that eventually. By Monday, she would have the police reports if nothing else. With Mouse under tight security, it was unlikely the same kind of accident could befall him as it had Parino.

For the answers she needed, she would bargain with Mouse, just as she would have bargained with the devil.

She gave her statement, wearily waited while it was typed for her signature. On Saturday night, the station was hopping. Hookers and pimps, dealers and mugging victims, gang members and harried public defenders. It was reality, an aspect of the system she represented and believed in. But it was with relief that she stepped outside.

"Long night," she murmured.

"You handled yourself very well." He laid a hand on her cheek. "You must be exhausted."

"Actually, I'm starving." Her lips curved. "We never did have dinner."

"I'll buy you a hamburger."

With a laugh, she threw her arms around him. Perhaps some things, some very precious things, could be simple. "My hero."

He pressed his lips to the side of her throat. "I'll buy you a dozen hamburgers," he murmured. "Then for God's sake, Deborah, come home with me."

"Yes." She turned her lips to his. "Yes."

* * *

He knew how to set the stage. Perfectly. When Deborah walked into the bedroom beside him, there was moonlight drifting through the windows, stardust filtering through the skylight, candle glow warming the shadows. Roses—the scent of them sweetened the air. The sound of a hundred violins romanced it.

She didn't know how he'd managed it all with the single phone call he'd made from the noisy little diner where they had eaten. She didn't care. It was enough to know he would have thought of it.

"It's lovely." She was nervous, she realized, ridiculously so after the passion of the previous night. But her legs were unsteady as she crossed to where a bottle of champagne sat nestled in a crystal bowl of ice. "You thought of everything."

"Only of you." His lips brushed her shoulder before he poured the wine. "I've pictured you here a hundred times. A thousand." He offered her a glass.

"So have I." Her hand trembled as she lifted her glass. Desire, fighting to break free. "The first time you kissed me, up in the tower, whole worlds opened up. It's never been like that for me before."

"I nearly begged you to stay that night, even though you were angry." He slipped off one of her earrings, then let his fingers rub over the sensitive lobe. "I wonder if you would have."

"I don't know. I would have wanted to."

"That's almost enough." He drew off her other earring, set them both on the table. Slowly he slid out one of her hairpins, then another, watching her. Always watching her. "You're shivering."

His hands were so gentle, his eyes so urgent. "I know."

He took the glass from her limp fingers and set it aside. With his eyes on hers, he continued to free her hair. The whisper of his fingertips on the nape of her neck. "You're not afraid of me?"

"Of what you can do to me."

Something flared in his eyes, dark and dangerous. But he lowered his head to gently kiss her temple.

Heavy eyed and sultry, she looked up at him. "Kiss me, Gage."

"I will." His mouth trailed over her face, teasing, never satisfying her. "I am."

Her breath was already coming fast. "You don't have to seduce me."

He ran a finger up and down her bare spine, smiling when she shuddered. "It's my pleasure." And he wanted it to be hers.

The night before, all the passion, all the fierce and angry needs had clawed their way out of him. Tonight he wanted to show her the softer side of love. When she swayed against him, he withstood the swift arrows of desire.

"We made love in the dark," he murmured as his fingers flicked open the trio of buttons at the back of her neck. "Tonight I want to see you."

The dress shimmered down her, a glittery blue pool at her feet. She wore only a lacy woman's fancy that lifted her breasts and skimmed transparent to her hips. Her beauty struck him breathless.

"Every time I look at you, I fall in love again."

"Then don't stop looking." She reached up to undo the formal tie. Her fingers slid down to unfasten the unfamiliar studs. "Don't ever stop." She parted his shirt with her hands, then pressed her mouth to the heated skin beneath. The tip of her tongue left a moist trail before she lifted her head, let it fall back in invitation. Her eyes were a rich blue gleam beneath her lashes. "Kiss me now."

As seduced as she, he branded her lips with his. Twin moans, low and throaty, shuddered through the room. Her hands slid slowly up his chest to his shoulders to push the dinner jacket aside. Her fingers tightened, then went bonelessly lax as he softened the kiss, deepened it, gentled it.

He lifted her into his arms as though she were fragile crystal rather than flesh and blood. With his eyes on hers, he held her there a moment, letting his mouth tease and torment hers. He continued those feather-light kisses as he carried her to the bed.

He sat, holding her cradled in his lap. His mouth continued its quiet devastation of her reason. He could almost see her float. Her eyes drifted shut. Her limbs were fluid. In arousing contrast, her heart pounded under his hand. He wanted her like this. Totally pleasured. Totally his. As he drew more and more of that warm exotic flavor from her mouth, he thought he could stay just so for hours. For days.

She felt each impossible tender touch, the stroke of a fingertip, the brush of his palm, the oh-so-patient quest of his lips. Her body seemed as light as the rose-scented air, yet her arms were too heavy to lift. The music and his murmurs merged in her mind into one seducing song. Beneath it was the violent roar of her own speeding pulse.

She knew she had never been more vulnerable or more willing to go wherever he chose to take her.

And this was love—a need more basic than hunger, than thirst.

One quiet, helpless gasp escaped her when his lips whispered over the tops of her breasts. Slowly, erotically, his tongue slid under the lace to tease her hardened nipples. His fingers played over the skin above her stockings, lightly, so lightly, gliding beneath the sheer triangle of material.

With one touch, he sent her over the first towering peak. She arched like a bow, and the pleasure arrowed out of her into him. Then she seemed to melt in his arms.

Breathless, almost delirious, she reached for him. "Gage, let me..."

"I will." He covered her next stunned cry with his mouth. And while she was still shuddering, he laid her on the bed.

Now, he thought. He could take her now, while she lay hot and damp in surrender. There was moonlight on her skin, on her hair. The white lace she wore was like an illusion. When she looked at him from beneath those heavy lashes, he saw the dark flicker of desire.

He had more to show her.

His knuckles brushed her skin, making her jolt as he unhooked her stocking. Almost lazily, he slid it down her leg, following the route with soft, openmouthed kisses. His tongue glided over the back of her knee, down her calf until she was writhing in mindless pleasures.

Trapped in gauzy layers of sensation, she reached for him again, only to have him evade and repeat each devastating delight on her other leg. His mouth journeyed up, lingering, pausing, until it found her. His name burst from her lips as she reared up. Nearly weeping, she grasped him against her.

And at the first touch, the strength seemed to pour into her.

Furnace hot, her flesh met his. But it wasn't enough. Urgent, her fingers pulled at his open shirt, tearing seams in her desperation to find more of him. As she ripped the silk away, her teeth nipped into his shoulder. She felt his stomach muscles quiver, heard the quick intake of his breath as she pulled at the waistband of his trousers. Buttons popped off.

"I want you." Her mouth fixed ravenously to his. "Oh, Lord, I want you."

The control he had held so tightly slipped through his tensed fingers. Desire overpowered him. She overpowered him with her desperate hands, her greedy mouth. The breath was clogging in his lungs, burning as he struggled out of his clothes.

Then they were kneeling in the middle of the ravaged bed, bodies trembling, eyes locked. He hooked a hand in the bodice of the lace and rent it ruthlessly down the center. With his fingers digging into her hips, he pulled her against him.

During the rough, reckless ride, she arched back. Her hands slid down his slick shoulders, then found purchase. She sobbed out his name as she tumbled off the razor's edge of sanity. He gripped her hair in his hand and drove her up again. Again. Then he closed his mouth over hers and followed.

Weak, she lay on the bed, one arm tossed across her eyes, the other hanging limply off the mattress. She knew she couldn't move, wasn't sure she could speak, doubted that she was even breathing.

Yet when he pressed a kiss to her shoulder, she shuddered again.

"I meant to be gentle with you."

She managed to open her eyes. His face was close. She felt his fingers move in her hair. "Then I guess you'll just have to try again until you get it right."

A smile curved his mouth. "I have a feeling that's going to take a long time."

"Good." She traced his smile with a fingertip. "I love you, Gage. That's the only thing that seems to matter tonight."

"It's the only thing that matters." He put a hand over hers. There was a bond in the touch, every bit as deep and as intimate as their lovemaking. "I'll get you some wine."

With a contented sigh, she settled back as he got up. "I never thought it could be like this. I never thought I could be like this."

"Like what?"

She caught a glimpse of herself in the wide mirror across the room—sprawled naked over pillows and rumpled sheets. "So wanton, I guess." She laughed at her choice of words. "In college I had a reputation for being very cool, very studious and very unapproachable."

"School's out." He sat on the bed, handed her a glass then tapped his against it.

"I guess. But even after, when I started in the D.A.'s office, the reputation remained." She wrinkled her nose. "Earnest O'Roarke."

"I like it when you're earnest." He sipped. "I can see you in a law library, poring over thick, dusty books, scribbling notes."

She made a face. "That's not exactly the image I prefer at the moment."

"I like it." He lowered his head to capture her chin gently between his teeth. "You'd be wearing one of those conservatively tailored suits, in those very unconservative colors you like." She frowned a bit, making him chuckle. "Sensible shoes and very discreet jewelry."

"You make me sound like a prude."

"And under it all would be something thin and sexy." He hooked a finger in a torn swatch of lace and lifted it to the light. "A very personal choice for a very proper attorney. Then you'd start quoting precedents and making me crazy."

"Like *Warner v. Kowaski?*"

"Mmm." He switched to her ear. "Just like. And I'd be the only one who knew that it takes six pins to hold your hair back in that very proper twist."

"I know I can be too serious," she murmured. "It's only because what I do is so important to me." She looked down at her wine. "I have to know what I'm doing is right. That the system I represent works." When he drew away to study her, she sighed. "I know part of it's ego and ambition, but another part of it is so basic, Gage, so ingrained. That's why I worry how you and I are going to resolve this."

"We won't resolve it tonight."

"I know, but—"

"Not tonight," he said, laying a finger over her lips. "Tonight it's just you and me. I need that, Deborah. And so do you."

She nodded. "You're right. I'm being too earnest again."

"We can fix that." He grinned and held up his glass to the light. The champagne bubbled.

"By getting drunk?" she said, brow lifted.

"More or less." When his eyes met hers, there was a smile in them. "Why don't I show you a...less serious way to drink champagne?" He tilted his glass and had a trickle of cool wine sliding over her breast.

Chapter 10

Gage lost track of time as he watched her sleep. The candles had gutted out in their own hot, fragrant wax so that their scent drifted, quiet as a memory. She had a hand in his, holding lightly even in sleep.

The shadows lifted, fading in the pearl gray of dawn. He watched the growing light fall over her hair, her face, her shoulders. Just as softly, he followed its path with his lips. But he didn't want to wake her.

There was too much to be done, too much he still refused to make her a part of. He knew that over a matter of weeks, the goals he carried inside him for more than four years had become mixed. It was not enough now to avenge his partner's death. It was not enough now to seek and find payment for the time and the life that had been stolen from him. Even justice, that driving force, was not enough.

He would have to move quickly now, for each day that passed without answers was another day Deborah was in jeopardy. There was nothing more important than keeping her safe.

He slid away from her, moving soundlessly from the bed to dress. There was time to make up, all the hours he had spent with her rather than on the streets or at his work. He glanced back when she shifted and snuggled deeper into the pillow. She would sleep through the morning. And he would work.

He pushed a button beneath the carved wood on the wall farthest from the bed. A panel slid open. Gage stepped into the dark and let it close again at his back.

With the husky morning greeting still on her tongue, Deborah blinked sleepily. Had she been dreaming? she wondered. She would have sworn Gage had stepped into some kind of secret passageway. Baffled, she pushed up on her elbows. In sleep she had reached for him and, finding him gone, had awakened just at the moment when the wall had opened.

Not a dream, she assured herself. For he wasn't beside her, and the sheets where he had lain were already cooling.

More secrets, she thought and felt the sorrow of his distrust envelop her. After the nights they had spent together, the love he had shown her, he still wouldn't give her his trust.

So she would take it, Deborah told herself as she pushed herself out of bed. She would not sit and sulk or wish and whine, but demand. Fumbling in his closet, she located a robe. Soft cotton in steel gray, it hit her mid-calf. Impatient, she bundled the sleeves up out of her way and began to search for the mechanism that opened the panel.

Even knowing the approximate location, it took her ten frustrating minutes to find it and another two to figure out how it worked. Her breath hissed out in satisfaction as the panel slid open. Without hesitation, she stepped into the dark, narrow corridor.

Keeping one hand on the wall for guidance, she started forward. There was no dank, disused smell as she might have expected. The air was clean, the wall smooth and dry. Even when the panel behind her closed her completely into the dark, she wasn't uneasy. There would be no scratching or skittering sounds here. It was obvious Gage used the passage, and whatever it led to, often.

She picked her way along, straining her eyes and ears. Corridors veered off, twisting like snakes from the main passage, but she followed instinct and kept to the same straight path. After a moment, she saw a dim glow up ahead and moved a bit more quickly. A set of stone stairs with pie-shaped treads curved into a tight semicircle as it plunged downward. With one hand tight on the thin iron rail, she wove her way to the bottom, where she was faced with three tunnels leading in different directions.

The lady or the tiger, she thought, then shook her head at her own fancy. "Damn you, Gage. Where did you go?" Her whisper echoed faint and hollow, then died.

Bracing her shoulders, she started through one archway, changed her mind and backtracked to the middle. Again she hesitated. Then she heard it, dim and dreamy down the last tunnel. Music.

She plunged into the dark again, following the sound, moving cautiously down the sloping stone floor. She had no idea how deep she was traveling underground, but the air was cooling rapidly. The music grew in volume as degree by faint degree the tunnel's light increased. She heard a mechanical hum, and a clatter—like typewriter keys hitting a platen.

When she stepped into the mouth of the tunnel, she could only stand and stare.

It was an enormous room with curving stone walls. Cavernlike with its arching ceiling and echoes, it spread more than fifty feet in every direction. But it wasn't primitive, she thought as she gathered Gage's robe close around her throat. Rather than appearing gloomy, it was brilliantly lit, equipped with a vast computer system, printers and monitors blinking away. Television screens were bolted to one wall. An enormous topographic map of Urbana spread over another. Music, eerily romantic, poured out of speakers she couldn't see. Granite-gray counters held work stations, telephones, stacks of photographs and papers.

There was a control panel, studded with switches and buttons and levers. Gage sat in front of it, his fingers moving. Over the map, lights blinked on. He shifted, working the controls. On a computer screen, the map was reproduced.

He looked like a stranger, his face grimly set and intense. She wondered if his choice of a black sweater and jeans had been deliberate.

She stepped forward, down a trio of stone steps. "Well," she began as he turned quickly, "you didn't include this on my tour."

"Deborah." He stood, automatically turning off the monitor. "I'd hoped you'd sleep longer."

"I'm sure you did." She stuck her tensed hands into the deep pockets of his robe. "Apparently I've interrupted your work. An interesting . . . getaway," she decided. "Nemesis's style, I'd say. Dramatic, secretive." She moved past a bank of computers toward the map. "And thorough," she murmured. "Very thorough." She whirled around. "One question. Just the one that seems to matter the most at the moment. Who am I sleeping with?''

"I'm the same man you were with last night."

"Are you? Are you the same man who told me he loved me, who showed me he did in dozens of beautiful ways? Is that the same man who left me in bed to come down here? How long are you going to lie to me?"

"It isn't a matter of lying to you. This is something I have to do. I thought you understood that."

"Then you were wrong. I didn't understand that you would keep this from me. That you would work without me, holding information from me."

He seemed to change before her eyes, growing distant and cool and aloof. "You gave me two weeks."

"Damn you, I gave you more than that. I gave you everything." Her eyes were brilliant with emotion as hurt and anger battled for priority. But she flung up a hand before he could cross to her. "No, don't. You won't use my feelings this time."

"All right." Though his own were straining for release. "It isn't a matter of feelings, but logic. You should appreciate that, Deborah. This is my work. Your presence here is as unnecessary as mine would be in the courtroom with you."

"Logic?" She spat out the word. "It's only logical if it suits your purposes. Do you think I'm a fool? Do you think I can't see what's happening here?" She gestured sharply toward one of the monitors. "And we'll keep it strictly professional. You have all the information I've been painfully digging up. All the names, all the numbers, and more, much more than I've been able to uncover. Yet you haven't told me. And wouldn't have."

The cloak came around him again, impenetrable. "I work alone."

"Yes, I'm aware of that." The bitterness seeped into her voice as she walked toward him. "No partners. Except in bed. I'm good enough to be your partner there."

"One has nothing to do with the other."

"Everything," she all but shouted. "One has everything to do with the other. If you can't trust me, in every way, respect me, in every way and be honest with me, in every way, then there's nothing between us."

"Damn it, Deborah, you don't know everything." He gripped her arms. "You don't understand everything."

"No, I don't. Because you won't let me."

"Can't let you," he corrected, holding her still when she would have pulled away. "There's a difference between lying to you and holding back information. This isn't black-and-white."

"Yes, it is."

"These are vicious men. Without conscience, without morals. They've already tried to kill you, and you'd hardly broken the surface. I won't risk you. If you want black-and-white, there it is." He shook her, punctuating each word. "I will not risk you."

"You can't prevent me from doing my job, or what I feel is right."

"By God, if I have to lock you upstairs until I'm done with this to keep you safe, I will."

"And then what? Will the same thing happen the next time, and the next?"

"I'll do whatever it takes to protect you. That won't change."

"Maybe you've got a nice little plastic bubble you could stick me in." She put her hands on his forearms, willing him to understand. "If you love me, then you have to love the whole person I am. I demand that, just as I demand to know and love the whole person you are." She saw something flicker in his eyes and pushed her point. "I can't become something different for you, someone who sits and waits to be taken care of."

"I'm not asking you to."

"Aren't you? If you can't accept me now, you never will. Gage, I want a life with you. Not just a few nights in bed, but a life. Children, a home, a history. But if you can't share with me what you know, and who you are, there can't be a future for us." She broke away from him. "And if that's the case, it would be better for both of us if I left now."

"Don't." He reached out for her before she could turn away. However deep his own need for survival ran, it was nothing compared to the possibility of life without her. "I need your word." His fingers tightened on hers. "That you won't take any chances, and that you'll move in here with me at least until it's over. Whatever we find here has to stay here. You can't risk taking it to the D.A. Not yet."

"Gage, I'm obligated to—"

"No." He cut her off. "Whatever we do, whatever we find stays here until we're ready to move. I can't give you more than that, Deborah. I'm only asking for a compromise."

And it was costing him. She could see that. "All right. I won't take anything to Mitchell until we're both sure. But I want it all, Gage. Everything." Her voice calmed, her hands gentled. "Don't you see I know you're holding something back from me, something basic that has nothing to do with secret rooms or data? I know, and it hurts me."

He turned away. If he was to give her everything, he had no choice but to begin with himself. The silence stretched between them before he broke it. "There are things you don't know about me, Deborah. Things you may not like or be able to accept."

The tone of his voice had her mouth growing dry and her pulse beating irregularly. "Do you have such little faith in me?"

He was putting all his faith in her, he thought. "I've had no right to let things go as far as they have between us without letting you know what I am." He reached out to touch her cheek, hoping it wouldn't be the last time. "I didn't want to frighten you."

"You're frightening me now. Whatever you have to tell me, just tell me. We'll work it out."

Without speaking, he walked away from her, toward the stone wall. He turned and, with his eyes on her, vanished.

Deborah's mouth opened, but the only sound she could make was a strangled gasp. With her eyes riveted to where Gage should be—had to be, her confused brain insisted—she stumbled back. Her unsteady hand gripped the arm of a chair as she let her numbed body slide into it.

Even while her mind rejected what her eyes had seen, he returned—materializing ten feet from where he had disappeared. For an instant she could see through him, as if he were no more than the ghost of the man who stood in front of her.

Deborah started to rise, decided against it, then cleared her throat. "It's an odd time for magic tricks."

"It isn't a trick." Her eyes were still huge with shock as he walked toward her, wondering if she would stiffen or jerk away. "At least not the way you mean."

"All these gadgets you've got down here," she said, clinging desperately to the lifeline of logic in a sea of confusion. "Whatever you're using, it produces quite an optical illusion." She swallowed. "I imagine the Pentagon would be very interested."

"It's not an illusion." He touched her arm, and though she didn't pull away as he'd feared she would, her skin was cold and clammy. "You're afraid of me now."

"That's absurd." But her voice was shaking. She forced herself to stand. "It was just a trick, an effective one, but—"

She broke off when he placed his hand, palm down on the counter beside them. It vanished to the wrist. Dark and dazed, her eyes lifted to his.

"Oh, God. It's not possible." Terrified, she pulled his arm and was almost faint with relief when she saw his hand, whole and warm.

"It's possible." He brought the hand gently to her face. "It's real."

She lifted her trembling fingers to his. "Give me a minute." Moving carefully, she turned and walked a few steps away. Rejection sliced through him, a dull, angry blade.

"I'm sorry." With great effort he controlled his voice, kept it even. "I didn't know of a better way, an easier way, to show you. If I had tried to explain, you wouldn't have believed me."

"No, no, I wouldn't have." She had seen it. Yet her mind still wanted to argue that she could not have seen it. A game, a trick, nothing more. Though there was a comfort in the denial, she remembered how time and again, Nemesis had seemed to vanish before her eyes.

She turned back and saw that he was watching her, his body tensed and ready. No game. When she accepted the truth her trembling only increased. Briskly, she rubbed her hands up and down her arms, hoping to warm and steady the muscles.

"How do you do this?"

"I'm not completely sure." He opened his hands, stared at them, then fisted them to push them impotently into his pockets. "Something happened to me when I was in the coma. Something changed me. A few weeks after I came back I discovered it, almost by accident. I had to learn to accept it, to use it, because I know it was given to me for a reason."

"And so—Nemesis."

"Yes, and so Nemesis." He seemed to steady himself. Deborah saw that his eyes were level and curiously blank when he looked at her. "I have no choice in this, Deborah. But you do."

"I don't think I understand." She lifted a hand to her head and gave a quick, shaky laugh. "I know I don't understand."

"I wasn't honest with you, about what I am. The man you fell in love with was normal."

Baffled, she let her hand fall to her side again. "I'm not following you. I fell in love with you."

"Damn it, I'm not normal." His eyes were suddenly furious. "I'll never be. I'll carry this thing with me until I die. I can't tell you how I know, I just do."

"Gage—" But when she reached out to him, he backed away.

"I don't want your pity."

"You don't have it," she snapped back. "Why should you? You're not ill. You're whole and you're healthy. If anything, I'm angry because you held *this* back from me, too. And I know why." She dragged both hands through her hair as she paced away from him. "You thought I'd walk, didn't you? You thought I was too

weak, too stupid, or too fragile to handle it. You didn't
trust me to love you." Her fury built so quickly, she was
all but blind with it. "You didn't trust me to love you,"
she repeated. "Well, the hell with you. I do, and I always will."

She turned, sprinting for the stairs. He caught her at
the base of them, turning her back to him and pulling
her close while she cursed at him and struggled.

"Call me anything you like." He grabbed her shoulders and shook once. "Slap me again if you want. But
don't leave."

"You expected me to, didn't you?" she demanded.
She tossed her head back as she strained away from him.
"You expected me to turn around and walk away."

"Yes."

She started to shout at him. Then she saw what was in
his eyes, what he held back with such rigid control. It
was fear. Accusations melted away. "You were wrong,"
she said quietly. With her eyes still on his, she lifted her
hands to his face, rose on her toes and kissed him.

A shudder. From him, from her. Twin waves of relief. He drew her closer, crushing, consuming. As huge
as his fear had been, a need sprang up to replace it. It
was not pity he tasted on her lips, but passion.

Small, seductive sounds hummed in her throat as she
struggled out of the robe. It was more than an offering
of herself. It was a demand that he take her as she was,
that he allow himself to be taken. With an oath that
ended in a groan, he moved his hands over her. He was
caught in the madness, a purifying madness.

Impatient, she tugged at his shirt. "Make love with
me." Her head fell back and her eyes were as challeng-
ing as her voice. "Make love with me now."

She pulled at his clothes even as they lowered to the floor.

Frenzied and frantic. Heated and hungry. They came together. Power leaped like wind-fed flames. It was always so between them, she thought as her body shuddered, shuddered, shuddered. Yet now there was more. Here was a unity. Here was compassion, trust, vulnerability to mix with hungers. She had never wanted him more.

Her hands clenched in his dark hair as she rose above him. She needed to see his face, his eyes. "I love you." The breath tore in her throat. "Let me show you how I love you."

Agile, quick, greedy, she moved over him, taking her mouth down his throat, over his chest, down to where his taut stomach muscles quivered under her moist, seeking lips. The blood pounded in his head, his heart, his loins.

She was a miracle, the second he'd been given in a lifetime. When he reached for her, he reached for love and for salvation.

They rolled, a tangle of limbs and needs, unmindful of the hard, unyielding floor, the clatter and hum of machines blindly working. Breath came fast, heartbeats galloped. Each taste, each touch seemed more potent, more pungent than ever before.

His fingers dug into her hips when he lifted her. She sheathed him, surrounded him. The pleasure speared them both. Their hands slid toward each other's, palm against palm, then fingers locked tight.

They held on, eyes open, bodies joined, until they took the final leap together.

Boneless, she slid down to him. Her mouth brushed his once, then again, before she lay her head on his shoulder. Never had she felt more beautiful, more desirable, more complete, than in feeling his heart thunder wildly beneath hers.

Her lips curved as she turned and pressed them to his throat. "That was my way of saying you're stuck with me."

"I like the way you get your point across." Gently he ran a hand up and down her spine. She was his. He'd been a fool to ever doubt it, or her. "Does this mean I'm forgiven?"

"Not necessarily." Bracing her hands on his shoulders, she pushed herself up. "I don't understand who you are. Maybe I never will. But understand this. I want all, or I want nothing. I saw what evasions, denials, refusals did to my parents' marriage. I won't live with that."

He put a hand on hers, very lightly. "Is that a proposal?"

She didn't hesitate. "Yes."

"Do you want an answer now?"

Her eyes narrowed. "Yes. And don't think you can get out of it by disappearing. I'll just wait until you come back."

He laughed, amazed that she could joke about something he'd been so sure would repel her. "Then I guess you'll have to make an honest man out of me."

"I intend to." She kissed him briefly, then shifted away to bundle into the robe. "No long engagement."

"Okay."

"As soon as we put a cap on this thing and Cilla and Boyd can arrange to bring the kids out, we get married."

"Agreed." Humor danced in his eyes. "Anything else?"

"I want children right away."

He hitched on his jeans. "Any particular number?"

"One at a time."

"Sounds reasonable."

"And—"

"Shut up a minute." He took her hands. "Deborah, I want to be married to you, to spend the rest of my life knowing when I reach out, I'll find you there. And I want a family, our family." He pressed his lips to the fingers that curled over his. "I want forever with you." He watched her blink back tears and kissed her gently. "Right now I want something else."

"What?"

"Breakfast."

With a strangled laugh, she threw her arms around him. "Me, too."

They ate in the kitchen, laughing and cozy, as if they always shared the first meal of the day together. The sun was bright, the coffee strong. Deborah had dozens of questions to ask him, but she held them back. For this one hour, she wanted them to be two ordinary people in love.

Ordinary, she thought. Strange, but she felt they were and could be ordinary, even with the very extraordinary aspects of their lives. All they needed were moments like this, where they could sit in the sunshine and talk of inconsequential things.

When Frank walked in, he paused at the kitchen doorway and gave Deborah a polite nod. "Is there anything you need this morning, Mr. Guthrie?"

"She knows, Frank." Gage laid a hand over Deborah's. "She knows everything."

A grin split Frank's wide, sober face. "Well, it's about time." All pretense of formality dropped as he lumbered across the room to pluck up a piece of toast. He took a seat at the semicircular breakfast nook, bit into the toast and gestured with the half that was left. "I told him you wouldn't head for the hills when you found out about his little vanishing act. You're too tough for that."

"Thank you. I think." Deborah chuckled and the rest of the toast disappeared in one healthy bite.

"I know people," Frank said, taking the tray of bacon Gage passed him. "In my profession—my former profession—you had to be able to make somebody quick. And I was good, real good, right, Gage?"

"That's right, Frank."

"I could spot a patsy two blocks away." He wagged a piece of bacon at Deborah. "You ain't no patsy."

And she'd thought of him as the strong, silent type, Deborah mused. She was fascinated by the way he made up for lost time, rattling quickly as he steam-shoveled food away. "You've been with Gage a long time."

"Eight years—not counting the couple of times he sent me up."

"Kind of like Kato to his Green Hornet."

He grinned again, then let out a series of guffaws. "Hey, I like her, Gage. She's okay. I told you she was okay."

"Yes, you did. Deborah's going to be staying, Frank. How would you like to be best man?"

"No kidding?" Deborah didn't think Frank's grin could stretch any wider. Then she saw the gleam of tears in his eyes. At that moment, her heart was lost to him.

"No kidding." She shifted, took his big face in her hands and kissed him firmly on the mouth. "There, you're first to kiss the bride-to-be."

"How about that." Deborah had to bite back a chuckle as a beet-red blush stained Frank's face. "How about that."

"I'd like Deborah to move in a few things today," Gage put in.

She glanced down at the robe. Besides the borrowed garment, she had an evening dress, a pair of stockings and an evening bag. "I could use a few things." But she was thinking of the big room downstairs, the computers, the information Gage had at his fingertips.

Gage had little trouble following the direction of her thoughts. "Do you have someone who could put what you need together? Frank could go by your apartment and pick them up."

"Yes." She thought of Mrs. Greenbaum. "I'll just make a call."

Within a half an hour, she was back in Gage's secret room, wearing a pair of his jeans hitched up with the belt of his robe and a crisply pressed linen shirt skimming her thighs. Hands on her hips, she studied the map as Gage explained.

"These are drop points, major drug deals. I've been able to run makes on a handful of the messengers."

"Why haven't you fed this information to the police?"

He glanced at her briefly. On this point they might never agree. "It wouldn't help them get any closer to the top men. Right now, I'm working on the pattern." He moved to one of the computers and, after a moment, signaled to her. "None of the drops are less than twenty blocks apart." He motioned to the reproduction on the monitor. "The time span between them is fairly steady." He punched a few buttons. A list of dates rolled onto the screen. "Two weeks, sometimes three."

Frowning in concentration, she studied the screen. "Can I have a printout of this?"

"Why?"

"I'd like to run it through my computer at the office. See if I can find any correlation."

"It isn't safe." Before she could argue, he took her hand and led her to another work station. He tapped a code in the keyboard and brought up a file. Deborah's mouth opened in surprise as she saw her own work reproduced on the screen.

"You've tapped into my system," she murmured. "In more ways than one."

"The point is, if I can, so can someone else. Anything you need, you can find here."

"Apparently." She sat, far from sure how she felt about Gage or anyone else peeking over her shoulder as she worked. "Am I on the right track?"

Saying nothing, he tapped in a new code. "You've been going after the corporations, and the directors. A logical place to start. Whoever set up the organization knows business. Four years ago, we didn't have the information or the technology to get this close, so we had to go in and physically infiltrate." Names flipped by, some she recognized, some she didn't. They were all tagged Deceased. "It didn't work because there was a leak. Someone who knew about the undercover operation passed the information to the other side. Montega was waiting for us, and he knew we were cops." Though Deborah felt a chill, he said it calmly. "He also had to know exactly how we were set up that night, to the man. Otherwise he could never have slipped through the backup."

"Another cop?"

"It's a possibility. We had ten handpicked men on the team that night. I've checked out every one of them, their bank accounts, their records, their life-style. So far, I haven't found a thing."

"Who else knew?"

"My captain, the commissioner, the mayor." He made a restless movement with his shoulders. "Maybe more. We were only cops. They didn't tell us everything."

"When you find the pattern, what then?"

"I wait, I watch, and I follow. The man with the money leads me to the man in charge. And he's the one I want."

She suppressed a shudder, promising herself she would somehow convince him to let the police take over when they had enough information. "While you're looking for that, I'd like to concentrate on finding names—that common thread."

"All right." He ran a hand over her hair until it rested on her shoulder. "This machine is similar to the one you use in the office. It has a few more—"

"How do you know?" she interrupted.

"How do I know what?"

"What machine I use in the office?"

He had to smile. "Deborah…" Lightly, lingering, he bent down to kiss her. "There's nothing about you I don't know."

Uncomfortable, she shifted away, then rose. "Will I find my name programmed on one of these machines?"

He watched her, knowing he would have to tread lightly. "Yes. I told myself it was routine, but the truth was I was in love with you and greedy for every detail. I know when you were born, to the minute, and where. I know you broke your wrist falling off a bike when you were five, that you moved in with your sister and her husband after the death of your parents. And when your sister divorced, you moved with her. Richmond, Chicago, Dallas. Finally Denver where you zipped through college in three years, *cum laude,* drove yourself through law school to graduate in the top five percent of your class, and passed your bar on the first attempt. With enough finesse to bring you offers from four of the top law firms in the country. But you chose to come here, and work in the D.A.'s office.''

She rubbed her palms over the thighs of her jeans. "It's odd to hear an encapsulated version of my life story."

"There were things I couldn't learn from the computer." The important things, he thought. The vital things. "The way your hair smells, the way your eyes go to indigo when you're angry or aroused. The way you make me feel when you touch me. I won't deny I invaded your privacy, but I won't apologize for it."

"No, you wouldn't," she said after a moment. She let out a little breath. "And I suppose I can't be overly offended, since I ran a make on you, too."

He smiled. "I know."

She laughed, shaking her head. "Okay. Let's get to work."

They had hardly settled when one of the three phones on the long counter rang. Deborah barely glanced over as Gage lifted a receiver.

"Guthrie."

"Gage, it's Frank. I'm at Deborah's apartment. You'd better get over here."

Chapter 11

Her heart beating erratically, Deborah sprinted out of the elevator and down the hall one step in front of Gage. Frank's phone call had had them shooting across town in Gage's Aston Martin in record time.

The door was open. Deborah's breath stopped as she stood on the threshold and saw the destruction of her apartment. Curtains slashed, mementos crushed, tables and chairs viciously broken and tossed in pieces on the floor. The first groan escaped before she spotted Lil Greenbaum propped on the remains of the torn and tattered sofa, her face deathly white.

"Oh, God." Kicking debris aside, she rushed over to drop to her knees. "Mrs. Greenbaum." She took the cold, frail hand in hers.

Lil's thin lids fluttered up, and her myopic eyes struggled to focus without the benefit of her glasses. "Deborah." Though her voice was weak, she managed a faint smile. "They never would have done it if they hadn't caught me by surprise."

"They hurt you." She looked up as Frank came out of the bedroom carrying a pillow. "Did you call an ambulance?"

"She wouldn't let me." Gently he slipped the pillow under Lil's head.

"Don't need one. Hate hospitals. Just a bump on the head," Lil said, and squeezed Deborah's hand. "I've had one before."

"Do you want me to worry myself sick?" As she spoke, Deborah slipped her fingers down to monitor Lil's pulse.

"Your apartment's in worse shape than I am."

"It's easy to replace my things. How would I replace you?" She kissed Lil's gnarled knuckles. "Please. For me."

Defeated, Lil let out a sigh. "Okay, I'll let them poke at me. But I won't stay in the hospital."

"Good enough." She turned, but Gage was already lifting the phone.

"It's dead."

"Mrs. Greenbaum's apartment is right across the hall."

Gage nodded to Frank.

"The keys—" Deborah began.

"Frank doesn't need keys." He crossed over to crouch beside Deborah. "Mrs. Greenbaum, can you tell us what happened?"

She studied him, narrowing and widening her eyes until she brought him into shaky focus. "I know you, don't I? You picked Deborah up last night, all spiffed up in a tux. You sure can kiss."

He grinned at her, but his hand slipped to her wrist just as Deborah's had. "Thanks."

"You're the one with pots of money, right?"

She may have had a bump on the head, Gage thought, but her mind seemed to work quickly enough. "Right."

"She liked the roses. Mooned over them."

"Mrs. Greenbaum." Deborah sat back on her heels. "You don't have to play matchmaker—we've taken care of it ourselves. Tell us what happened to you."

"I'm glad to hear it. Young people today waste too much time."

"Mrs. Greenbaum."

"All right, all right. I had the list of things you'd called for. I was in the bedroom, going through the closet. Neat as a pin, by the way," she said to Gage. "The girl's very tidy."

"I'm relieved to hear it."

"I was just taking out the navy pin-striped suit when I heard a sound behind me." She grimaced, more embarrassed now than shaken. "I'd have heard it before, but I turned on the radio when I came in. That'll teach me to listen to the Top 40 countdown. I started to turn, and, boom. Somebody put my lights out."

Deborah lowered her head to Lil's hand. Emotions screamed through her, tangled and tearing. Fury, terror, guilt. She was an old woman, Deborah thought as she struggled for control. What kind of person strikes a seventy-year-old woman?

"I'm sorry," she said as levelly as she could. "I'm so sorry."

"It's not your fault."

"Yes, it is." She lifted her head. "This was all for my benefit. All of it. I knew they were after me, and I asked you to come in here. I didn't think. I just didn't think."

"Now, this is nonsense. I'm the one who got bashed, and I can tell you I'm damn mad about it. If I hadn't been caught off guard, I'd have put some of my karate training into use." Lil's mouth firmed. "I'd like to have another go at it. Wasn't too many years ago I could deck Mr. Greenbaum, and I'm still in shape." She glanced up as the paramedics came through the door. "Oh, Lord," she said in disgust. "Now I'm in for it."

With Gage's arm around her shoulders, Deborah stood back while Lil ordered the paramedics around, complaining about every poke and prod. She was still chattering when they lifted her onto a stretcher and carried her out.

"She's quite a woman," Gage commented.

"She's the best." When tears threatened, she bit her lip. "I don't know what I'd do if..."

"She's going to be fine. Her pulse was strong, her mind was clear." He gave her a quick squeeze then turned to Frank. "What's the story?"

"The door wasn't locked when I got here." The big man jerked his thumb toward the opening. "They did a messy job forcing it. I walked into this." He gestured around the chaos of the living room. "I thought I should check out the rest of the place before I called you, and found the lady in the bedroom. She was just coming to. Tried to take a swing at me." He smiled at Deborah. "She's one tough old lady. I calmed her down, then I called you." His mouth tightened. There had been a time he hadn't been above pinching a purse from a nice little old lady, but he'd never laid a finger on one. "I figure I missed them by ten or fifteen minutes." His big fists bunched. "Otherwise they wouldn't have walked out of here."

Gage nodded. "I have a couple of things I'd like you to do." He turned back to Deborah, gently cradling her face in his hands. "I'll have him call the police," he said, knowing how her mind worked. "Meanwhile, why don't you see if you can salvage anything you might need until tomorrow?"

"All right." She agreed because she needed a moment alone. In the bedroom, she pressed her hands to her mouth. There had been such viciousness here, such fury, yet there was a cold kind of organization to the destruction that made it all the more frightening.

Her clothes were torn and shredded, the little antique bottles and jars she'd collected over the years broken and smashed over the heaps of silk and cotton. Her bed had been destroyed, her desk littered with ugly words someone had carved deeply in the wood with a knife. Everything she owned had been pulled out or torn down.

Kneeling, she picked up a ragged scrap of paper. It had once been a photograph, one of the many of her family she had treasured.

Gage came in quietly. After a moment, he knelt beside her and laid a hand on her shoulder. "Deborah, let me take you out of here."

"There's nothing left." She pressed her lips together, determined to keep her voice from shaking. "I know they're only things, but there's nothing left." Slowly she curled her fingers around the remains of the photograph. "My parents—" She shook her head, then turned her face into his shoulder.

His own anger was a bright steady flame in his chest. He held her, letting her grieve while he promised himself he would find the men who had hurt her. And all the while he couldn't get past the sick terror that lodged in his throat.

She might have been there. She might have been alone in this room when they'd come in. Instead of trinkets and mementos, he could have found her broken on the floor.

"They'll pay," he promised her. "I swear it."

"Yes, they will." When she lifted her head, he saw that her grief had passed into fury. It was just as deep, just as sharp. "Whatever I have to do, I'm going to bring them down." After pushing back her hair, she stood up. "If they thought they could scare me away by doing this, they're going to be disappointed." She kicked at the remains of her favorite red suit. "Let's go to work."

They spent hours in the cavern beneath his house, checking data, inputting more. Deborah's head was throbbing in time with the machines, but she continued to push. Gage busied himself across the room, but they rarely spoke. They didn't need to. Perhaps for the first time, their purposes meshed and their differences in viewpoints no longer seemed to matter.

They were both anxious to make up the time lost while talking to the police—and evading the enterprising Wisner, who had shown up at the apartment in their wake. She'd be a Monday-morning headline again, Deborah thought impatiently. The press would only bring more pressure from City Hall. She was ready for it.

She no longer swore when she slammed into a dead end, but meticulously backtracked with a patience she hadn't been aware of possessing. When the phone rang, she didn't even hear it. Gage had to call her name twice before she broke out of her concentrated trance.

"Yes, what?"

"It's for you." He held up the receiver. "Jerry Bower."

With a frown for the interruption, she walked over to take the call. "Jerry."

"Good God, Deborah, are you all right?"

"Yes, I'm fine. How did you know where I was?"

She could hear him take two long breaths. "I've been trying to reach you for hours, to make sure you were okay after last night. I finally decided just to go by your place and see for myself. I ran into a pack of cops and that little weasel Wisner. Your place—"

"I know. I wasn't there."

"Thank God. What the hell's going on, Deb? We're supposed to have a handle on these things down at City Hall, but I feel like I'm boxing in the dark. The mayor's going to blow when he hears this. What am I supposed to tell him?"

"Tell him to concentrate on the debates next week." She rubbed her temple. "I already know his stand on this, and he knows mine. You're only going to drive yourself crazy trying to arbitrate."

"Look, I work for him, but you're a friend. There might be something I can do."

"I don't know." She frowned at the blinking lights on the map. "Someone's sending me a message, loud and clear, but I haven't worked out how to send one back. You can tell the mayor this. If I manage to work this out before the election, he's going to win by a landslide."

There was a slight hesitation. "I guess you're right," Jerry said thoughtfully. "That might be the best way to keep him from breathing down your neck. Just be careful, okay?"

"I will."

She hung up, then tilted her head from one side to the other to work out kinks.

Gage glanced over. "I wouldn't mind taking out a full page ad in the *World* to announce our engagement."

Confused, she blinked. Then laughed. "Jerry? Don't be stupid. We're just pals."

"Mmm-hmm."

She smiled, then walked over to hook her arms around his waist. "Not one big, sloppy kiss between us. Which is exactly what I could use right now."

"I guess I've got at least one in me." He lowered his head.

When his lips met hers, she felt the tension seep out of her, layer by layer, degree by degree. With a murmur, she slid her hands up his back, gently kneading the muscles, soothing them as his lips soothed her.

Quiet, content, relaxed. She could bring him to that, just as she could make him shudder and ache. With a soft sound of pleasure, he changed the angle of the kiss and deepened it for both of them.

"Sorry to break this up." Frank came through the tunnel, bearing a large tray. "But since you're working so hard . . ." He grinned hugely. "I figured you should eat to keep up your strength."

"Thanks." Deborah drew away from Gage and took a sniff. "Oh, Lord, what is it?"

"My special burn-through-the-ribs chili." He winked at her. "Believe me, it'll keep you awake."

"It smells incredible."

"Dig in. You got a couple of beers, a thermos of coffee and some cheese nachos."

Deborah rolled a chair over. "Frank, you are a man among men." He blushed again, delighting her. She took her first bite, scorched her mouth, her throat and her stomach lining. "And this," she said with real pleasure, "is a bowl of chili."

He shuffled his feet. "Glad you like it. I put Mrs. Greenbaum in the gold room," he told Gage. "I thought she'd get a kick out of the bed curtains and stuff. She's having some chicken soup and watching *King Kong* on the VCR."

"Thanks, Frank." Gage scooped up his own spoon of chili.

"Just give me a ring if you need anything else."

Deborah listened to the echo of Frank's footsteps in the tunnel. "You had her brought here?" she said quietly.

"She didn't like the hospital." He shrugged. "Frank talked to the doctor. She only had a mild concussion, which was a miracle in someone her age. Her heart's strong as an elephant. All she needs is some quiet and pampering for a few days."

"So you had her brought here."

"She shouldn't be alone."

She leaned over and kissed his cheek. "I love you very much."

When they had finished and were back to work, Deborah couldn't stop her mind from wandering in his direction. He was such a complicated man. Arrogant as the devil when it suited him, rude when it pleased him, and as smooth and charming as an Irish poet when the mood struck him. He ran a multimillion-dollar business. And he walked the streets at night to ward off muggers, thieves, rapists. He was the lover every woman dreamed about. Romantic, erotic, yet solid and dependable as granite. Yet he carried something intangible inside him that allowed him to vanish like smoke into the wall, slip without a shadow through the night.

She shook her head. She was far from ready, far from able to dwell on that aspect of him.

How could he, a man she knew to be flesh and blood, become insubstantial at will? Yet she had seen it with her own eyes. She pressed her fingers against those eyes for a moment and sighed. Things weren't always what they seemed.

Straightening her shoulders, she doubled her concentration. If numbers began to blur, she downed more coffee. Already she had a half dozen more names, names she was sure she would find attached to death certificates.

It seemed hopeless. But until this avenue was exhausted, she had no other. Mumbling to herself, she punched up screen after screen. Abruptly she stopped. Cautious, eyes sharpened, she backtracked—one screen, two. She held back a smile, afraid to believe she'd finally broken through. After another five minutes of careful work, she called Gage.

"I think I've found something."

So had he, but he chose to keep his information to himself. "What?"

"This number." When he bent over her shoulder, she ran a finger below it on the screen. "It's all mixed with the corporation number, the tax number, and all the other identification numbers of this company." When he lifted a hand to rub at the base of her neck, she leaned back into the massage gratefully. "A supposedly bankrupt corporation, by the way. Out of business for eighteen months. Now look at this." She punch up a new screen. "Different company, different location, different names and numbers. Except...this one." She tapped a finger on the screen. "It's in a different place here, but the number's the same. And here." She showed him again, screen after screen. "It's the corporation number on one, the company branch on another, tax ID here, a file code there.''

"Social security number," Gage muttered.

"What?"

"Nine digits. I'd say it's a social security number. An important one." He turned to walk quickly to the control board.

"What are you doing?"

"Finding out who it belongs to."

She blew out a breath, a bit annoyed that he hadn't seemed more enthusiastic about her find. Her eyes were all but falling out of her head, and she didn't even get a pat on the back. "How?"

"It seems worth going to the main source." The screen above him began to blink.

"Which is?"

"The IRS."

"The—" She was out of her chair like a shot. "You're telling me you can tap into the IRS computers?"

"That's right." His concentration was focused on the panel. "Almost got it."

"That's illegal. A federal offense."

"Mmm-hmm. Want to recommend a good lawyer?"

Torn, she gripped her hands together. "It's not a joke."

"No." But his lips curved as he followed the information on the screen. "All right. We're in." He shot her a look. The internal war she was waging showed clearly on her face. "You could go upstairs until I've finished."

"That hardly matters. I know what you're doing. That makes me a part of it." She closed her eyes and saw Lil Greenbaum lying pale and hurt on her broken couch.

"Go ahead," she said, and put a hand on his arm. "We're in this together."

He tapped in the numbers she had found, pushed a series of buttons and waited. A name flashed up on the screen.

"Oh, God." Deborah's fingers dug into Gage's shoulder.

He seemed to be made of stone at that moment, unmoving, almost unbreathing, his muscles hard as rock.

"Tucker Fields," he murmured. "Son of a bitch."

Then he moved so quickly, Deborah nearly stumbled. With a strength born of desperation, she grabbed him. "Don't. You can't." She saw his eyes burn, as she had seen them behind the mask. They were full of fury and deadly purpose. "I know what you want," she said quickly, clinging. "You want to go find him right now. You want to tear him apart. But you can't. That isn't the way."

"I'm going to kill him." His voice was cold and flat. "Understand that. Nothing's going to stop me."

The breath was searing and clogging in her lungs. If he left now, she would lose him. "And accomplish what? It won't bring Jack back. It won't change what happened to you. It won't even finish what you both started that night on the docks. If you kill Fields, someone will replace him, and it'll go on. We need to break the back of the organization, Gage, to bring it all out to the public so that people will see. If Fields is responsible—"

"If?"

She took a careful, steadying breath and kept her grip on him tight. "We don't have enough, not yet. I can build a case if you give me time, and bring them down. Bring them all down."

"My God, Deborah, do you really think you'll get him in court? A man with that much power? He'll slip through your fingers like sand. The minute you start an investigation, he'll know, and he'll cover himself."

"Then you'll do the investigating here, and I'll throw dust in his eyes from my office." She spoke quickly, desperate to convince him and, she was sure, to save them both. "I'll make him think I'm on the wrong track. Gage, we have to be sure. You must see that. If you go after him now, like this, everything you've worked for, everything we've started to build together, will be destroyed."

"He tried to have you killed." Gage put his hands to her face, and though his touch was light, she could feel the tension in each finger. "Don't you understand that nothing, not even Jack's murder, signed his death warrant more indelibly?"

She brought her hands to his wrists. "I'm here, with you. That's what's important. We have more work to do, to prove that Fields is involved, to find out how far down the line the corruption runs. You'll have justice, Gage. I promise."

Slowly he relaxed. She was right—at least in some ways she was right. Killing Fields with his bare hands would have been satisfying, but it wouldn't complete the job he had begun. So he could wait for that. There was another stone to uncover, and he had less than a week to wait until he did so.

"All right." He watched the color seep slowly back into her face. "I didn't mean to frighten you."

"Well, I hope you never mean to, because you scared me to death." She turned her head, pressing her lips to his palm, then managed a shaky smile. "Since we've already broken a federal law, why don't we go a step forward and look at the mayor's tax records for the last few years?''

Minutes later, she was seated beside Gage at the console.

"Five hundred and sixty-two thousand," she murmured, when she read Fields's declared income for the previous tax year. "A bit more than the annual salary for Urbana's mayor."

"It's hard to believe he's stupid enough to put that much on record." Gage flipped back another year. "I imagine he's got several times that much in Swiss accounts."

"I never liked him, personally," Deborah put in. "But I always respected him." She rose to pace. "When I think about the kind of position he's been in, a direct line to the police, to the D.A.'s office, to businesses, utilities. Nothing goes on in Urbana he doesn't know about. And he can put his people everywhere. How many city officials are on his private payroll, how many cops, how many judges?"

"He thinks he's got it covered." Gage pushed away from the console. "What about Bower?"

"Jerry?" Deborah sighed and rubbed her stiff neck. "Loyal to the bone, and with political aspirations of his own. He might overlook a few under-the-table machinations, but nothing so big as this. Fields was clever enough to pick someone young and eager, with a good background and unblemished reputation." She shook her head. "I feel badly that I can't pass this along to him."

"Mitchell?"

"No, I'd bet my life on Mitch. He's been around a long time. He's never been Fields's biggest fan but he respects the office. He's by the book because he believes in the book. He even pays his parking tickets. What are you doing?"

"It doesn't hurt to check."

To Deborah's consternation, he pulled up Jerry's then Mitchell's tax returns. Finding nothing out of the ordinary, he moved toward another console.

"We can start pulling up bank accounts. We need a list of people who work at City Hall, the department, the D.A.'s office." He glanced up at her. "You've got a headache."

She realized she was rubbing at her temple. "Just a little one."

Instead of turning on the machine, he shut the others down. "You've been working too hard."

"I'm fine. We've got a lot to do."

"We've already done a lot." And he was cursing himself for pushing her so hard for so long. "A couple of hours off won't change anything." He slipped an arm around her waist. "How about a hot bath and a nap?"

"Mmm." She leaned her head against his shoulder as they started down the tunnel. "That sounds incredible."

"And a back rub."

"Yes. Oh, yes."

"And why don't I give you that foot rub that's long overdue."

She smiled. Had she ever really been worried about something as foolish as other women? "Why don't you?"

Deborah was already half-asleep by the time they came through the panel into Gage's bedroom. She stopped in mid-yawn and stared at the boxes covering the bed.

"What's all this?"

"At the moment all you have is my shirt on your back. And though I like it—" he flicked a finger down the buttons "—a lot, I thought you might want some replacements."

"Replacements?" She pushed at her tumbled hair. "How?"

"I gave Frank a list. He can be very enterprising."

"Frank? But it's Sunday. Half the stores are closed." She pressed a hand to her stomach. "Oh, God, he didn't steal them, did he?"

"I don't think so." Then he laughed and caught her in his arms. "How am I going to live with such a scrupulously honest woman? No, they're paid for, I promise. It's as easy as making a few calls. You'll notice the boxes are from Athena's."

She nodded. It was one of the biggest and slickest department stores in the city. And the light dawned. "You own it."

"Guilty." He kissed her. "Anything you don't like can go back. But I think I know your style and your size."

"You didn't have to do this."

From the tone of her voice, he understood she wished he hadn't done it. Patient, he tucked her tumbled hair behind her ear. "This wasn't an attempt to usurp your independence, Counselor."

"No." And she was sounding very ungrateful. "But—"

"Be practical. How would it look for you to show up at the office tomorrow in my pants?" He tugged the belt loose and had the jeans sliding to her feet.

"Outrageous," she agreed, and smiled when he lifted her up and set her down beside the heap of denim.

"And my shirt." He began to undo the buttons.

"Ridiculous. You're right, you were being very practical." She took his hands to still them before he could distract her. "And I appreciate it. But it doesn't feel right, you buying my clothes."

"You can pay me back. Over the next sixty or seventy years." He cupped her chin when she started to speak again. "Deborah, I've got more money than any one man needs. You're willing to share my problems, then it should follow that you'll share my fortunes."

"I don't want you to think that the money matters to me, that it makes any difference in the way I feel about you."

He studied her thoughtfully. "You know, I didn't realize you could come up with anything quite that stupid."

She lifted her chin, but when he smiled at her she could only sigh. "It is stupid. I love you even though you do own hotels, and apartment buildings, and department stores. And if I don't open one of these boxes, I'm going to go crazy."

"Why don't you keep your sanity then, and I'll go run the bath?"

When he walked into the adjoining room, she grabbed one at random, shook it, then pulled off the lid. Under the tissue paper she found a long, sheer sleeping gown in pale blue silk.

"Well." She held it up, noting the back was cut below the waist. "Frank certainly has an eye for lingerie. I wonder what the boys in the office will say if I wear this in tomorrow."

Unable to resist, she stripped off the shirt and let the cool thin silk slide over her head and shoulders. A perfect fit, she mused, running her hands over her hips.

Delighted, she turned to the mirror just as Gage came back into the room.

He couldn't speak any more than he could take his eyes from her. The long, sleek shimmer of silk whispered against her skin as she turned to him. Her eyes were dark as midnight and glistening with a woman's secret pleasure.

Her lips curved slowly. Was there a woman alive who didn't dream about having the man she loved stare at her with such avid hunger? Deliberately she tilted her head and lifted one hand to run her fingertips lazily down the center of the gown—and just as lazily up again—watching his eyes follow the movement.

"What do you think?"

His gaze trailed up until it met hers again. "I think Frank deserves a very large raise."

As she laughed, he came toward her.

Chapter 12

Over the next three days and the next three evenings, they worked together. Piece by steady piece they built a case against Tucker Fields. At her office Deborah pursued avenues she knew would lead nowhere, carefully laying a false trail.

As she worked, she continued to fight the rugged tug-of-war inside her. Ethics versus instinct.

Each night, Gage would slip out of bed, clothe himself in black and roam the streets. They didn't speak of it. If he knew how often Deborah lay awake, anxious and torn until he returned just before dawn, he offered no excuses or apologies. There were none he could give her.

The press continued to herald Nemesis's exploits. Those secret nocturnal activities were never mentioned and stood between them like a thick, silent wall that couldn't be breached on either side.

She understood, but couldn't agree.

He understood, but couldn't acquiesce.

Even as they worked toward a single goal, their individual beliefs forced them at cross-purposes.

She sat in her office, the evening paper beside a stack of law books.

Nemesis Bags East End Ripper

She hadn't read the copy, couldn't bring herself to read it. She already knew about the man who had killed four people in the past ten days, with his favored weapon, a hunting knife. The headline was enough to tell her why she had found traces of blood in the bathroom sink.

When was it going to end? she asked herself. When was he going to stop? A psychotic with a knife had nothing to do with Fields and the drug cartel. How much longer could they go on pretending that their relationship, their future, could be normal?

He wasn't pretending, Deborah admitted with a sigh. She was.

"O'Roarke." Mitchell slapped a file on her desk. "The city doesn't pay you this princely salary to daydream."

She looked at the file that had just landed on a pile of others. "I don't suppose it would do any good to remind you that my caseload has already broken the world's record."

"So's the city's crime rate." Because she looked exhausted, he walked over to her coffee machine to pour her a cup of the bitter bottom-of-the-pot brew. "Maybe if Nemesis would take some time off, we wouldn't be so overworked."

Her frown turned into a grimace as she sipped the coffee. "That sounded almost like a compliment."

"Just stating facts. I don't have to approve of his methods to like the results."

Surprised, she looked up into Mitchell's round, sturdy face. "Do you mean that?"

"This Ripper character carved up four innocent people and was starting on a fifth when Nemesis got there. It's hard to complain when anybody, even a misguided masked wonder, drops a creep like that in our laps and saves the life of an eighteen-year-old girl."

"Yes." Deborah murmured. "Yes, it is."

"Not that I'm going out and buying a T-shirt and joining his fan club." Mitchell pulled out a cigar and ran it through his stubby fingers. "So, making any progress on your favorite case?"

She shrugged evasively. "I've got another week."

"You're hardheaded, O'Roarke. I like that."

Her brows rose. "Now, that was definitely a compliment."

"Don't let it swell your pinstripes. The mayor's still unhappy with you—and the polls are happy with him. If he knocks Tarrington out in the debates tomorrow, you could have a hard road until the next election."

"The mayor doesn't worry me."

"Suit yourself. Wisner's still pumping your name into copy." He held up a hand before she could snarl. "I'm holding Fields off, but if you could keep a lower profile—"

"Yeah, it was really stupid of me to have my apartment trashed."

"Okay, okay." He had the grace to flush. "We're all sorry about that, but if you could try to keep out of trouble for a while, it would make it easy on everyone."

"I'll chain myself to my desk," she said between her teeth. "And the minute I get the chance, I'm going to kick Wisner right in his press card."

Mitchell grinned. "Get in line. Hey, ah, let me know if you need a few extra bucks before the insurance takes over."

"Thanks, but I'm fine." She looked at the files. "Besides, with all this, who needs an apartment?"

When he left her alone, Deborah opened the new case file. And dropped her head in her hands. Was it a twisted kind of irony or fate that she'd been assigned to prosecute the East End Ripper? Her chief witness, she thought, her lover, was the one man she couldn't even discuss it with.

At seven Gage waited for her at a quiet corner table in a French restaurant skirting City Park. He knew it was almost over and that when it was, he would have to explain to Deborah why he hadn't trusted her with all the details.

She would be hurt and angry. Rightfully so. But he preferred her hurt and angry, and alive. He was well aware how difficult the past few days—and nights—had been for her. If there had been a choice, he would have given up everything, including his conscience, to keep her happy.

But he had no choice, hadn't had a choice since the moment he'd come out of the coma.

He could do nothing but tell her and show her how completely he loved her. And to hope that between the very strong and opposing forces that drove each of them, there could be a compromise.

He saw her come in, slim and lovely in a sapphire-colored suit trimmed and lined with chartreuse. Flashy colors and sensible shoes. Was there lace or silk or satin beneath? He had an urge to sweep her up then and there, take her away and discover the answer for himself.

"I'm sorry I'm late," she began, but before the mâitre d' could seat her, Gage had risen to pull her to him. His kiss was not discreet, not brief. Before he released her, nearby diners were looking on with curiosity and envy.

The breath she hadn't been aware of holding rushed out between her parted lips. Her eyes were heavy, her body vibrating.

"I—I'm awfully glad I wasn't on time."

"You worked late." There were shadows under her eyes. He hated seeing them. Knowing he'd caused them.

"Yes." Still breathless, she took her seat. "I had another case dumped on my desk just before five."

"Anything interesting?"

Her gaze came to his and held. "The East End Ripper."

He watched her unwaveringly. "I see."

"Do you, Gage? I wonder if you do." She drew her hand from his and laid it in her lap. "I felt I should disqualify myself, but what reason could I give?"

"There is no reason, Deborah. I stopped him, but it's your job to see that he pays for the crimes. One does not have to interfere with the other."

"I wish I could be sure." She took up her napkin, pleating it between her fingers. "Part of me sees you as a vigilante, another part a hero."

"And the truth lies somewhere in between." He reached for her hand again. "Whatever I am, I love you."

"I know." Her fingers tightened on his. "I know, but, Gage—" She broke off when the waiter brought over the champagne Gage had ordered while waiting for her.

"The drink of the gods," the waiter said in a rich French accent. "For a celebration, *n'est-ce pas?* A beautiful woman. A beautiful wine." At Gage's nod of approval, he popped the cork with a flourish that had the bubbling froth lapping at the lip of the bottle before teasingly retreating. "*Monsieur* will taste?" He poured a small amount into Gage's glass.

"Excellent," Gage murmured, but his eyes were on Deborah.

"*Mais, oui.*" The waiter's gaze slid approvingly over Deborah before he filled her glass, then Gage's. "*Monsieur* has the most exquisite taste." When the waiter bowed away, Deborah chuckled and touched her glass to Gage's.

"You're not going to tell me you own this place, too?"

"No. Would you like to?"

Though she shook her head, she had to laugh. "Are we celebrating?"

"Yes. To tonight. And to tomorrow." He took a small velvet box from his pocket and offered it to her. When she only stared at it, his fingers tensed. Panic rushed through him, but he kept his voice light. "You asked me to marry you, but I felt this privilege was mine."

She opened the box. In the candlelight, the center sapphire glittered a deep and dark blue. Surrounding that bold square was a symphony of ice-white diamonds. They flashed triumphantly in the setting of pale gold.

"It's exquisite."

He'd chosen the stones himself. But he had hoped to see pleasure in her eyes, not fear. Nor had he thought to feel fear himself.

"Are you having doubts?"

She looked up at him and let her heart speak. "Not about the way I feel about you. I never will. I'm afraid, Gage. I've tried to pretend I'm not, but I'm afraid. Not only of what you do, but that it might take you away from me."

He wouldn't make her promises that could be impossible to keep. "I was brought out of that coma the way I was brought out for a reason. I can't give you logic and facts on this one, Deborah. Only feelings and instinct. If I turned my back on what I'm meant to do, I'd die again."

Her automatic protest clogged in her throat. "You believe that?"

"I know that."

How could she look at him and not see it, too? How many times had she looked in his eyes and seen—something? Different, special, frightening. She knew he was flesh and blood, yet he was more. It wouldn't be possible to change that. And for the first time, she realized she didn't want to.

"I fell in love with you twice. With both sides of you." She looked down at the ring, took it out of its box where it flashed like lightning in her hand. "Until then, I was sure of my direction, of what I wanted, needed, and was working for. I was certain, so certain that when I fell in love it would be with a very calm, very ordinary man." She held the ring out to him. "I was wrong. You didn't come back just to fight for your justice, Gage. You came back for me." Then she smiled and held her hand out to him. "Thank God."

He slipped the ring on her finger. "I want to take you home." Even as he brought her hand to his lips, the waiter bounced back to their table.

"I knew it. Henri is never wrong." Deborah chuckled as he made a business out of topping off their glasses. "You have chosen my table. So, you have chosen well. You must leave the menu to me. You must! I will make a night such as you will never forget. It is my pleasure. Ah, *monsieur,* you are the most fortunate of men." He grabbed Deborah's hand and kissed it noisily.

Deborah was still laughing as he hurried away, but when she looked at Gage, she saw his attention was elsewhere. "What is it?"

"Fields." Gage lifted his glass, but his eyes followed the mayor's progress across the room. "He just came in with Arlo Stuart and a couple of other big guns with your friend Bower bringing up the rear."

Tensed, Deborah turned her head. They were heading for a table for eight. She recognized a prominent actress and the president of a major auto manufacturer. "Power meeting," she muttered.

"He's got the theater, industry, finance and the art worlds all represented neatly at one table. Before the evening's over, someone will come along and take a few 'candid' shots."

"It won't matter." She covered Gage's hand with hers. "In another week, it won't matter."

In less than that, he thought, but nodded. "Stuart's coming over."

"Well, now." Stuart clamped a hand on Gage's shoulder. "This is a nice coincidence. You look stunning as always, Miss O'Roarke."

"Thank you."

"Great restaurant this. Nobody does snails better." He beamed at both of them. "Hate to waste them talking business and politics. Now, you've got the right idea here. Champagne, candlelight." His sharp gaze fell on

Deborah's ring hand. "Well, that's a pretty little thing."
He grinned at Gage. "Got an announcement to make?"

"You caught us in the act, Arlo."

"Glad to hear it. You take your honeymoon in any of
my hotels." He winked at Deborah. "On the house."
Still grinning, he signaled to the mayor. It wouldn't hurt
Fields's image, he thought, to be in on the first congratulations to one of the city's top businessmen and the
most recognizable D.A.

"Gage, Deborah." Though Fields's smile was broad,
his nod of greeting was stiff. "Nice to see you. If you
haven't ordered, perhaps you'd like to join us."

"Not tonight." Stuart answered before Gage could.
"We've got ourself a newly engaged couple here, Tuck.
They don't want to waste the evening talking campaign
strategy."

Fields glanced down at Deborah's ring, the smile still
in place. But he wasn't pleased. "Congratulations."

"I like to think we brought them together." Always
exuberant, Stuart tossed an arm around Fields's shoulder. "After all, they met at my hotel during your fund-
raiser."

"I guess that makes us one big, happy family." Fields
looked at Gage. He needed Guthrie's support. "You're
marrying a fine woman, a tough lawyer. She's given me
a few headaches, but I admire her integrity."

Gage's voice was cool, but perfectly polite. "So do I."

Stuart gave another booming laugh. "I've admired
more than her integrity." He winked at Deborah again.
"No offense. Now we'll get back to politics and leave
you two alone."

"Bastard," Deborah mumbled when they were out of
earshot. She snatched up her wine. "He was sucking up
to you."

"No." Gage tapped his glass to hers. "To both of us." Over her shoulder, he saw the minute Jerry Bower heard the news. The man jolted, glanced up and over. Gage could almost hear him sigh as he stared at Deborah's back.

"I can't wait until we nail him."

There was such venom in her voice that Gage covered her hand with his and squeezed. "Just hold on. It won't take much longer."

She was so lovely. Gage lingered in bed, just looking at her. He knew she was sleeping deeply, sated by love, exhausted from passion. He wanted to know that she would dream content until morning.

He hated knowing there were times she woke in the middle of the night to find him gone. But tonight, when he could all but feel the danger tripping through his blood, he needed to be sure she would sleep, safe.

Silently he rose to dress. He could hear her breathing, slow and steady, and it soothed him. In the sprinkle of moonlight, he saw his reflection in the mirror. No, not a reflection, he thought. A shadow.

After flexing his hands in the snug black gloves, he opened a drawer. Inside was a .38, a regulation police issue revolver whose grip was as familiar to him as a brother's handshake. Yet he had not carried it since the night on the docks four years before.

He had never needed to.

But tonight, he felt that need. He no longer questioned instinct, but tucked the gun into a holster and belted it on so that the weapon fit at the small of his back.

He opened the panel, then paused. He wanted to see her again, sleeping. He could taste the danger now—

bitter on his tongue, in his throat. His only respite from it was knowing she wouldn't be affected. He would come back. He promised himself, and her. Fate could not deal such a killing blow twice in one lifetime.

He slipped away in the dark.

More than an hour later, the phone rang, pulling Deborah from sleep. Out of habit, she groped for it, murmuring to Gage as she rattled the receiver from the hook.

"Hello."

"Señorita."

The sound of Montega's voice had her icy and awake. "What do you want?"

"We have him. The trap was so easily sprung."

"What?" Panicked, she reached out for Gage. But even before her hands slid over empty sheets, she knew. Terror made her voice shake. "What do you mean?"

"He's alive. We want to keep him alive, for now. If you wish the same you'll come, quickly and alone. We'll trade him for all your papers, all your files. Everything you have."

She pressed a hand to her mouth, trying to stall until she could think. "You'll kill us both."

"Possibly. But I will surely kill him if you don't come. There is a warehouse on East River Drive. Three twenty-five East River Drive. It will take you thirty minutes. Any longer and I remove his right hand."

A rancid sickness heaved her stomach. "I'll come. Don't hurt him. Please, let me talk to him first—"

But the phone went dead.

Deborah sprang out of bed. Dragging on a robe, she rushed out to Frank's room. When one glance told her it was empty, she bounded down the hall to find Mrs.

Greenbaum sitting up in bed with an old movie and a can of peanuts.

"Frank. Where is he?"

"He went out to the all-night video store, and for pizza. We decided to have a Marx Brothers festival. What's wrong?"

But Deborah only covered her face with her hands and rocked. She had to think.

"He'll be back in twenty minutes."

"That's too late." She dropped her hands. She couldn't waste another moment. "You tell him I got a call, I had to go. Tell him it involves Gage."

"You're in trouble, tell me."

"Just tell him, please. The moment he comes in. I've gone to 325 East River Drive."

"You can't." Lil was climbing out of bed. "You can't go there at this time of night by yourself."

"I have to. Tell Frank I had to." She gripped Lil's hands. "It's life or death."

"We'll call the police—"

"No. No, just Frank. Tell him everything I said, and tell him what time I left. Promise me."

"Of course, but—"

But Deborah was already racing out.

It took several precious minutes to throw on clothes and to push stacks of printouts in her briefcase. Her hands were slick with sweat when she reached her car. In her mind, like a chant, she said Gage's name over and over as she streaked down the streets. Sickness stayed lodged in her throat as she watched the clock on the dash tick away the minutes.

Like a ghost, Nemesis watched the exchange of drugs for money. Thousands of bills for thousands of pounds of pain. The buyer slit one sample bag open, scooped out a touch of white powder and tapped it into a vial to test the purity. The seller flipped through stacks of bills.

When both were satisfied, the deal was made. There were few words exchanged. It was not a friendly business.

He watched the buyer take his miserable product and walk away. Even though Nemesis understood he would find the man again, and quickly, there was regret. If he had not been stalking larger game, it would have given him great pleasure to have thrown both merchants and their product into the river.

Footsteps echoed. The acoustics were good in the high, spreading cinderblock building. Boxes and crates were piled beside walls and on long metal shelves. Tools and two-by-fours crowded workbenches. A large fork-lift was parked by the aluminum garage doors, there to lift the stacks of lumber stored within. Though the scent of sawdust remained, the enormous saws were silent.

He saw, with blood-boiling fury, Montega walk into the room.

"Our first prize tonight." He strode to the suitcase of cash, waving the underlings aside. "But we have richer coming." He closed the suitcase, locked it. "When he comes, show him here."

As he stood, as insubstantial as the air he breathed, Nemesis fisted his hands. It was now, he thought. It was tonight. A part of him that thirsted only for revenge burned to take the gun he carried and fire it. Cold-blooded.

But his blood was too hot for such a quick and anonymous solution. His lips curved humorlessly. There were better ways. More judicious ways.

Even as he opened his mouth to speak, he heard voices, the sound of shoes rushing over the concrete floor. His heart froze to a ball of ice in his chest.

He had left her sleeping.

While his blood ran cold, the sweat of terror pearled on his brow. The danger he had tasted. Not for himself. Dear God, not for himself, but for her. He watched Deborah rush into the room, followed by two armed guards. For an instant, he slipped, wavering between Nemesis's world of shadows and hers.

"Where? Where is he?" She faced Montega like a tigress, head back, eyes blazing. "If you've hurt him, I'll see you dead. I swear it."

With an inclination of his head, Montega tapped his hands together in applause. "Magnificent. A woman in love."

There was no room for fear of him, not when all her fear was for Gage. "I want to see him."

"You are prompt, *señorita,* but have you come with what I asked for?"

She heaved the briefcase at him. "Take it to hell with you."

Montega passed the briefcase to a guard and, with a jerk of his head, had the man take it into an adjoining room.

"Patience," Montega said, holding up a hand. "Would you like to sit?"

"No. You have what you want, now give me what I came for."

The door opened again. Eyes wide, she stared. "Jerry?" Over surprise came the first wave of relief. Not Gage, she thought. They had never had Gage. It had been Jerry. Moving quickly, she went over to take his hands. "I'm sorry, I'm so sorry this happened. I had no idea."

"I know." He squeezed her hands. "I knew you'd come. I was counting on it."

"I wish I thought it was going to help either of us."

"It already has." He put an arm around her shoulder as he faced Montega. "The deal went smoothly, I take it."

"As expected, Mr. Bower."

"Excellent." Jerry gave Deborah's shoulder a friendly pat. "We have to talk."

She knew the color had drained from her face. She had felt it. "You—you're not a hostage here at all, are you?"

He allowed her to step away, even holding up a hand to signal the guards back. There was nowhere for her to go, and he was feeling generous. "No, and unfortunately, neither are you. I regret that."

"I don't believe it." Shaken, she lifted both hands to her temples. "I knew, I knew how blindly you stood behind Fields, but this— in the name of God, Jerry, you can't possibly let yourself be a part of this. You know what he's doing? The drugs, the murders? This isn't politics, it's madness."

"It's all politics, Deb." He smiled. "Mine. You don't honestly believe that a spineless puppet like Fields is behind this organization?" This time he laughed and signaled for a chair. "But you did. You did, because I laid a nice, neat trail of bread crumbs for you and anyone else who decided to look." Putting a hand on her shoulder, he pushed her into the chair.

"You?" She stared at him, head reeling. "You're telling me you're in charge? That Fields—"

"Is no more than a pawn. For more than six years I've stood two paces behind him, picking up all the flack—and pushing all the buttons. Fields couldn't run a dime store much less a city. Or the state..." He took a seat himself. "As I will in five years."

She wasn't afraid. Fear couldn't penetrate the numbness. This was a man she had known for nearly two years, one she had considered a friend and who she had judged as honest, if a bit weak. "How?"

"Money, power, brains." He ticked the three points off on his fingers. "I had the brains. Fields supplied the power. Believe me, he's been more than willing to leave the details, administrative and otherwise, to me. He makes a hell of a speech, knows whose butt to kick and whose to kiss. The rest of it, I do, and have since I was put in his office six years ago."

"By whom?"

"You are sharp." Still smiling, he gave her an admiring nod. "Arlo Stuart—he's the money. The problem has been that his businesses—the legitimate ones—dug a bit deeper into his profits than he cared for. Being a businessman, he saw another way to make that profit margin sing."

"The drugs."

"Right again." Casually he crossed his legs and gave an almost disinterested glance at his watch. There was time yet to indulge her, he thought. Since this was the last time. "He's been the head man on the East Coast for over twelve years. And it pays. I worked my way up in the organization. He likes initiative. I had the knowledge—law, political science—and he had Fields."

Questions, she ordered herself. She had to think of questions and keep him answering. Until...would Gage come? she wondered. Was there a way for Frank to contact him?

"So the three of you worked together," she said.

"Not Fields—I'd hate to give him credit in your mind, because I do respect your mind. He's nothing but a handy pawn and he hasn't a clue about our enterprise. Or if he does, he's wise enough to overlook it." He moved his shoulders. It didn't matter either way. "When the time is right, we'll expose the tax information and so forth that you've already discovered. No one will be more surprised than Fields. Since I'll be the one who righteously and regretfully exposes him, it should be very simple to step into his place. Then beyond."

"It won't work. I'm not the only one who knows."

"Guthrie." Jerry linked his fingers over his knee. "Oh, I intend to see to Guthrie. I ordered Montega to remove him four years ago, and the job was incomplete."

"You?" she whispered. "You ordered?"

"Arlo leaves that kind of detail to me." He leaned forward so only she could hear him. "I like details— such as what your new fiancé does in his spare time." His lips curved when her color drained. "You led me to him this time, Deborah."

"I don't know what you're talking about."

"I'm a good judge of people. I have to be. And you are a very predictable person. You, a woman of integrity, intelligence and fierce loyalties, involved with two men? It didn't seem likely. Tonight, I became sure of what I've suspected for several weeks. There's only one man, one man who would have recognized Montega, one man who would have won your heart, one man with enough reason to fanatically pursue me." He patted her

hand when she remained silent. "That's our little secret. I enjoy secrets."

His eyes chilled again as he rose. "And though I regret it, sincerely, only one of us can walk out of here tonight with that secret. I've asked Montega to be quick.
For old times' sake."

Though her body was shaking, she made herself
stand. "I've learned to believe in destiny, Jerry. You
won't win. He'll see to that. You'll kill me, and he'll
come after you like a Fury. You think you know him,
but you don't. You don't have him, and you never will."

"If it gives you comfort." He stepped away from her.
"We don't have him—at the moment."

"You're wrong."

Every head in the room turned at the voice. There was
nothing but blank walls and piles of lumber. Deborah's
knees went so weak she almost folded to the ground.

Then everything seemed to happen at once.

A guard standing beside the wall jerked back, his eyes
bright with surprise. While his body struggled and
strained, the rifle he was holding began to spray bullets.
Men shouted, diving for cover. The guard screamed,
stumbled away from the wall. His own men cut him
down.

Dashing behind a line of shelves, Deborah searched
frantically for a weapon. Laying her hands on a crowbar, she stepped back, ready to defend herself. Before
her astonished eyes, a weapon was grappled away from
a goggle-eyed guard. Mad with fear, he raced away,
screaming.

"Stay back." The voice floated out toward her.

"Thank God, I thought that—"

"Just stay back. I'll deal with you later."

She stood, gripping the crowbar. Nemesis was back, she thought, and gritted her teeth. And as arrogant as ever. Sliding a box aside, she peeked through the opening to the melee beyond. There were five men left—the guards, Montega and Jerry. They were firing wildly, as terrified as they were confused. When one of the bullets plowed into the wall a scant foot from her head, she crouched lower.

Someone screamed. The sound made her squeeze her eyes shut. A hand grabbed her hair, dragging her up.

"What is he?" Jerry hissed in her ear. Though his hand was shaking, it maintained a firm grip. "What the hell is he?"

"He's a hero," she said, looking defiantly into his wild eyes. "Something you'll never understand."

"He'll be a dead one before this is over. You're coming with me." He jerked her in front of him. "If you try anything, I'll shoot you in the back and take my chances."

Deborah took a deep breath and slammed the crowbar into his stomach. When he keeled over, retching, she raced out, weaving and dodging around workbenches and shelving. He recovered quickly, half running, half crawling until his hand reached out and slipped over her ankle. Cursing, she kicked him off, knowing any minute she could feel a bullet slam into her back. She scrambled up a graduated hack of lumber, thinking if she could climb to safety, he couldn't use her as a shield.

She could hear him clambering behind her, gaining ground as he got back his wind. Desperate, she imagined herself like a lizard, quick and sure, clinging to the wood. She couldn't fall. All she knew was that she couldn't fall. Splinters dug into her fingers, unfelt.

With all her strength, she heaved the crowbar at him. It struck him on the shoulder, making him curse and falter. Knowing better than to look back, she set her teeth and jumped from the stack of lumber to a narrow metal ladder. Sweaty, her hands slipped, but she clung, climbing up to the next level. Her breath was coming fast as she raced across the steel landing crowded with rolls of insulation and building material.

But there was no place to go. As she reached the far side, she saw that she was trapped. He had nearly reached the top. She couldn't go down, had no hope of making the five-foot leap to the overhang of metal shelving that held more supplies.

He was breathing hard, and there was blood on his mouth. And a gun in his hand. Deborah took an unsteady step back, looking down twenty-five feet to where Nemesis battled three to one. She couldn't call to him, she realized. To distract him even for an instant could mean his death.

Instead, she turned and faced her one-time friend. "You won't use me to get him."

With the back of his hand he wiped blood and spittle from his lip. "One way or another."

"No." She stepped back again and bumped into a hoist chain. It was thick and hooked and heavy, used, she realized quickly, to lift the huge stacks of material to the next level for storage. "No," she said again and, using all her strength, swung the chain at his face.

She heard the sound of bones breaking. And then his scream, one horrible scream before she covered her own face.

He had whittled things down to Montega when Nemesis looked up and saw her, white as a ghost and swaying on the brink of a narrow metal ledge. He didn't spare a glance for the man who had fallen screaming to the concrete below. As he sprinted toward her, he heard a bullet whistle past his head.

"No!" she shouted at him, pushing aside the faintness. "He's behind you." She saw with relief, and Montega with disbelief, that he veered left and disappeared.

Cautious, wanting to draw Montega's attention from Deborah, Nemesis moved along the wall. He would call tauntingly, then move right or left before Montega could aim his trembling gun and fire.

"I will kill you!" Shaking with fear, Montega fired again and again into the walls. "I've seen you bleed. I will kill you."

It wasn't until he was certain Deborah was down and safely huddled in the shadows that he reappeared, six feet from Montega. "You've already killed me once." Nemesis held his gun steady at Montega's heart. He had only to pull the trigger, he thought. And it would be over. Four years of hell would be over.

But he saw Deborah, her face white and sheened with sweat. Slowly his finger relaxed on the trigger.

"I came back for you, Montega. You'll have a long time to wonder why. Drop your weapon."

Speechless, he did so, sending it clattering onto the concrete. Pale but steady, Deborah stepped forward to pick it up.

"Who are you?" Montega demanded. "What are you?" A scream of warning burst from Deborah's lips as Montega slipped a hand into his pocket.

Two more gunshots ripped the air. Even as they echoed, Montega sprawled lifelessly on the floor. Staring at him, Nemesis stepped closer. "I'm your destiny," he whispered, then turned and caught Deborah in his arms.

"They said they had you. They were going to kill you."

"You should have trusted me." He turned her away, determined to shield her from the death surrounding them.

"But you were here," she said, then stopped. "Why were you here? How did you know?"

"The pattern. Sit down, Deborah. You're shaking."

"I have a feeling it's going to be from anger in a minute. You knew they would be here tonight."

"Yes, I knew. Sit. Let me get you some water."

"Stop it, just stop it." She snatched at his shirtfront with both hands. "You knew, and you didn't tell me. You knew about Stuart, about Jerry."

"Not about Jerry." And he would always regret it. "Until he walked in here tonight and I heard what he told you, I was focused on Fields."

"Then why were you here?"

"I broke the pattern a few days ago. Every drop had been made in a building Stuart owned. And each drop was at least two weeks apart in a different section of the city. I spent a couple of nights casing a few other spots, but honed in here. And I didn't tell you," he continued when her eyes scraped at him, "because I wanted to avoid exactly what happened here tonight. Damn it, when I'm worried about you I can't concentrate. I can't do my job."

Her body was braced as she held out her hand. "Do you see this ring? You gave this to me only hours ago. I'm wearing it because I love you, and because I'm teaching myself how to accept you, your feelings and your needs. If you can't do the same for me, you'll have to take it back.''

Behind his mask his eyes were dark and flat. ''It's not a matter of doing the same—''

''It's exactly that. I killed a man tonight.'' Her voice shook, but she pushed him away when he would have held her again. ''I killed a man I knew. I came here tonight ready, willing to exchange not only my ethics but my life for yours. Don't you ever protect me, pamper me, or think for me again.''

''Are you through?''

''No.'' But she did lean against the chair. ''I know you won't stop what you do. That you can't. I'll worry about you, but I won't stand in your way. You won't stand in mine, either.''

He nodded. ''Is that all?''

''For now.''

''You're right.''

She opened her mouth, shut it, then blew out a long breath. ''Would you say that again?''

''You're right. I kept things from you and instead of protecting you, I put you in more danger. For that, I'm sorry. And besides admitting that, I think you should know I wasn't going to kill him.'' He looked down at Montega, but cupped Deborah's chin in his hand before she could follow his direction. ''I wanted to. For an instant, I tasted it. But if he had surrendered, I would have turned him over to the police.''

She saw the truth of it in his eyes. ''Why?''

''Because I looked at you and I knew I could trust you to see there was justice.'' He held out a hand. ''Deborah, I need a partner.''

She was smiling even as her eyes overflowed. ''So do I.'' Instead of taking his hand, she launched herself into his arms. "Nothing's going to stop us," she murmured. In the distance, she heard the first sirens. "I think Frank's bringing the cavalry." She kissed him. "I'll explain later. At home. You'd better go." With a sigh, she stepped back. "It's going to take a good lawyer to explain all of this."

At the sound of rushing feet, he moved back, then into the wall behind her. "I'll be here."

She smiled, spreading her palm on the wall, knowing he was doing the same on the shadowy other side. "I'm counting on it."

* * * * *

SILHOUETTE'S "BIG WIN"
SWEEPSTAKES RULES & REGULATIONS

NO PURCHASE NECESSARY TO ENTER OR RECEIVE A PRIZE

1. To enter the Sweepstakes and join the Reader Service, scratch off the metallic strips on all your BIG WIN tickets #1-#6. This will reveal the potential values for each Sweepstakes entry number, the number of free book(s) you will receive and your free bonus gift as part of our Reader Service. If you do not wish to take advantage of our Reader Service but wish to enter the Sweepstakes only, scratch off the metallic strips on your BIG WIN tickets #1-#4. Return your entire sheet of tickets intact. Incomplete and/or inaccurate entries are ineligible for that section or sections of prizes. Torstar Corp. and its affiliates are not responsible for mutilated or unreadable entries or inadvertent printing errors. Mechanically reproduced entries are null and void.

2. Whether you take advantage of this offer or not, on or about April 30, 1992, at the offices of Marden-Kane Inc., Lake Success, NY, your Sweepstakes numbers will be compared against the list of winning numbers generated at random by the computer. However, prizes will only be awarded to individuals who have entered the Sweepstakes. In the event that all prizes are not claimed, a random drawing will be held from all qualified entries received from March 30, 1990 to March 31, 1992, to award all unclaimed prizes. All cash prizes (Grand to Sixth), will be mailed to the winners and are payable by check in U.S. funds. Seventh prize will be shipped to winners via third-class mail. These prizes are in addition to any free, surprise or mystery gifts that might be offered. Versions of this Sweepstakes with different prizes or approximate equal value may appear at retail outlets or in other mailings by Torstar Corp. and its affiliates.

3. The following prizes are awarded in this sweepstakes: ★ Grand Prize (1) $1,000,000; First Prize (1) $25,000; Second Prize (1) $10,000; Third Prize (5) $5,000; Fourth Prize (10) $1,000; Fifth Prize (100) $250; Sixth Prize (2,500) $10; ★ ★ Seventh Prize (6,000) $12.95 ARV.

   ★ This presentation offers a Grand Prize of a $1,000,000 annuity. Winner will receive $33,333.33 a year for 30 years without interest totalling $1,000,000.

   ★ ★ Seventh Prize: A fully illustrated hardcover book published by Torstar Corp. Approximate Retail Value of the book is $12.95.

   Entrants may cancel the Reader Service at anytime without cost or obligation to buy (see details in center insert card).

4. This Sweepstakes is being conducted under the supervision of an independent judging organization. By entering this Sweepstakes, each entrant accepts and agrees to be bound by these rules and the decisions of the judges, which shall be final and binding. Odds of winning in the random drawing are dependent upon the total number of entries received. Taxes, if any, are the sole responsibility of the winners. Prizes are nontransferable. All entries must be received at the address printed on the reply card and must be postmarked no later than 12:00 MIDNIGHT on March 31, 1992. The drawing for all unclaimed Sweepstakes prizes will take place on May 30, 1992, at 12:00 NOON, at the offices of Marden-Kane, Inc., Lake Success, New York.

5. This offer is open to residents of the U.S., the United Kingdom, France and Canada, 18 years or older, except employees and their immediate family members of Torstar Corp., its affiliates, subsidiaries, and all the other agencies, entities and persons connected with the use, marketing or conduct of this Sweepstakes. All Federal, State, Provincial and local laws apply. Void wherever prohibited or restricted by law. Any litigation within the Province of Quebec respecting the conduct and awarding of a prize in this publicity contest must be submitted to the Régie des Loteries et Courses du Québec.

6. Winners will be notified by mail and may be required to execute an affidavit of eligibility and release, which must be returned within 14 days after notification or an alternate winner will be selected. Canadian winners will be required to correctly answer an arithmetical skill-testing question administered by mail, which must be returned within a limited time. Winners consent to the use of their names, photographs and/or likenesses for advertising and publicity in conjunction with this and similar promotions without additional compensation. For a list of our major prize winners, send a stamped, self-addressed ENVELOPE to: WINNERS LIST, c/o Marden-Kane Inc., P.O. Box 701, SAYREVILLE, NJ 08871. Requests for Winners Lists will be fulfilled after the May 30, 1992 drawing date.

If Sweepstakes entry form is missing, please print your name and address on a 3" ×5" piece of plain paper and send to:

In the U.S.	**In Canada**
Silhouette's "BIG WIN" Sweepstakes	Silhouette's "BIG WIN" Sweepstakes
3010 Walden Ave.	P.O. Box 609
P.O. Box 1867	Fort Erie, Ontario
Buffalo, NY 14269-1867	L2A 5X3

Offer limited to one per household.

LTY-S391D

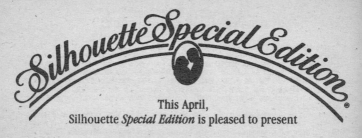

Silhouette Special Edition

This April,
Silhouette *Special Edition* is pleased to present

ONCE IN A LIFETIME
by Ginna Gray

the long-awaited companion volume to her bestselling duo

Fools Rush In (#416)
Where Angels Fear (#468)

Ever since spitfire Erin Blaine and her angelic twin sister Elise stirred up double trouble and entangled their long-suffering brother David in some sticky hide-and-seek scenarios, readers clamored to hear more about dashing, debonair David himself.

Now that time has come, as straitlaced Abigail Stewart manages to invade the secrecy shrouding sardonic David Blaine's bachelor boat—and creates the kind of salty, saucy, swashbuckling romantic adventure that comes along only once in a lifetime!

**Even if you missed the earlier novels,
you won't want to miss**

ONCE IN A LIFETIME #661

Available this April, only in Silhouette *Special Edition*.   OL-1